No Sorrow to Die

No Sorrow to Die

Gillian Galbraith

First published in 2010 by Polygon
an imprint of Birlinn Ltd
West Newington House
10 Newington Road, Edinburgh EH9 1QS

www.birlinn.co.uk

ISBN: 978-1-84697-164-8

British Library Cataloguing-in-Publication Data
A catalogue record for this book is available from
the British Library

Set in Italian Garamond BT at Birlinn Ltd

Printed and bound in the UK by
CPI Mackays, Chatham ME5 8TD

ACKNOWLEDGEMENTS

Maureen Allison
Colin Browning
Douglas Edington
Lesmoir Edington
Robert Galbraith
Daisy Galbraith
Diana Griffiths
Jinty Kerr
Roger Orr
Dr Sandra Smith
Aidan O'Neill

Any errors in the text are my own.

DEDICATION

To Douglas, with all my love

I

Saturday night

'I am doing nothing wrong,' Heather Brodie told herself, trying to silence the unwelcome voice in her head which was busy telling her that she certainly was – doing something shameful, in fact. A few bars of 'Jerusalem', hummed loudly, finally smothered it.

Craning towards the mirror she began to apply her lipstick, conscious, as she did so, of every flaw and imperfection on her careworn, middle-aged face. True, the blue of the irises was as deep as ever, but crows-feet had begun to clamber across her cheekbones and her brow was no longer smooth, one corrugated fold following another like sand on a beach at low tide. She smiled humourlessly at her own reflection, and as she did so taut lines appeared on either side of her mouth, extending from nose to chin, multiplying when the smile widened and producing a dimple on the left. An eyelash caught in the corner of her eye distracted her, making her blink convulsively until, with a fingertip, she was able to remove it. Relieved, she turned her attention back to her lips, dabbing them with a paper hankie to remove the outer layer of scarlet gloss in an attempt to make herself look less predatory, less like a hawk.

'Life must go on.' Everybody said it, and she could only agree. When younger, greener, she had thought that

1

the cliché had a pitiless ring to it, the mantra of a ruthless survivor, the living sloughing off illness and death in their determination to kick their heels and enjoy the remainder of their allotted span. But, after nearly half a century on this earth, she knew better, understood the saying only too well. Now she positively embraced it.

The wardrobe door was already open and she looked inside, fingering the material of the black dress that she had decided to wear, then took the soft garment out. She had planned ahead, no goodbyes were now required, she had attended to them before she had begun to get ready. Previous experience had taught her that the spring in her step, never mind the warm scent of her perfumed body, was likely to disturb him, to provoke some kind of incoherent fury or, worse still, deeper withdrawal. So she stepped out of the front door as quietly as she was able, the icy air tingling her tender cheeks, and pulled it tight closed behind her.

———

The decision to walk had been a good one, she decided. The sound of her heels clicking on the pavement made her feel alive, part of the human race once more, and she studied the other pedestrians as they ambled along, taking in their clothes and imagining their destinations. None of them, she thought, were likely to be as delightful, as exhilarating as her own. The farther she got from the hushed interior of her house in India Street, with its stale air and faded colours, the more she allowed the excitement rising in her to grow unchecked until she felt herself almost crackling with energy, as if champagne had been transfused into her veins. She was off the leash again, and must make full use of her freedom.

2

Both Heather Brodie and her lover knew that it was foolish to choose a restaurant on Dublin Street for their illicit rendezvous, but neither had been able to resist the charms of *Il Gattopardo*. Edinburgh might be a capital city, but it was a small one, an intimate one, one where words travelled easily and secrets were seldom kept. The place remained little more than a series of interlinked villages, and scandalous tales, usually of infidelity or embezzlement, knew no boundaries; they passed from Bruntsfield to Ravelston, Corstorphine to Comely Bank as easily as the air itself. Nowhere was completely safe.

But standing under a street-light in the marrow-chilling cold outside the eating house as one leaden minute piled on another, exposed to the gaze of every passer-by, she regretted the recklessness of their choice. And after a further fifteen minutes of waiting she no longer met the eyes of anyone, her gaze fixed steadfastly on the pavement, afraid that she might again be confronted by a former colleague or acquaintance, a playful smile on their lips as they cocked a quizzical eyebrow at her.

She pushed a strand of damp hair off her forehead and looked up the hill, scanning the horizon, her eyes coming to rest on the red Dumfries sandstone of the National Portrait Gallery. But she was blind to its gothic grandeur; one thing only was now on her mind. Where the hell *was* he? She inspected her watch – seven-twenty – and felt a surge of desperate, impotent anger. They had agreed on seven, had agreed on *Il Gattopardo* and, crucially, that they would meet outside it. He must know how exposed she would be, waiting for him on the street, attracting curious glances, vulnerable to the cruel winter weather.

Someone tapped her arm and she spun round, her anger already forgotten, expecting to look into his dark eyes, but instead found herself face to face with Miss Guild's thick spectacles and whiskery chin. The old school-mistress's pleasure on bumping into a former pupil was clear from her broad, buck-toothed smile.

'Hevver . . .' she hesitated briefly, 'Hevver Burns!' she exclaimed, triumphant at having remembered the elusive name.

'Heather Brodie, now,' her ex-pupil corrected irritably, glancing over the old lady's shoulder in search of the man, not bothering to hide her preoccupation.

'So, Hevver, you married. And you're as lovely as ever. Did you continue with your drama course? I've never forgotten your Ophelia, you were a star . . .'

Before their conversation could go any further, unseen clouds in the black, starless sky above them burst, unleashing a deluge, and raindrops as large as cherries began to fall on their heads, splattering on the ground round about them. In seconds they were both drenched, tiny rivulets forming on the old teacher's spectacles and running down her cheeks. Fumbling ineffectually with a folded polythene rain-hat, she mumbled, 'I must be off, dear. I'm not dressed for vis kind of wevver!' and, like an anxious duck, she waddled speedily down Dublin Street, her flat feet splashing from side to side on the streaming pavement.

Heather Brodie ran down the steps to *Il Gattopardo* and pushed open its door. She was certain that he would not be inside, but she had to have shelter, both from any more prying eyes and the cold rain. She wandered into the dining area and, absentmindedly, put a finger to her cheek to wipe away another drip. Her mascara had mingled with the water, so she would be looking a fright.

As she became accustomed to the subdued lighting, a flickering candle on each table, she noticed a familiar figure sitting in a corner, hunched over a menu and nursing a beer glass in his left hand.

'Let him not see me yet' she prayed, embarrassed by her wet, flattened hair and besmirched eyes, now hunting frantically for a sign to the toilets, and quickly spotting it. Hastily, she threaded her way between the tables heading for the *Donne*, but her lover caught sight of her and immediately began to wave, semaphoring his presence. When she did not respond, he shouted in ever-increasing volume, 'Heather! Heather! I'm over here', broadcasting to the world her arrival, and with it his own.

Flustered, and desperate to shut him up, she waved back and changed course towards his table. She reached him, all poise now gone, sodden and flushed, and instantly he rose to greet her, planted a kiss on her cold, wet cheek and attempted to help her out of her coat. Sitting down opposite him, she imagined the impression that she must be making with her black, smudged eyes and sopping hair, the dim light not dim enough for her now. But he seemed, simply, pleased to see her, and showed no signs of being dismayed or disappointed by her appearance.

'I thought we were supposed to be meeting outside,' she began, leaving her sentence unfinished, but meaning, 'That was what we arranged. I stayed there to ensure we would not miss each other, and that's why I'm now soaking wet.'

'Yep, I know,' he answered, blithely unaware of what had not been said, 'but it was freezing. I got here early and it seemed sensible to wait inside.'

And, of course, she had to agree, and in the act of doing so, she felt herself relax in his company, unfurling like a damp flower in full sunlight.

They did not eat a great deal, being too immersed in each other to savour, or even notice, the food, but the wine flowed freely enough, loosening their tongues and making them less fearful of discovery. And every so often, when their eyes met, he smiled delightedly at her, like a fellow conspirator privy to some wonderful, shared secret.

Once, when her companion had left in search of the *Uomini*, Heather Brodie allowed her gaze to roam freely around the room, inspecting her fellow customers and the staff scurrying around them. A couple close to their table caught her attention. Holding hands with an unshaven student was a petite, blonde girl, and they were looking at each other so fondly, so intently, that they seemed oblivious to their surroundings, to the chatter of their fellow guests, to anything other than each other, certainly to her scrutiny. Other lovers, she thought, just like us. And they appeared so young and attractive, untouched, unscarred by life, that she remained enchanted by the sight of them until the spell was broken by a waiter accidentally dropping her dessert plate onto the floor, where it spun on its axis until it fell, smashing itself on the cold tiles. Hearing the noise, the fair girl looked up and caught her eye, smiling shyly at her, as she might have done at a benign aunt.

'Coffee, back at my place?' her companion asked, stuffing a receipt for the bill into his jacket pocket, confident that she would accompany him home. She hesitated momentarily before replying. Not because the question had not been unexpected, she had long anticipated it, well aware that 'Coffee' did not mean coffee.

And why should she not go back with him, spend the night once more in his company? Once an adulteress, always an adulteress. She was only human after all, had the same needs as everyone else and, so far, so good. Their secret had remained undiscovered by everyone, including the children. So what was there to hold her back? Nothing whatsoever. Certainly, 'Coffee' had been on her mind throughout the day: while doing the housework; in the bath; walking along the street and, most of all, while sitting opposite him, inhaling his particular scent and feeling the pressure of his hand on hers. So she smiled her reply wordlessly and rose to leave, turning her hips sideways, ready to navigate her way through the narrow spaces leading to the exit.

She had been often enough to his flat in Mansfield Place to know her way around it, but she still enjoyed its strangeness, its faint aroma of stale cigar smoke, the casual, bachelor untidiness of the place, with a squash-racket propped up by the door and post-it notes stuck on the bathroom mirror.

Waiting for him to return from the kitchen, she wandered over to inspect his CD collection, unconsciously expecting it to resemble, to some extent at least, her own middle-aged, middle-of-the-road selection. But she found no Elton John, Genesis or David Bowie in his racks and her unfamiliarity with the New Romantics reminded her forcibly of the disparity in their ages. Of course. It was only to be expected. He would have been a small boy tucked up in his bed on the evening that she had swayed with thousands of others to the strains of 'Rocket Man' in the Usher Hall. He had probably never even seen a platform heel.

The realisation was accompanied by the recurrence of a doubt, a sinking feeling inside her as all her confidence slowly drained away. Who was she fooling? She was no longer young or good-looking, her flesh sagged and bulged in unnatural places and her skin had developed unsightly blemishes. This very morning she had been horrified by a glimpse of her own fat knees. She could only be a disappointment to any lover. And he must see young, firm flesh on a daily basis at his work. How stupid she had been to listen to him again, to come with him again.

Hurriedly she rose from the couch, intending to leave, but before she had taken a step her companion re-entered the room bearing two cups on a tray, two whisky glasses beside them.

As if in a dream, she sat down once more, and as she did so, he closed the curtains and dimmed the lights. To bolster her flagging spirits, she took a large mouthful of the Talisker, hoping that it would mix quickly with the half-bottle of Chianti she had already consumed, and help to dispel her doubts, make her less agonisingly self-conscious. If only he were ten years older, rather than ten years younger.

They sat close together, thighs touching and tingling, and he put his arm behind her neck until his hand dangled above her shoulder. Briefly he allowed it to rest it there, with his fingertips brushing the side of her breast. Taking another sip of her whisky, she turned to kiss him, desperate to forget about herself and all her flaws. But as they kissed, she found that instead of losing herself as she had hoped, she was becoming all too conscious of what was happening. The sneering voice in her head had begun to speak, telling her that she, a middle-aged wife and mother, should have known better than to cradle-snatch, and that this affair would never last.

Trying to ignore the voice's unpleasant, intrusive words, she closed her eyes and lay back, allowing her hands to ruffle his hair, trying to quieten her mind with her body, allow it to follow its own desires. Soon, she could hear nothing but their breathing, feeling her excitement mirroring his own as he removed her blouse and bra and placed his lips on her neck. And the knowledge that he, he of all men, wanted her, was enough, enough to banish all other thoughts from her mind.

When they had finished and sleep was just beginning to steal over her, she felt him move away, heard him get up and stride about the room, gathering his clothes together. And though he had said nothing to her, lying there she felt sure that he wanted her to do the same. So she rose and in the darkness started to pick up her own disordered garments. A single shoe proved elusive and she began searching for it, trying first behind an armchair and then dragging back one of the curtains in the belief that it would be revealed there.

While she continued her quest, the silence between them began to oppress her. He turned on the light to help her, its harsh illumination finally destroying the comforting ambience that had previously existed, and instantly she spotted the heel of the shoe protruding from beneath the sofa.

'See you next week?' he said brightly, holding it up in triumph for her to put on.

'Yes, maybe,' she replied in a thin voice, taking the shoe, the contrast between her fantasy leave-taking scene and the real thing disheartening her, making it difficult for her to say more without breaking down. This time she had hoped to spend the night beside him.

'Darling, think,' he said, as if he had read her mind, 'what would his carer make of it, finding him alone in the morning?'

'I know, but I love you,' she replied, speaking the words for the first time and looking into his eyes to see if he would flinch. But he did not, and his murmured response pleased her, sounding something like 'Love you too.'

He went with her to the main front door, holding her hand in his as they walked down the common stair together and planting a kiss on her cheek before they parted. As the door of the tenement building closed behind her, Heather Brodie leant against it for a moment, her eyes closed, breathing out in a long, heartfelt sigh. In middle-age, however ludicrous it might seem, to her as much as to anybody else, love had somehow got through her defences and managed to pierce her tired heart.

Still deep in thought, she set off at a slow pace along London Street, oblivious to the drizzle that had begun to fall on her unprotected head. Loving him was wonderful, still too good to be true, but how on earth had she managed to end up in this situation? How had she fallen? And, dear God, what would the world think of her if they knew? What would her mother have thought, or, worse yet, what would her mother-in-law think?

Actually, on reflection, old Mrs Brodie would feel entirely vindicated. She had been expecting some kind of nebulous 'worst' from the first day she had set eyes on her 'flighty' daughter-in-law. 'Flighty' indeed! If she had ever been flighty, she would have fled on the day of Gavin's diagnosis, in fact, would never have touched someone like him in the first place.

And none of them had any idea what it was like living with him on a daily basis – wiping him, feeding him, changing him, soothing his fears. It was like having a giant baby in the house, only one that regressed each day rather than progressed. Each week brought with it some new, negative milestone. And she had signed up to be his wife, not his mother. She was not cut out to be a bloody 'carer'. Thank God for that day-centre, unspeakable as it was, because old Ma Brodie could not be seen for dust nowadays, too busy with her bridge parties, or preparation for her bridge parties, and the odd bout of 'charity' work.

And who cared about her anymore, or the children for that matter? 'How's Gavin?' everyone asked in concerned tones, before getting on with their own lives.

Well, she was entitled to a life too, like everyone else. For far too long her needs, her wants, had been put on hold, and all the while the last of her youth was draining away. But this man wanted her and loved her, and such an amazing gift must be seized with both hands. Nothing and no-one should be allowed to stand in the way. After all, she was not to blame for the disease, any part of it. She would not accept any further punishment for it, or from it, either.

But despite her musings, her attempt to rationalise things and free herself from guilt, she felt a very different woman from the one who had flown along the same street earlier that same evening. Her feet, still damp from their earlier soaking outside the restaurant, were now cold, and her fallen arches ached with each step. Misjudging the speed of the traffic as she crossed Dundas Street in her high heels, a car hooted its horn derisively at her, several drunken ladettes popping their heads out of the windows and shouting obscenities in her direction.

Rattled by them, she stepped onto the kerb, hurrying onwards, and as she passed the end of the gardens in Royal Circus, a breeze came from nowhere, turning the rain horizontal and making the bare, leafless trees within the railings creak and groan.

A few minutes later and glad to reach shelter, she opened her own front door in India Street and slipped inside, quickly closing it again on the outside world. The light in the vestibule was still on and she tiptoed towards the kitchen, throwing down her jacket on a hall chair, intending to make herself a pot of tea.

Standing in the dark outside her husband's bedroom with her mug in hand, she waited, listening at the door, trying to make out whether his radio had been switched off or not. Thinking that she could hear a voice speaking, she pushed it open and took a single step inside. Instantly, the familiar, sweet scent of sickness hit her, and for a second she turned her head away in disgust, holding her breath. In the deep, black silence it was apparent that the radio was not on, and she took another step towards the bed before, changing her mind, she backed away from it. She would not take a look at him now, it might wake him, and besides, it would simply depress her further.

As she undressed in her own room, a photograph in a leather frame caught her eye and she picked it up, dusted it with her sleeve and then examined it closely. A handsome young man had his arms around a girl, and his head was thrown back in laughter as the girl squirmed helplessly in his arms, ostensibly trying to escape but, in fact, relishing the feel of his flesh enclosing hers. It was a picture of them taken on their first holiday alone together. A snapshot, preserving in celluloid a fleeting moment of happiness, and by its continuing existence falsifying their past. Because no images existed of the arguments, the sulks and silences, there was nothing tangible to chart or commemorate the slow decline of their relationship except the lines on their faces, the dullness of their smiles.

Coldly, she laid the photograph face down on the shelf. The truth had to be faced. Their marriage had not been a happy one, and the little store of goodwill upon which they had both relied had long ago been depleted. She was now running on empty.

No. Things simply could not go on as they were. The man she lived with was no longer a husband to her, bore little resemblance to the father of her children, and still less to the man whose hand she had held when they stood at the altar together. And the disease had, in its unremitting, malign way, changed her almost as much as it had changed him.

Something would have to be done, for all their sakes, otherwise they might all drift along aimlessly for another year, further damaged by the voyage and coming no closer to land. Her fate lay in her own hands and so, too, did his. The children's as well. From somewhere deep inside herself she would have to find the strength, because what everyone said was true: life must go on.

2

After escorting the tearful lady to her kitchen, the young constable pushed open the bedroom door with the tip of his highly polished boot and peeked gingerly round the side of it. Involuntarily he inhaled, and then whipped his head back into the hallway, retching convulsively, his hand now clamped over his mouth. His companion, PC Rowe, seeing the horrified expression on his mate's face, instantly and enthusiastically stuck his own head round the door and remained there, spellbound, taking in everything and relishing the sight before him as if at a show.

'We'd better phone the Sarge, eh?' he said excitedly, remaining fixed to the spot and continuing to drink in the scene before his eyes. 'Looks like there's been a fuckin' bloodbath in there, eh?'

Within twenty minutes, a small, overweight woman with a purposeful air, dressed in a paper suit and bootees, marched into the hallway of the Brodie's India Street flat. Immediately, and as if it were her own, she started taking control of the situation and issuing orders to the uniformed officers.

'Constable,' DCI Bell began, looking hard at Rowe, 'no-one seems to be at the door logging movements in

14

and out.' And though he had no idea who the middle-aged woman was, the young man said, 'No, Ma'am. I'll see to it the now,' and immediately disappeared, obeying her unspoken command.

Passing through the vestibule he cannoned, in his blind haste, into another detective, similarly clad in green paper, who had her head down and was perching on one foot like a heron, pulling on the final bootee. On impact, she careered over and fell heavily onto the tiled floor, cursing under her breath as she toppled. Appalled at what he had done, PC Rowe put out his hand to pull her up, but she stayed where she was, still fitting the overshoe, and only once it was on did she grasp his outstretched hand and allow herself to be hauled up by him.

To his surprise, once the woman was upright again, she towered over him, and seeing his worried expression she said with a grin, 'Don't look so worried. No bones broken.' She was pretty, even with a paper shower cap halfway down her forehead, and when she smiled at him he found himself relaxing and smiling in return.

DCI Elaine Bell, with DS Alice Rice now following in her footsteps like her shadow, strode towards the bed in Gavin Brodie's room. The bedroom shutters had been partly opened and the man himself lay motionless, his head tilted backwards, a crescent-shaped cut dividing his exposed neck in two. Blood, spurting from the wound, had been pumped by his heart onto the wall behind him, its final contractions creating a sprayed arc until, the pressure diminishing, it landed on the headboard and sides, the hoist, his pillows and his own head. A glass of water on the bedside table was stained a deep, dark red, and a framed photograph of a little boy playing on a beach had been showered too.

The face of the dead man was unnaturally pale, waxen, as if all blood had been siphoned out of the overly skull-like head. Clad in his light blue-and-white-striped pyjamas he resembled, Alice thought, one of the starved inmates of a concentration camp. Sharp bones protruded through his yellowish skin, and between his cracked lips his teeth were bared like a dog. She had seen worse, but not often, and at least if it had been in the open air, the fresh air, the smells of death would have dispersed. Here a strange cloying aroma enveloped them, as if the air itself was diseased.

As the two women bent over him, their heads a few inches from the glistening slice in his cartilaginous neck, a couple of photographers entered the room, one with a video camera at the ready, nattering to each other while awaiting their instructions. With her eyes still fixed on the wound, Elaine Bell said crisply, 'Get a move on, boys. Do *Homes and Gardens* . . . the whole house, outside and in. And I want mid-range and close-ups in here – the body and all the blood-spatters. All of them, mind. And . . .' she added, after a moment's hesitation 'get all the exits and entrances too. Doors and windows.'

'Alice?' she said, straightening up and raising the bed covers for them both to peer inside and inspect the whole cadaver.

'Yes, ma'am,' the sergeant replied, shifting her gaze from the emaciated torso to her boss's face.

'See what the constables have learned so far, eh? One of them should have spoken to Mrs Brodie by now. I'll need to talk to her myself later in the station, but get the rough sequence of events from them. I need to speak to the Super again. Our friend, the Prof, is due to arrive soon. Keep an eye out for him. Oh, and the Fiscal too, and bring them here the minute they come.'

PC Rowe was sitting stiffly at the wooden kitchen table, made uncomfortable by the heavy silence but unable to break it, and he glanced up as the sergeant approached. He looked fidgety and ill at ease, and as she came towards him he rose from his chair, relief transforming his features. In truth, he had no experience of the effects of shock and was embarrassed in the presence of grief, unable to think of anything to say, his limited repertoire of comforting platitudes having long since been exhausted. Any further questioning of the widow seemed unthinkable. She seemed unaware of his presence, remaining from minute to minute completely motionless, staring into space through sightless eyes.

'Could I see you for a second, constable?' Alice said, smiling at the woman as if asking her permission to borrow her companion for a moment. She did not look up, and showed no sign that she was aware that someone else had joined them. Without further invitation the young man raced out of the kitchen, closing the door behind him.

'Have you spoken to her yet?' Alice enquired.

'Not really. Just a quick chat when we first arrived.'

'And?'

'She found the body . . .' he began breathlessly. 'She went into his room. She's got her own one. Opened those shutter things as usual and found him lying there. Dead an' all. She got on the phone to us straight away. She reported it.'

'And you were the first on the scene?'

'Me and him,' he said, pointing to the passing figure of the other constable.

At the sound of approaching feet they moved away from the hall door to allow a group of SOCOs to enter.

Alice caught sight of a rotund, freckle-faced man ambling behind them, weighed down by an oversized black attaché case. Seeing her he beamed cheerily in her direction, adding a wave for good measure, and noting the constable's curious expression she said, 'That's the Crime Scene Manager, an old pal of mine. Now, did Mrs Brodie say when exactly she last saw her husband alive?'

'Yep. She saw him at about 4.30 p.m. yesterday. She spent the evening out and she didn't look in on him after that.'

'Anyone else see him after her, as far as she knows?'

'Erm . . .' the constable hesitated, and then said apologetically, 'I hadn't quite finished speaking to her, so I'm not sure about that one.'

Despatching a slightly crestfallen PC Rowe to see if the pathologist had arrived, Alice re-entered the kitchen, and sat down opposite Heather Brodie. A huge vase of red roses obscured her view of the woman's face. As she moved it to one side, she said, 'They're lovely – a present?'

'Yes, a gift,' the woman replied, looking at them. 'From . . . ah, my mother-in-law.'

'The constable who was with you, PC Rowe, says you last saw your husband at about 4.30 p.m. Would anyone else have seen him after that?'

Such a long silence followed the question that Alice was just about to pose it again, when in a dull voice the answer came.

'Una, I expect. She'd have given him his supper, his bath. Tidied him up . . .'

'And when would Una have done that?'

Another long pause followed, then the woman said, 'Seven . . . Quarter-past, maybe, that's her usual time.'

'And who is Una, exactly?'

'She's . . .' the woman hesitated, 'his carer. Una Reid, my husband's carer. We employ her. She comes from Abbey Park Lodge . . . you know, the home, the place in Comely Bank.'

DCI Bell swept into the kitchen, accompanied by a giant of a man with a pale moon-face, which rounded off, unexpectedly, into a luxuriant auburn beard. Once inside he stood erect, fingering his moustache-ends nervously, fashioning them into points by twirling their ends to and fro between his thumbs and index fingers.

'This is Thomas Riddell, our Family Liaison Officer, Mrs Brodie,' Elaine Bell announced, feeling the need to introduce him to the widow but not herself, she, apparently, needing no introduction. Sitting down next to the woman, and without any preamble, she started to fire a burst of staccato questions at her.

'Anything gone from this room? Anything sharp, like a knife, for example?'

'No.'

'You've checked then?'

'No, I haven't . . . I'll just check now, will I?' Heather Brodie asked, seeking the policewoman's leave before, looking slightly dazed, she got up slowly and walked towards an old-fashioned Welsh dresser, rummaging inside both its drawers before saying, almost apologetically, 'I don't think anything's missing from here. But,' she paused briefly, '. . . a knife's gone from the block. Usually there are five in it. Now it's only got four. I can see the space for it from here.'

'Could it be in the dishwasher, the sink, somewhere like that?' the DCI responded immediately.

'No,' Heather Brodie answered. 'I never use those knives. They were given to us as a wedding present, but

19

I didn't like them, so I never used them.' For the first time she lifted her deep blue eyes and looked directly into the Inspector's face, being met by an unblinking, rather stony, gaze.

'Have you noticed anything else missing – anything shifted, disarranged . . . out of place, as if a stranger had been at it?'

The woman nodded.

'Well?' the DCI shot back, not troubling to disguise her impatience, the need for further elaboration blindingly obvious to her. Riddell, the liaison officer, threw his boss a reproachful glance, wordlessly reminding her that shock could cause confusion, but he got no expression of understanding or remorse in return.

'My laptop's gone from in here. It was in its case . . . and Gavin, my husband, his wallet's been taken too, I think. It was always kept by his bed. Not that he ever used it, but he liked it to be there. It's not there now. It was always kept beside the water glass . . . but that's full of blood now. And it's gone. They've taken all his bottles of medicine, pills, everythi . . .' Her voice tailed off into a sob.

'Mrs Brodie?' Thomas Riddell said, 'have you got anyone you could stay the night with, or even for the next few days – children, or your mother? You won't want to spend any more time here than you need, I'm sure. And then we can get on with things . . . after that we'll get the place cleaned up for you.'

'Yes. A good idea. Leave the house,' Elaine Bell said curtly, before the widow had time to reply. She added, in a softer tone, 'We've a few more . . . er, things to attend to here. It'll take maybe another half an hour. Then it would be helpful, if you wouldn't mind, if you came with us to the station. We need a little more information from you. So I'll get a WPC to collect some overnight things for you right now.'

'Ma'am,' PC Rowe stuck his head round the door. 'That's Professor McConnachie here the now. I showed him into the victim's bedroom and he told me to come and get you.'

'One other thing,' Heather Brodie said, aware that the Inspector's attention was shifting away from her, 'I think my jewellery case's gone too. I looked for it last night when I got back, but I couldn't find it anywhere. I'd taken a bracelet out earlier that evening. None of it was good, but it was all of sentimental value. A photograph, one of my daughter, in an antique silver frame, it's gone too. My husband kept it by his bed.'

Professor Daniel McConnachie was leaning over the gash in the dead man's neck, examining it closely through his half-moon spectacles and humming Beethoven's 'Ode to Joy' rapidly through his teeth. Alerted by the rustling of Elaine Bell's paper suit he looked up as she bustled towards him, Alice following in her slipstream.

'Ah, the two lovely ladies have arrived. And how are you both?'

'Lets just get on with it, shall we?' the DCI answered, feeling out of sorts, unwilling to engage in their usual raillery.

'As you wish, Elaine,' he began, gesturing expansively at the blood-spatters on the wall as if it at a sample of Chinese silk wallpaper. 'It's obvious that this isn't an accidental death. The wound's not self-inflicted either, by the look of things. There is a hesitation mark, a tiny one . . .

but I don't doubt that we should treat this as a homicide nonetheless. Have you found the weapon?'

'Maybe,' the Inspector said cagily. 'A knife may be missing from the kitchen. Where's the hesitation mark?'

A latex-encased finger was pointed at a single minute slit-mark directly above the gash.

'What's that mean?' the policewoman asked.

'Just what it says – hesitation, dithering. In suicides it's usually a little experiment before the final cut, and much the same, really, in homicide. A moment of indecision before the deed's done.'

'So what d'you think we're dealing with here?'

'But that's your job, Elaine, isn't it?' he replied tartly, still smarting from her initial show of impatience. He continued his inspection of the dead man's fingernails, one of which was unnaturally long.

'OK, OK, I'm sorry. Please . . . it might be helpful. A fair amount of stuff seems to have been taken from the house, and presumably the injuries are consistent with that – with a botched robbery, I mean, with Brodie being killed in the course of it?'

'Possibly,' the professor answered, but his shrugged shoulders suggested that he was not persuaded.

'Well, if not that, why not that?' Elaine Bell asked, exasperated by his guarded response.

'Because of the knife – the throat-cutting,' a voice from the door said. PC Rowe had slipped into the room and been unable to stop himself from answering, alerting all to his presence despite knowing the likely consequences of his speech.

'What the hell are you doing in here?' The DCI spun round, glaring at the young man.

'But the boy's right, of course,' the professor said, magisterially. 'Your average thieving ned, robber and so on, doesn't cut throats, does he? If disturbed or whatever, he, or they, just grab the nearest weapon . . .' He hesitated, looking round the room. 'Something like that lamp over there or . . . or the carafe, even. They beat the person to a pulp, don't they? Beat them about the head. They don't come, like a surgeon, prepared with a knife.'

'These ones didn't come prepared either,' Elaine Bell interjected. 'They just used what they could find.'

'Even so . . .'

'And they took stuff, quite a lot of stuff.'

'Could be mementoes of the killing or something like that – who knows?'

'Mementoes! A wallet, a computer, a jewellery box? I don't think so.'

'All I'm saying,' the professor answered, gazing at the corpse, 'is that you'd best keep an open mind, Elaine, hadn't you? Remember what happened last time? Of course, this might well be the handiwork of an opportunist thief or thieves. But it might, just might, be that of a cold-blooded murderer. I wouldn't exclude that possibility quite yet.'

3

In the interview room at St Leonard's Police Station shortly before noon, Heather Brodie closed her eyes and tried to gather her wayward thoughts, to concentrate, ensure that she did not speak nonsense or worse. Lying was not easy at the best of times, and this would need to be a good performance. So much depended on it. Below the table, unconsciously, she was rubbing her hands together, washing them in accordance with her nurse training, linking her fingers at the knuckles, locking them and moving them from side to side, engaging her thumbs and then releasing them before starting the endless cycle once more. It was a nervous habit, like the clicking noise her tongue made on the roof of her mouth when she was over-anxious but pretending to be carefree.

She picked up her cup and took a gulp of tepid tea, trying to focus on her surroundings and the people with her. The stuff was so watery, it could have been China or Indian, it was impossible to tell from the taste.

'Mrs Brodie,' DCI Bell repeated irritably, trying for a second time to gain her attention. The woman had not appeared to hear a word of the policewoman's earlier set speech, the routine one apologising for 'intruding at such a time', her mind clearly elsewhere.

'Yes?'

'As I said before, you left your husband at 4.30 p.m.?'

'No,' the woman corrected her, forcing her mind to engage. 'I didn't leave him then. I last saw him then. I left our flat at more like 6.30 p.m., I think.'

The Inspector nodded and then looked enquiringly into Heather Brodie's eyes as if to nudge her into divulging more information. In particular, where she had gone when she left the flat.

'Well,' Heather Brodie continued, 'I had plans . . . had arranged, in fact, to meet up with my sister. We'd intended to go out for a meal, then on to the theatre, and I was going to spend the night with her, but I changed my mind and came home.'

'So what did you do instead?' the DCI asked, tapping her yellow biro on her cheekbone as she spoke.

'No, that's what I did do. We went shopping, had a meal and then went on to see the play. But, for some reason, I changed my mind about staying with her, and I came back here instead.'

'Getting home at?'

'At . . . about 11.30 p.m., I think.'

'Then I expect you looked in on your husband, him being an invalid and all?'

'No.'

'No. Why not?' The question was posed in a puzzled tone, with an air of false concern.

'I put my head round the door, but I didn't see him. It was too dark.'

'You could have put a lamp on or something, surely?' The DCI's brows were knitted and the speed of her cheek-tapping with the biro had increased.

'Yes, but, to be quite honest, I wasn't in the mood. I'd already said goodnight earlier. I didn't want to wake him, and the radio hadn't been left on, as it sometimes is. I was tired and I wanted to get to my bed.'

She suppressed an impulse to grab the ever-moving pen from her questioner's hand.

'When did you last lock the back door? Was it before you left, or when you came back, or the day before or when, exactly?'

'I couldn't really say. I try to remember to do it every night. My daughter, Ella, is always at me to check it, but it's just part of my routine. So sometimes I do forget. I know I do. I can't say when I last checked it. All I can say is that I try to remember to do it every night. Was it open or something?'

'Yes. Does anyone apart from you have keys to the property?'

'Una Reid. My son, Harry, my daughter, Ella, my mother in law . . . Pippa, my sister, as well. Then they can visit if I'm out. Gavin likes company, needs it, in fact. And I can't be there all the time, with him always . . .' she ended, defensively.

'Your husband's illness – what was wrong with him?'

'Huntingdon's Disease. In the old days it used to be called Huntingdon's Chorea. He's been virtually bed-ridden for the last year or so. Hasn't been able to work for longer than that.'

'What was his work?'

Silence followed. Heather Brodie did not answer because her attention had drifted once more, she had not heard the question, just as she did not see Thomas Riddell enter the room. Tears were now flowing unchecked down her cheeks, and she had no hankie with her to wipe them away.

As if aware of the spectacle she was making of herself,

she turned her head to the side, humiliated to be seen in such a state by strangers, and pretended to look out of the window. But, with vision blurred, she saw almost nothing of the traffic rattling by on St Leonards Street. Her nose began to run, and just as she was about to break the habits of a lifetime and use the back of her hand, a paper hankie was proffered. Sniffing self consciously, she took it and dabbed her nose and cheeks, alert once more to all the eyes on her. Thomas Riddell removed another hankie from his packet, offered it to her and then changed his mind, passing her the whole packet instead. She blinked her large blue eyes at him to express her gratitude. 'So, Mrs Brodie,' the DCI continued. 'Your husband's job?'

'He was an accountant. Initially he had his own business in Abercrombie Place. He employed three others. But, well . . . as the disease progressed things got more and more difficult. In the end it all fell to pieces . . .' Her voice tailed off.

'Fell to pieces?' the Chief Inspector repeated.

'Oh, his concentration went. He was on too many drugs, to stop the movements and so on. One of his clients sued him, something to do with underestimating tax liabilities or something. The woman went bust eventually. She was as mad as a hatter. The insurers handled it all for us, of course, but Gavin took fright. So did I, actually. I thought we'd lose the house, what with the legal expenses and everything.'

'One thing, Mrs Brodie,' Alice said, as they all rose to go. 'Why did you change your arrangements, decide not to stay with your sister, I mean?'

'I don't know. I wasn't in the right frame of mind. I just wasn't in the right mood, I wanted to be back in my own home.'

At 11 p.m. Alice Rice was still sitting at her desk in the incident room, both hands covering her eyes, feeling almost nauseous with fatigue. She had spent the past few hours staring at her computer screen, reading bulletins on the Scottish Intelligence database. Among the hundreds of opportunist thieves listed on there, only five seemed possible, and only one of those was suspected of having been recently 'active in the New Town area' of Edinburgh. He was a nineteen-year-old youth named Billy Wallace, who had rarely seen the inside of his own home, having been in a succession of foster homes, residential schools and penal institutions since the age of eight.

Tomorrow, she thought, she must become similarly 'active', not stealing things but buying them. Her lover's fortieth birthday, and nothing yet in the bag for him, despite his unsubtle reminders and hour upon hour spent in crowded shops seeking, but not finding, inspiration. Time must be made – no, stolen if need be, otherwise Ian would be hurt. A wet suit, maybe or . . . or what? Too late already to wake him up on his birthday-morning with his present, as she had envisaged.

Her eye-sockets ached and she was, she knew, no longer thinking clearly. Nonetheless, she turned back to the monitor, ready to try to scan the next page, hoping to achieve something before leaving. As she did so, a bleary-eyed Thomas Riddell returned to the room with DCI Bell bustling behind him, crunching noisily on a barley sugar and almost shooing him onwards with her hands in her impatience to get on. As he was collecting his coat from the back of a chair she said, her mouth still partly full, 'Alice, did you get the list of Brodie's prescription drugs from the GP?'

'Yes, it's on the system now. Plenty of saleable stuff amongst it, too.'

'Right. Any luck with the bulletins yet?'

'Only one real possibility so far, I'm afraid. Someone called Billy Wallace, if that name means anything to you.'

'"Braveheart"? Or "Softheid", as I prefer to call him.'

'You know him?'

'Mmm. He's a regular – a junkie,' she nodded. 'Anyway, you'd best get home now. You and Eric can see our hero first thing tomorrow.'

'Suppose, ma'am, it's not a thief, like the Prof said,' Thomas Riddell asked, yawning uncontrollably. 'Are we any further on, with the loony brigade, I mean?'

'No,' Bell replied, hesitating as she swallowed the remains of her sweet, 'we are not. Light-fingered bastards are two a penny, aren't they? Whereas, fortunately for all of us, your cold-blooded killer's a much rarer bird. Have you heard whether anything interesting's turned up from the door to doors in India Street?'

The large man shook his head and then, with old-fashioned gallantry, held up Alice's coat for her to put her arms into. Then he lumbered wearily towards the door, putting his hand to his mouth to conceal another huge yawn.

As soon as he had gone, the DCI asked, 'D'you know him, Alice? Ever worked with him before?'

'No. Why?' Alice replied, shaking her head.

'Isn't he the one that was following Susan Burton around – remember the one she couldn't shake off, until she managed to wangle a transfer to Fettes?'

'Gollum?'

'I think so. So watch yourself.'

29

Monday

The boy they had come to see was standing behind the bar, drying a white china water jug on a stained dishcloth and whistling to himself. Billy Wallace looked up on their approach, taking them for customers, and a winning smile transformed his sallow face.

'What can I get youse?' he asked, hanging the cloth over his shoulder, his hand already hovering playfully over the beer taps.

'Nothin', son,' DI Eric Manson replied. 'We just need to speak to you . . . get a wee bit of information off you.'

'Polis!' the boy hissed, sounding disgusted 'I've nothin' tae say tae youse. I dinnae hae tae speak tae youse neither, ye cannae make me,' and he deliberately turned his back on them and began stacking glasses noisily on a shelf, his sharp, boyish elbows visible below the sleeves of his short-sleeved green shirt.

'Oh?' Eric Manson said, and his intonation of the single syllable made it quite plain that he thought they could make him.

'Billy! Billy!' A loud female voice called through a doorway, above which was tacked a sign stating 'Kitchen Staff Only'

The boy turned; then, as if he had heard nothing, continued his stacking. Now he speeded up as if he was in a competition, or racing against the clock. A few seconds later, a dumpy woman with dyed plum-coloured hair and a bust straining to escape from a purple and black tartan waistcoat, marched through the doorway, nodded at the two plain-clothes police officers and tapped the boy's shoulder.

'Billy, did you no' hear me shoutin' oan you?'

'Em . . . no, Elsie,' he answered her, a look of injured innocence on his face. He continued with his job, studiously ignoring the sceptical expressions directed at him. His lie sounded completely convincing.

'Enjoyin' yer work tae much, eh, son?' she laughed good-naturedly. 'You'll need tae get oan an serve they customers, eh? Rab says aifter you've finished in here you're tae come an' help us in the kitchen. There's a party of fifteen comin' in fer bar lunches, an office outin' or somethin'. You'll be needed tae help wi' makin' the soup.'

The boy nodded, and pinching his cheek affectionately between her fingers and thumb, the woman bustled towards the doorway and disappeared once more.

'So, Billy,' Eric Manson said, 'better help us out the now. Right now. We wouldn't want to have to follow you about the place asking questions as you're busy chopping the carrots up, eh? Might look a wee bit strange. I wonder if Elsie, or whatever she's called, knows about you? Your record, I mean, your wee brushes with the law? I bet she's not aware that you're a thief, a druggie with a string of previous convictions long enough to hang your boxers on? Or that you're handy with knives, too – but slicing up people, not veg.'

Recognising that he was beaten, Billy Wallace looked the Inspector in the face, folded his arms defensively across his narrow chest and said, in a low, desperate voice, 'Naebody here kens, OK? So dae us a favour an' make this quick.'

DI Manson smiled, stretched across the bar and took a bag of peanuts. He made no attempt to pay for them, opened them and then, in a leisurely fashion, trawled his fingers through the bag before picking up a handful and putting it into his mouth. Crunching noisily, he dipped in for more and slowly began feeding himself individual nuts.

Watching him, the boy looked frantic.

'Where were you on Saturday night, Billy?' Alice asked, taking pity on him.

'Ma nicht aff, Saturdays,' he answered immediately, sniffing loudly and wiping his nose with the side of his hand. 'I'm always aff Saturday nichts.'

'What did you do on your night off?'

'A little light housebreaking, perhaps?' Eric Manson interjected, his voice slurred with masticated peanuts. Ignoring the remark, the boy continued. 'Eh . . . I wis in ma ain hoose, playin' oan ma gameboy 'n' that, then I watched a couple o' DVDs.'

A man with glazed eyes and skin as dry as paper slumped onto the bar stool at Alice's elbow, and crooked a nicotine-stained finger at Billy several times. Getting no response, he thumped the bar with his fist. As he did so, little snowflakes of dandruff sprinkled on his shoulders, a few cascading down his greasy, orange anorak and landing on his fleshless thighs.

'Billy!' he shouted 'Shift yer airse. Ah'm wantin' a drink ower here.'

First catching Alice's eye, the boy moved along the bar until he was directly opposite the new customer and pulled him a pint of Tartan Special, then set it in front of him. No sooner had the glass made contact with the coaster than it was raised to the drinker's mouth. Kissing its edge theatrically, he began to pour it down his throat, his Adam's apple bobbing up and down rhythmically as he did so. As Billy turned back towards the police officers, his young face now contorted with anxiety, the man took a breath and said crossly, 'An' ma chaser son – mind ma chaser.'

Billy placed the measure of Bells next to the half-empty beer glass and the customer rose unsteadily from his stool, a drink in either hand, and set out for a table, drawn to an old copy of the *Daily Record* lying on it.

'All evening – you spent the whole night in?' Alice asked the boy.

'Aye.' He sniffed again.

'On your own?'

'Naw'

'Who was with you?'

'Ma girlfriend, Tracey.'

'Tracey what? Where does she live?'

'Wi' me . . . in ma flat in Drylaw. She's there the now. She wis washin' her hair.'

'Maybe that's what she'll say,' Eric Manson cut in, shaking his head in disbelief, and adding in a loud voice, 'she'll say that you were with her. But know what I think? I think it's all rubbish. I think you cannae kick the habit, that you've been up to your old tricks lately, Billy boy.'

Grinning now with false bonhomie, he helped himself to a stray bowl of last night's Bombay mix and chewed a mouthful slowly, all the while keeping his eyes fixed on the boy. Never shifting his gaze, he took another handful and inadvertently put a used matchstick into his mouth, crunched it, then grabbed a paper napkin and spat the mouthful onto it.

'Naw, I've not,' the boy answered, his face contorted with disgust at Manson's eating habits, forgetting to pretend that he did not know what his old tricks might be.

'I heard,' the inspector continued, wiping saliva from the edge of his lips with the soiled napkin, 'that you nipped into a flat in St Stephen's Street a couple of weeks ago – you and one of your wee pals, maybe?'

'Nah,' the boy began, shaking his head. 'I'm clean. I've a job now. I dinnae need tae knock oaf other folk's stu . . .' but he never completed his sentence, stopping the instant he caught sight of the manageress's burly figure bearing down on him, a scowl on her face.

'No' finished in here yet, son?' she asked. Then tipping her head in the direction of the two police officers, she added, 'Who're they? They pals of yours or somethin'? They're no' drinkin'. They holdin' you up?'

Billy Wallace threw a pleading glance at the officers, begging them to remain silent. Eric Manson winked at him, as if to say he had got the message, then replied to the woman, 'No, we're not pals of his, dear. And we can't take a drink . . . not whilst we're on duty, you understand.'

—

In Wallace's spotless council flat in Wester Drylaw Avenue, Tracey nodded her slick, black ponytail up and down and said: 'He was wi' me – like what he said.'

Having answered their question, she leaned back in the leather settee where a small, dark-featured man sat next to her, and returned her attention to her crisps and the television.

'How do you know he told us that?' Eric Manson demanded, a complacent smile playing on his lips as he stood, legs apart, towering over the seated girl.

'Well . . . he would, wouldn't he, if you'd asked him.'

'But how d'you know we asked him anything?' the inspector shot back. 'He phoned you, eh? Told you we'd been round. Told you what to say and all.'

'Funnily enough, "officer", I didnae come up the Clyde oan a banana boat. Ye're asking aboot him, aren't ye? No me, really, no interested in me are ye? I am right aboot that, eh? So, ye'll have asked him first. That's how it works, how it aye works. An' no, fer the record, like, he didnae phone me.'

'All night? He was here, with you, all night?' Alice asked, but her voice was drowned out by the sound of excited applause from the studio audience on the TV.

'You were together all night?' she repeated loudly.

'Aye! What dae ye think I am? Think I'd sneak aff in the middle o' the night tae sleep wi' somebody else or somethin'? The fuckin' cheek o' it!'

'They botherin' you, chick?' the ferrety little man sitting beside the girl asked, raising his eyes from the screen to look menacingly at the two officers.

'Naw,' she replied idly, drawing deeply on her cigarette and flicking the snake's tail of ash into her empty coffee cup.

''Cause if they are,' the man said, putting his arm around her and fixing Eric Manson's eyes with his own bloodshot gaze, 'I'll just ask them to leave . . . politely like.'

'Is there anyone who saw you and Billy here, on the Sunday night?' Alice persisted.

'Aye,' the girl answered sarcastically, rolling her eyes at the stupidity of the question.

'Who?'

'Him,' she said, tweaking the fingers of the hand that was resting on her fleshy arm.

'"Him"? Sorry, but who is "him"? I mean what's his name?'

'*Him*. Meet ma lodger, Mr Ecky . . . naw, Mr Alistair

Cockburn – pronounced "Coburn",' she giggled, adding, 'the cock's silent, see?'

'Ma cockle doodle you . . .' the ferret guffawed, stroking the girl's ponytail.

'You can confirm that Billy Wallace was here all night?'

'Aye, you've ma word oan it . . . as a gentleman,' the man replied, laughing, his eyes back on the screen, pressing a button on the remote control and changing channels.

———

Catching sight of the clock in the Astra in which they were travelling, Alice asked her companion if the time shown was correct. Eric Manson nodded, but said nothing, his mind miles away, thinking of events earlier that day. What was his wife playing at? She had got up before him, dressed, and by the time he had wandered, sleepy-eyed, into the kitchen, she was already on the phone to someone. When she saw him, the smile on her face froze and she whispered, 'That's Eric. Got to go.'

When he questioned her she became angry with him, telling him to mind his own business, remarking crossly that she was not one of his suspects. Really, she wasn't behaving like the Margaret he knew at all. And nowadays she was always out, had some excuse or other for evenings away, jaunts taken here, there and everywhere, but always without him.

'Bugger!' Alice said.

'What's the matter?' he said, the concern in her voice interrupting his train of thought.

'I was supposed to be at the mortuary at twelve with the DCI.'

'Phone them. Tell them that we're running late but we're on our way.'

'They'll be all togged up, gloved up . . . probably left their phones in the changing room. Would you mind putting your foot down, Sir?'

'No problem, pet, but I reckon it's past praying for. We can be there in fifteen . . . no, make that thirteen minutes.' And so saying, he clamped the blue light onto the roof of the car and pressed down hard on the accelerator. They sped down Ferry Road, overtaking a juggernaut on Inverleith Row before screeching straight over the roundabout at Canonmills, just managing to jump an amber light from Broughton Street onto York Place, siren screaming like a banshee and drawing the attention of all the passers-by. North Bridge passed in a flash, then they jinked eastwards, in short bursts, turning left down the Mile, rumbling over the cobbles down to St Mary's Street past the Ben Line Building and, finally, entering the sunless corridor of the Cowgate.

By the time they bumped to a halt, Alice was feeling thoroughly shaken up and on edge, expecting a bollocking from the DCI for her lateness and still seeing in her mind's eye the face of the startled pedestrian who was brushed by their car mirror at a zebra crossing. But adrenalin was coursing through her driver's veins, making him bubble with excitement and goodwill, his earlier anxieties temporarily banished by the rush. Eleven minutes!

Shouting her thanks, she dashed from the car, only to find herself blocked at the entry-phone. There she waited for a few more precious minutes, stamping her feet impatiently on the greasy tarmac, the urgency in her voice insufficient to persuade the man on the door to adopt anything other than his usual sloth's pace. He knew her, of course, and could see her on the CCTV monitor, but there were procedures to be followed, otherwise any Tom,

Dick or Harry might gain access to the place. She caught the DI's eye as he sat, engine revving intermittently to warm the air, waiting for her in case she had missed the show completely. Watching her, he shook his head slowly in disbelief at her treatment.

When, finally, the heavy black door opened, Elaine Bell came striding out, pulling on her coat as she walked. Seeing Alice she said tersely, 'Fat lot of use you are now. The party's over. The parcel's open, the cake's been cut. So, where the hell have you been?'

'Billy Wallace had an alibi – his girlfriend. We had to check it out.'

'And my calls? Why didn't you answer them?'

An angry red line encircled Elaine Bell's brow from the over-tight paper cap she had worn in the mortuary, and as she spoke, she distractedly fingered its contour with the tips of her fingers.

'I never got any calls, there can't have been any reception. I'm sorry, Ma'am.'

'You didn't have to go to check it out there and then, you could have waited until after the P.M., couldn't you?'

'Seemed safer to follow it up. Wallace told us that she was in the flat, if we'd waited she might have gone out.'

'Alright, alright. Fine. What did she have to say?'

'She said that he was with her, but I'm not convinced. I've checked with Alistair and she's got form too. A junkie, in and out of Cornton Vale like a yo-yo, so she knows the ropes. She might say almost anything. How did you get on with the Professor?'

'Never mind that now. Is that Eric, sitting wasting time, twiddling his thumbs in the car?' asked the DCI, looking up at the grey sky and holding out her palms to catch the first few drops of rain.

'Mmm.'

'Good. He can take us back to the station. I want to speak to the whole squad – before lunch.'

———

Elaine Bell paced up and down while addressing her team, her notebook open and held at arm's length as she squinted at it with her longsighted eyes.

'Let me see . . . well, McConnachie wasn't prepared to stick his neck out, as bloody usual, so we've a window of nine hours at the moment. Time of death sometime between 4.30 pm, when the victim was last seen alive, and 2 or 3 am.'

'Why such a long period?' Alistair Watt asked, crossing his long legs.

'"Little rigor mortis, but a very thin corpse", it says here. God only knows.'

'And the cause of death?' DI Manson asked, rubbing his chin thoughtfully.

'Cause is . . . "exsanguination". The poor bastard bled to death, hence his colourless appearance – and the spray-paint on the walls, of course.'

She turned over the page and stared hard at it, screwing up her eyes and trying to make out her own brief notes, then mumbled, 'He said "wound inflicted from front . . . starting on left", so the attacker's probably left-handed . . . "complete transaction" – sorry, *"transection* of right jugular and common carotid".'

'The missing kitchen-knife?' Alice asked, her tummy rumbling in anticipation of lunch.

'He said "a sharp-ended thing", which I think's his usual code for a knife. Toxicology's to follow, but even that's going to be problematic, apparently, because there was so little blood left in the man's system. So, they'll have to analyse bits of the heart and liver as well,' she added, closing her notebook decisively with a business-like snap.

'That's it?' DI Manson said, in a tone of disbelief.

'That's it, yes, all we've got. They may be able to firm up on the time of death after they've done a stomach contents. Otherwise, that's it for now at least.'

'So, Wallace's got an alibi then has he?' DC Littlewood mused, leaning back on his seat, his hands clasped over his rounded belly, and looking enquiringly at Alice.

'An alibi worth doodly squat, or, as we might say, fuck all,' Eric Manson butted in. 'It consists of Tracey's word, backed up by the boy's favourite partner in crime.'

'True enough,' the DCI said wearily, 'it's not worth much, but for the moment he's our only lead. No report back from the lab as yet. And you've still got nothing from the door-to-doors, eh, Alistair?'

DS Alistair Watt shook his head. 'Nothing so far. Saturday was a pretty hellish night, weather-wise, everybody seems to have been tucked up indoors with their tellies. Uniforms are re-doing the whole area in case they manage to catch someone new in, but so far, nothing. The dogs have been all round India Street, the Jamaica Street lanes and Gloucester Lane and Terrace, but they've drawn a blank too.'

'What about Una Reid, the man's carer, has she been tracked down? Until we find her, we don't even know when, precisely, he was last seen alive.'

'Nope,' the sergeant shook his head. 'Her flat's deserted, apparently she's away for a few days – somewhere in the Aberdeen area. But her work have no idea where exactly, and nor does Heather Brodie.'

40

Back in her office, Elaine Bell gazed out of her window, her attention caught briefly by a man on Arthur's Seat trailing a kite behind him, its tail writhing sinuous as a snake while it rose slowly heavenwards, caught by a gust of wind. Sighing, she moved back to her desk. She had already passed such news as there was on to the Superintendent, desperately trying to dress up the truth to make it sound less feeble.

But when he heard the update, unimpressive despite her best efforts, her superior had sounded positively pleased. Of course, it made perfect sense. Disliking her as heartily as he did, and due to retire in less than five months, news like this was music to his oversized ears. After all, what would be more likely to stymie her prospects of promotion to his post than an unsuccessful murder investigation?

Thinking about him and his malevolence towards her, the findings of the review team on the Dyce killing came to mind, and as she reflected on them she unconsciously started to chew her bottom lip. Yes, she had missed one line of enquiry on it, that was undeniable, but it had made no difference whatsoever to the end result. They had still got their man, hadn't they? And the brass knew that too, and would put it down on her tab. But, she thought, a sudden, uncharacteristic doubt assailing her, maybe I am losing my touch. Perhaps I'm not as sharp as I was, and Chief Inspector is my limit – my ceiling. Perhaps this is it, as far as I can go.

D.C. Littlewood put his head round the door and waggled a long brown envelope at her. 'A present from the Super,' he said brightly, as he handed it over. The second he left the room she tore it open. Her eyes scanned the first page of her annual appraisal hungrily, but halfway down it, a feeling of dread had begun to overwhelm her, making her stomach churn and her mouth feel dry. But by the time she had worked her way to the end of the document, her mood had changed again and she was incensed, almost trembling with fury. It was outrageous. The bastard had finally done it, shown his true colours, and well and truly shafted her in the process.

'Fuck!' she said out loud, throwing the papers onto her desk in disgust. The report was late, as always, but had not been prepared in haste. Its author had carefully chosen his words in order to produce the perfect hatchet-job. The appraisal narrated dutifully all that she had accomplished, conscientiously listed all her responsibilities and skills, and made it plain that she had achieved only what was asked of her, and not a jot more. It told everyone that there was nothing exceptional about her, that she had no outstanding qualities, and that she fulfilled only the most basic requirements of a Chief Inspector's post. And by its excessive restraint, its glaring omissions, it trumpeted to the world her professional inadequacy. The promotion board would likely take one glance at it and then drop it on the 'Not to Be Interviewed' pile.

Thinking of the fight ahead of her, of all the time she would have to spend trying to overturn his conclusions, Elaine covered her face with her hands. Every second was precious, needed for the investigation in hand, and her energy was in short supply. And he knew that too.

'Ma'am?' Alice said, stopping by the open door but, on seeing the distraught figure, reluctant to enter.

'Yes.'

'We've just heard that a man called Norman Clerk was released from Carstairs about a month ago. He was in for slitting the throat of an old lady. He comes from Edinburgh and his victim lived in the city too.'

'Why was he put in the bin rather than the jail?' Elaine Bell asked, her face still hidden.

'Supposedly he was schizophrenic. Eric says he remembers the case. Clerk cut the old lady's throat but claimed that a voice had ordered him to do it or something. He told me all about it.'

'And he's cured?'

'Apparently.'

'And he's back in the city now?' the DCI said, straightening up and uncovering her face.

'Somewhere in the Haymarket area. Eric's busy tracking down his address.'

'Well, we've nothing to lose, have we?' the DCI replied, almost jauntily. 'Go and see him, talk to him, get a handle on him. This minute. If nothing else, the timing's right, and it might, it just might, be more than coincidence. Take Tom Littlewood with you.'

4

Chewing on her scotch pie, Alice walked along Morrison Street with the rotund constable trotting beside her, his short, denim-clad legs taking two strides to her every one. He was busily explaining to her how to make the perfect beef madras, unaware that, above the roar of the traffic, she could only catch occasional isolated words like 'fenugreek' and then, a little later, 'scotch bonnet'.

As they crossed the junction with Dewar Place, a gust of chill wind hit her, sending a crumpled sheet of newsprint in the gutter spiralling upwards towards her head, and she dodged it, accidentally dropping her pie onto the pavement. She cursed, but her companion said smugly, 'Better for you,' taking his last mouthful of sushi and wiping his lips.

Turning eastwards, they crossed the busy road, dodging between the lanes of speeding traffic, heading for the blackened tenement building on the corner. Once there, they began hunting for 'Clerk' among the dozens of names on the doorbells. A young man wheeled his bicycle out of the main door, allowing Alice to walk into the common stair, and she signalled as she did so for her colleague to follow. In the absence of any glimmers of sunlight, the air inside seemed, if possible, colder and damper than that outside on the street, and she shivered, pulling the ends of her coat together and wishing it had not lost all its buttons.

'Here's an "R. Clerk" the DC said excitedly, his knuckles raised to knock on the door. She shook her head. 'Norman Arthur Clerk', the conviction sheet had said, so they continued upwards, checking every landing until on the third floor she saw a scrap of paper tacked onto the lintel with 'N. A. CLERK' written on it in large, uneven capitals. The door itself had the word 'Nonce' hacked into it with the blade of a knife. Standing there, they exchanged glances.

'What a depressing hole,' the constable remarked, absentmindedly dropping his empty sushi packet onto the stone floor where it joined the rest of the litter. The air trapped in the tenement smelt of stale, fried food, and flakes of cream paint were peeling off the ancient piping that snaked along its walls. Someone had taken the trouble to splash purple gloss paint onto the ceiling, and a few shiny stalactites hung down from it.

'If this is him, let's go in, eh?' Tom Littlewood said, eager to get on and finish the job, get out of the building and back out into Torphichen Street and daylight.

She nodded again, but said nothing, still trying to gather her thoughts and work out what she would ask the man. This might be their one and only chance. While she was still deep in thought, the door opened and their quarry appeared, his hand on the shoulder of an ancient crone, her spine so crooked that she could see nothing but the floor in front of her.

Looking directly at the police officers, he whispered, 'Bye, bye, Mum,' and released her to teeter towards the banister, which she gripped with a bony claw before looking anxiously down at the flights of stone stairs she would have to descend. Keeping his gaze fixed on Alice, Clerk nodded his head in the direction of his flat and said,

45

'Come on in. Your Inspector Manson told me the pair of you would be coming.'

A Sidney Devine record was playing on an old-fashioned gramophone. Clerk lowered the volume just enough to produce background music, before sitting down and raising a cloud of talcum powder from the seat of his chair, further scenting the already unsavoury air. Coughing theatrically, he fanned it away with his hands. Looking at them, Alice noticed how pudgy they were, his fingers like large, pale sausages. As he stared at her expectantly, he absent-mindedly conducted the music, jerking his thick forefingers to and fro in time with the beat. He was middle-aged and plump, thick cushions of flesh rippling when he moved, so that he reminded her, in his tight pink pullover, of an oversized marshmallow.

'Do you know someone called Gavin Brodie?' she began.

'No. The dead man, you mean? I don't know any dead people. You can't, can you?' he said, earnestly, his tongue protruding from the side of his mouth.

'How did you know he was dead?'

'Indeed, how did I know that he was dead?' he repeated.

'Yes. How did you know he was dead?' Was he deaf as well as schizophrenic, perhaps?

'I read it in the *Evening News*, "Accountant Found Murdered",' he answered, his tongue protruding once more from the side of his mouth.

'Did you know him – when he was alive, I mean?'

'You know what? I am parched, really parched. Dry as a bone,' he said, ignoring her question and, unexpectedly, rising to his feet and offering to make them both a cup of tea too.

Without waiting for an answer, he disappeared into his kitchenette, murmuring that it would do them good. Within minutes, a tray with three stained floral teacups and a plate of biscuits was placed in front of them and, as if they had accepted his offer, he proceeded to pour out tea and milk for them both, handing it over with a polite nod. When Alice took it and put it to her mouth, he smiled at her as if in encouragement or, perhaps, in recognition of some small victory, a wide grin dimpling his fat cheeks.

Carstairs, he said, sipping daintily from his own cup, had changed him completely, com-plete-ely.

When Alice enquired in what respect, he replied, 'Fish fingers. I enjoy them now, I didn't used to, you see. Oh, and I prefer a shower nowadays. I used to like baths, you see.'

'Anything else of any importance?' DC Littlewood chipped in sarcastically.

'I'm alright now, in *technical*, *medical* terms, I mean. Like everyone else. Indeed, right as rain. Don't hear voices in my head any more. Of course, I used to have to take medication for my condition when I was in the Big House, but not now. I stopped them myself a little while ago. I don't need any pills to keep me right nowadays.'

'Glad to be out of Carstairs, I expect, on your own again,' Alice said.

'Glad to be free of luncheon meat,' he said vehemently, puckering his lips. 'Glad to be able to get my teeth into something else. I had so much of that stuff it was coming right out of my ears. But that's what happens when you lose your human rights, of course. No Coca-Cola either… just Pepsi.'

'So, did you know Gavin Brodie . . . in life?'

'No . . . in life, no . . . the after-life? Well, I'm not there yet, heaven or . . .'

'Where were you on Saturday night from 5 o' clock onwards?' she interrupted him, determined to take hold of their rambling exchange.

Crunching a custard cream, he leant towards her and said excitedly that on that very night, the night she was interested in, the Saturday, he had undergone a life-changing experience. He had gone with a pal from the centre to an evening service in the nearby church, but the minister celebrating it had been a woman, and a fairly young one at that.

'Imagine that,' he said brightly to DC Littlewood, smacking his lips. 'A young woman!'

She had been attractive, too, with long blonde hair and a complexion like Queen Elizabeth's, all peaches and cream. Oh, she could minister to him anytime, he purred. In fact, the sooner the better. Perhaps, if she heard that he was 'sick', he'd get a home visit from her! And he'd been told often enough that he was sick . . . sick in the head, he giggled, pointing at his temple.

Then, seeing that his visitors were not laughing, he ostentatiously swept his hand from his forehead to his chin, transforming his expression into a deadly serious one as it passed over his face. He muttered out of the side of his mouth to the policeman, 'Bit of a killjoy, isn't she?'

'After the service, where did you go?' Alice continued.

'Home Sweet Home. Here.'

'And you were here throughout the whole of Saturday night?'

'Indeed no, sweetie. At about eight I went to my brother's flat. It's on the ground floor of this building, you see.'

'So, were you with him for the rest of the night, or did you come back here, or what?'

'Aha. I was with him.'

'All night?'

'All night?' he repeated, extending his tongue again and adding, 'Aha. I was with him.'

'That,' Alice said, 'would be your brother Robert, I suppose?'

'Yes, indeed, Robert. My, you may be no fun but you've fairly done your homework, haven't you?' he replied, taking a final swig from his cup.

'The same Robert who was prepared to give you an alibi at your trial for the night the old lady was killed by you?' DC Littlewood interjected.

'Yes. Good old Bob,' Clerk answered, unconcerned, rising from his chair and waiting behind it for them to do the same.

'One last thing, Mr Clerk. Did the voice, the one in your head, did it tell you to take the stuff from the old lady's flat – the TV and the little clock?' Alice asked.

'Well,' he said, opening the door for her and stroking his chin in thought, 'it did, you know. But no one's ever asked me about that before. The voice said, "Take the TV, Norman. Go on, take the telly." I heard it ordering me, as clear as a bell. Indeed I did. The clock, too. It was very taken with the clock for some reason or other, even though I said "it's not particularly valuable". I argued with it and argued with it, but it won – it always does, you see.'

'Your brother's flat. Where is it?'

'I told you,' he answered, 'on the ground floor. Number 3, if you must know. But I'm afraid you can't speak to him.'

'Why?'

'Because,' he replied, gesturing for them to leave, 'for one thing, he's still away at the Day Centre in Raeburn Place. He goes there every day. Well, every day since he got out of the hospital.'

'What's wrong with him?'

'He doesn't talk much any more,' Norman Clerk answered. 'In fact, since he had his stroke he's hardly uttered a single thing, in Queen's English, anyway. He's paralysed on the right side too. That's why I go along and look after him – help feed him, undress him, keep him company. Spend the night in his spare room. Mum used to do it, but, well, she's way past that now. He's got a carer, too, but she can't be there all the time, can she?'

Once they were back out on the street, Alice asked 'So, what's the verdict, Tom?'

'In *technical*, *medical* terms?'

'Indeed.'

'A mad tosspot of the first order.'

—

The Raeburn Day Centre was housed in a converted church on the main thoroughfare through Stockbridge, an unending stream of traffic passing close to its doors, deepening the black of its soot-stained masonry and making the very walls vibrate.

Inside, one of the swing-doors leading into the main hall was jammed open with a bucket. Alice peered self-consciously into the hall, her eyes eventually homing in on the only male in a wheelchair in the room. People sat in little groups about the place, some asleep, some knitting, a few talking in low voices to themselves or others.

Occupying the middle of the floor was a ring of office chairs, each with a bored old lady sitting in it. In the centre of the circle, like the bulls-eye, was a gargantuan man, his flesh seeping over the sides of his wheelchair. His partially-shaved head lolled to one side, but when prompted by a member of staff, he threw a tennis ball in the approximate direction of one of the circle, laughing loudly as it missed its target and bounced off the back of someone's chair.

A female cleaner, clad in a denim jacket and jeans and carrying a mop, attempted delicately to squeeze past Alice, stepping over the bucket into the hall. Moving out of the way, the Sergeant apologised and then asked, 'Is the man in the middle Robert Clerk?'

'Aye – he's like a big bairn,' the woman replied, rinsing her mop in the bucket and beginning to swab the lino closest to the door, adding as an afterthought, 'he's wan o' ma favourites.'

'Does he speak at all? Can he speak any more?'

'A wee bit, but I dinnae think he understan's a word said tae him. But he's aye in guid spirits, laughin', the life an' soul o' the party, like . . .'

Once the game was finished, a helper wheeled the man to the side of the hall, where he sat, smiling to himself, looking round at the others brightly and flexing one bandaged hand in and out to some internal rhythm.

When Alice approached him, bending down beside his wheelchair, he appeared not to notice her until she said, 'Excuse me, but are you Robert Clerk?'

Still looking straight ahead, he nodded his head up and down vigorously. A woman with childish features and the distinctive eye-folds of Down's syndrome ambled over and put her arm around the man's broad shoulders, tickling the back of his neck affectionately with her fingers. Her head was level with his, and when their eyes met the man chuckled delightedly.

51

'You want a biscuit, Bob?' she asked him. Once more he nodded, and when she asked whether he wanted a digestive or a bourbon or a piece of shortbread he assented to each suggestion in the same way.

'He likes them all? Every type?' Alice said conversationally to the small figure.

'No,' she said, looking fondly at him, 'he doesn't, but it's good manners, eh? To ask him. He only likes jammy dodgers really, don't you, Bob?'

And in response to the further question he nodded excitedly, his eyes never leaving his friend's figure as she set off for the tea-trolley on his behalf.

On impulse, Alice asked the man, 'Are you . . . Gordon Brown?' and as before, the man's head bobbed up and down, communicating that he was, indeed, the Prime Minister.

Alice's phone went, and she took it from her pocket.

'Alice, where are you?' It was DCI Bell, and she sounded rattled.

'I'm at the Day Centre on Raeburn Place, checking up on Clerk's alibi for the Saturday night. Tom's on his way back to the station.'

'And?'

'And . . . it's not up to much. He says he was with his brother, but the brother's had a stro . . .' Her voice became inaudible as loud cha-cha music started up, a few elderly people taking to the floor. She moved towards the entrance.

'Jammy Dodger?' the little Down's syndrome woman asked, offering her one from a plateful.

She shook her head, speaking into the phone again. 'The man's had a stroke, so he can't tell us whether his brother was with him on the Saturday night or not. There's a mother, I was going to go and . . .'

'Never mind that now. Clerk's a long shot. I need you to meet Eric at the bank by Saughtonhall Drive. The Fraud Squad's just tipped us the wink that someone's used Brodie's card at an ATM machine on the Corstorphine Road. The CCTV footage reveals that it's Ally Livingstone.'

'I thought he was still inside.'

'Well, he isn't. So speak to the manager, then go pick him up and bring him straight here.'

———

Usually, having his wife's fingertips resting on the handle of the supermarket trolley, restraining it, blatantly attempting to control it, maddened him. But this morning Ally Livingstone did not mind, he even allowed himself to be cajoled into traipsing up and down all the aisles, including the pet food one, although they owned neither dog nor cat. Seeing his heavily pregnant wife helping herself from the shelves, unconcerned about the cost and indulging in needless extravagances, pleased him, and on the only occasion on which she hesitated, he nodded at her indulgently, signalling for her to add the item to their load, just as a rich man would.

At the till he stood, legs crossed and arms folded, watching as the women packed the carrier bags, Frankie talking to the check-out girl as if they were old friends and surreptitiously adding some last-minute purchases, a couple of packets of chewing gum for each of them. Juicy Fruit for him and Wrigley's Spearmint for her. Only at the kiosk did he lose his temper, after waiting for seven other people to be served before them and then being told that they had no Lambert and Butler left.

Back in the car, the three measures of whisky that he had downed in O'Riordan's Bar earlier that day warmed him still, making him feel good-humoured once more, content with the world and all its works. As they approached the traffic lights on Gorgie Road, he had a sudden idea, a truly inspired one. He had bought loads of stuff for Frankie and the wee man, so now it was his turn!

'Stop the car a minute, hen,' he commanded, and obediently she flicked on the indicator and drew slowly to the pavement, coming to a halt on the double yellow lines opposite the pet shop.

'Dinnae go an' get another o' them fish now, Ally,' she said wearily, looking over at the pet store as he let himself out the Nissan. She added, 'The pump's no' workin', an' all they cherry barbs 'n' tiger barbs are deid, mind.'

'Aha,' he said, slamming the car door and lumbering eagerly along the pavement, heading straight for 'Furry Friends', his mouth curving into a wide smile in his glee. In his absence his wife watched the endless stream of pedestrians dawdling along, heads sunk into their shoulders and their carrier bags half-empty, wondering why only old people were out and about at this time of day. The Credit Crunch maybe?

When she inadvertently caught the eye of a prowling traffic warden, she smiled meekly at him, dropping her eyes to her distended belly, drawing his attention to it by way of excuse for parking illegally. Frowning, he nodded back at her, ostentatiously returning his notebook into his unbuttoned front pocket. Thanks, ye wee Hitler, she mouthed, eyelashes fluttering at him.

After ten minutes she began to feel restive, her swollen belly slightly compressed by the steering wheel and her back beginning to ache. She shifted her position, forcing herself to sit up straight, leaving a few inches between her tummy and the wheel. She was, she decided, looking down at the disappearing curve, nothing more than a monstrous bag of flesh, some kind of childbearing pod. Even her fingers had become fat, so thick that she could feel her pulse throbbing in the one encircled by her new engagement ring. An antique, no less, Ally had boasted that morning as he had wrestled to push it over her knuckle, after first fastening the matching chain of pearls around her neck. Old-fashioned crap, she had thought to herself. A band of white gold with a single diamond had been what she had expected, what she wanted.

The loud noise made by her husband as he clambered into the back seat, shuffling the bulging Mothercare bags along it with his hip, ended her musing. Glancing in the rear-view mirror she saw on his lap a cardboard box. It had tipped on its side, and his head and shoulders seemed to be disappearing inside it.

'C'mon, back here, ye wee sod . . .' he muttered, grasping at air, and then, pushing the box to one side, he bent over to look under the passenger seat, laughing uproariously to himself as he did so.

'What you get?' she asked idly, heading off into the traffic again and concentrating on her driving. He did not answer her, so she tried again 'What d'you get? No' another of they tortoise things?'

'Naw,' he replied. 'Em, just a wee . . .' he hesitated, breathless from being bent double, 'em . . . just a wee . . . eh, snake.'

'A snake! A snake! Fer fuck's sake, Ally, tell me there's no' a snake loose in ma car?'

'Naw,' replied Ally. 'Naw, hen – no' loose, really. It's gone an' trapped itsel' under the mat.'

'Is it poisonous? A poisonous wan? 'Cause if it is, ah'm oot o' here.'

When they got home, she pulled the handbrake on sharply and made to leave the car, but as she was doing so he shouted at her, his hands scrabbling wildly under the passenger's seat. 'Keep your bloody door shut, mind, or it'll be oot an' a'!'

'Ally,' she said, close to tears, 'I'm no' staying here, getting a snake's fangs in ma ankle, just because you . . .'

'Frankie, Frankie, it's OK, Frankie. Honest, it's OK,' he interrupted her. 'He'll no' bite ye, I promise. Armageddon's a python – squeezes his prey tae death, and he cannae squeeze you tae death yet darlin'. He's too sma', he's less than two foot long. We've tae feed him once we get home, then he'll no' be looking for prey anyway. He's tae get his dinner on Mondays.'

'But whit aboot the baby, Ally?' she demanded, dully.

'Whit aboot him?' he answered, now fumbling under the driver's seat.

'Well, she'll just be wee. Will Armadillo no' be able to squeeze the life oot o' her?'

'Em . . .' her husband said, playing for time. 'Em . . . him, pet, the life oot o' him. The bairn's a him. But Armageddon'll not . . .'

Their conversation ended abruptly with a loud knock on the driver's steamed-up window. Frankie rolled it down slowly, to see herself beckoned out of the car by a couple of uniformed policemen. Standing by them was a young woman, and beside her was a middle-aged man in a beige raincoat, shouting loudly, ordering the constables around.

—

Sitting alone at the table in the interview room Ally Livingstone stroked his jaw up and down, up and down, feeling the springy stubble beneath his fingertips and listening to the rasping noise made by his fingers. Seeing a chewed biro at his left hand he picked it up, and absentmindedly put it into his mouth. He sucked on it, thinking things over as he did so. He reckoned he knew why they wanted to speak to him and he told himself he must try to concentrate, prepare himself to answer their questions.

The money that they had found on him, and any recently spent, could be explained away easily enough by a win on the horses. Frankie had fallen for that one after all, no bother. All he needed to do was multiply his actual stake twenty-fold, and that would account for his record winnings. 'Whispering Wind' had, genuinely, won the 2.30 at Doncaster. And if they could be fobbed off with that, then maybe he would be able to use the card again, please God, because the Parks Department paid only peanuts.

If they were after the card itself then he had an explanation for that, too, although they might not believe him. If he could just get another two hundred pounds or three hundred maybe, then they could buy the cot or the buggy and a couple of corn-snakes, or better yet, a baby African Grey parrot. He could teach it to speak along with the little one, when he arrived. They'd both learn to say, 'Fuck off ye wee twat' in unison.

Now deep in thought, he closed his jaws on the biro, accidentally biting into it and splitting its plastic casing into smithereens in his mouth. He tried to spit the tiny fragments out, but a few obstinate ones stuck to his tongue. As he attempted to remove them with his fingers, the young policewoman entered the room and sat down opposite him, catching him in the act. A couple of seconds later, the middle-aged man joined them, muttering gruffly as he sat down, 'On you go, Alice, love . . .'

'Can you tell me where you were from about six o'clock onwards last Saturday, the day before yesterday, Mr Livingstone?' the woman asked, watching him as he wiped his sticky fingers on the shoulders of his leather jacket.

'Eh?' he answered, still trying to remove a stray splinter from his mouth and genuinely taken aback by the question. This was not one that he had expected, and he had no answer planned for it. She repeated it, her eyes on his fingers as he examined them for bits of pen.

'Em . . . I was at home with ma wife, Frankie – I think.' That would have to do for now.

'Have you ever been to the house of a Mr Gavin Brodie in India Street?'

'Naw.'

'Have you ever met that man, Gavin Brodie?'

'Naw.'

'Do you know him?'

'Naw.'

'Then can you tell me how you got hold of his Royal Bank card?'

At last the fight could begin, he thought, feeling the inside of his cheek with his tongue, unpleasantly aware of another piece of plastic. Then another thought crossed his mind – perhaps the biro had belonged to a junkie? Christ! He could get Aids from it!

'I dinnae ken whit you're oan about, hen . . . you've got the wrong man this time, hen,' he said, spitting forcefully onto the floor and ridding his mouth of the final splinter.

'Don't do that!' Inspector Manson said, shaking his head, his lips pursed in disdain.

'And it's Detective Sergeant Rice, Mr Livingstone, not "hen", thanks,' the woman corrected him, looking down at the gob of spittle. 'We have CCTV footage of the ATM machine on Corstorphine Road, taken yesterday between 3 pm and 4 pm, and it quite clearly shows you using Mr Brodie's card. You withdrew £200 from his account on that occasion, and I understand that today you drew out another £200.'

Fucking spies in the sky were everywhere nowadays, Ally Livingstone thought to himself, desperately trying to work out if there was a way out of this trap, or if, somehow, it could be avoided entirely. Well, the old ones were the best ones, he decided. So he scratched his head as if in puzzlement, and then said, 'Em . . . no, miss, it disnae show me. It cannae show me. Must be somewan who looks like me, ken, but isnae me at a'. I was wi' Frankie yesterday at Asdas, we were buyin' stuff for the wee yin. Well, for when he's born, like. It must be somebody else in the pictures. Somewan who looks like me but isnae me.'

He picked up the split biro and began twirling it between his fingers like a tiny baton, surreptitiously glancing up at the policewoman's face to see how she was reacting to his story. Then, remembering that it might be contaminated, he dropped the pen. As he did so, their eyes met. Holding his gaze, she said, 'I've now seen the footage myself, Mr Livingstone, and others have identified you from it personally. It was you. Gavin Brodie, the owner of the card, was murdered late on Saturday . . . as I'm sure you know.'

'Eh?' Ally Livingstone said, pushing the biro off the table, and noting in passing that his fingers were now stained blue with ink.

'I said, the owner of . . .'

'I heard you,' he interrupted, 'and I've nothing tae dae wi' any o' that, hen. I've no' hurt nobody.'

'Fine,' she replied coolly. 'Then, perhaps, you could explain to me how the murdered man's bank card ended up in your hands?'

'I wull, but you'll no' believe me. I found the caird, OK? In a wallet.'

'And how did you get the pin number?'

'It wis in there an a', in the wallet. Oan a wee piece of paper. I tried it an' it worked first time. Ye'd think folk wid be more careful.'

'Where did you find the wallet?'

'I found it oan the ground, ken, on the path under the big, high bridge. Yesterday.'

'You seriously expect us to believe that, son?' the inspector said. 'You'll be telling us next that you've turned over a new leaf – gone respectable, going straight!'

'Aye. I expect youse tae believe us.'

'The big, high bridge?' Alice picked up the thread once more.

'Aha. The wan o'er the Water o' Leith.'

'The Dean Bridge, is that the one you mean?'

'Maybe . . . Aha.'

'Where exactly under that bridge did you find it?'

'Under the bridge,' he repeated impatiently, 'by some bushes just as you go under it.'

'On which side?'

'Em . . .' he racked his brain, trying to think of something further to identify the location. 'Em . . . on the Princes Street side. I could take you there, tae the place.'

'Why were you there?'

'Why no'? It's for the public, isn't it? I'm the public. I was taking my pal's wee dug for a walk in the morning. It's a bull terrier pup, if you need tae ken. No' wan o' they dangerous dogs neither.'

'Where is it – the wallet, I mean?'

'In the Water o' Leith, I chucked it in there.'

'After you'd taken out what from it?'

'Em . . . now let me think. Em . . . a' the cairds, a' the notes and the change, the wee bit o' paper . . . and a driver's licence. That's a'.'

'And where is the card now?'

Ally fingered its thin plastic edge in his pocket. Frankie would not want the police in their flat, dirtying the carpets with their mucky boots and pulling everything out of their drawers. Well, he thought to himself, the policewoman had asked for it, so she could have it. Slowly, he pulled a clear plastic sachet from his trouser pocket, containing a single, white, half-frozen mouse, which he laid on the table. Then he extracted the card and carefully slid it below the tiny corpse.

'What on earth is that?' Alice asked, peering at the little corpse but making no attempt to take the card on which it lay.

'Em . . . that's Armageddon's tea. I've been thawing it oot fer him,' he answered, smiling broadly. 'You no' like mice then, hen?' he added.

DI Manson, who had been sitting back from the table with his arms crossed, pulled in his chair and leant over to take a look. Seeing the card sticking out from below the dead rodent, he pulled his jacket sleeve over his hand as a glove and nudged the mouse off it.

The door opened and DC Littlewood's head appeared. Looking at Alice, he said, 'Sorry to interrupt, but the DCI's just heard that Una Reid's been traced. She says that you've to go and see her, Sarge. She's at her work, at the Abbey Park Lodge, that home in Comely Bank.'

'This very minute?' Alice said, looking at her watch, feeling suddenly tired. Five o' clock, and still she had not found time to buy a present for Ian's birthday. It was past praying for now.

'Aye. Pronto.'

'Off you go, Alice,' the Inspector said faintly, waving for her to leave. 'I'll finish off this . . .' he pointed at Livingstone, 'wee, sleekit, cowran, tim'rous . . . shitie.'

But Eric Manson did not want to take over the interview. He had stopped listening to Livingstone's words early on, had allowed his thoughts free range, and as always, of late, they had returned home to Margaret. His preoccupation. What was going on? Why did she no longer have any time for him, why was she always out and about, too busy to sit with him, talk to him even? Something must be happening to her, to them.

But, for the moment, he would have to try and concentrate on the matter in hand. So, the wee shitie would just have to begin all over again. Teach him for gobbing on the station floor, anyway.

5

Two things struck Alice Rice as she walked through the doors of the Abbey Park Lodge in search of Una Reid. The first was the unnatural warmth of the place, enveloping her like a soft blanket, and the second was the institutional smell. Her nose told her that it was composed of a blend of yesterday's mince, floral air freshener and stale human urine, and in the competition between the three ingredients the last emerged as a clear victor. Initially, she attempted to make the supply of fresh air in her lungs last unnaturally long, but by the time she reached the bottom of the main stair they were crying out for oxygen and she had no alternative but to breathe in and inhale the place's foetid atmosphere.

Entering the residents' lounge, she almost walked into a paper banner which hung loosely from one side of the room to the other, proclaiming in huge, multi-coloured letters, 'HAPPY BIRTHDAY, RHONA'. As she stood in front of it, a female resident sidled up to her, looked timidly into her eyes, and then, unexpectedly, grasped her hand and began pulling her towards the Formica-topped table at one end of the room.

Seated at it were five elderly women, three of them fast asleep with their chins resting on their bony chests, another one apparently awake but staring blankly into the middle distance. The last was cleaning her paintbrush by sucking it in her toothless mouth. A male care assistant was busily engaged in painting a giant birthday card, dipping his brush in and out of the paint pots, apparently oblivious to the fact that most of his helpers had dozed off. Assuming she was related to the resident clasping her hand, he gave Alice a friendly nod and began sprinkling glitter on the lettering of the homemade card.

'Excuse me,' Alice began, 'but I've come to see Una Reid, could you tell me where I'd find her?' As she spoke, she tried to free herself from her captor, but the bony hand was immovable.

'Aye,' answered the attendant, blowing away loose sparkles before turning his attention to the stranger, 'she's . . . ah,' he hesitated as the last specks flew off the table and onto the floor, 'she's giving Miss Swire her tea.'

Thanking him, Alice turned to leave the group, but found that she was unable to do so, the old lady still firmly attached to her and leaning back on her heels, straining to prevent any escape. Seeing Alice's discomfort and realising his own mistake, the assistant said, 'Come on now, Betty, let the nice lady go.'

Betty, however, had no intention of releasing her new friend, and making her defiance plain, simply clamped her other hand over Alice's already entrapped one.

'Maybe she could just go with you as far as Miss Swire's door?' the assistant asked tentatively. His attention was now divided, as he busied himself doing up the buttons on the blouse of his nearest neighbour, as she resolutely and as quickly unbuttoned them.

'Aye, I'll just come along to Miss Swire's ro . . .' Betty declared, ready to go, but before she had finished her sentence, an over-vigorous movement on the part of the yellow-lipped painter sent the paint-water jar crashing on its side, flooding the table and ruining the card. Within seconds, the thin khaki liquid began to drip over the edge of the Formica onto the laps of those sitting at it.

Alice silently nodded to the assistant. After all, he only had one pair of hands and the air was now filled with shrill cries of horror, as the three sleepers were woken by the cold water pouring onto their sunken laps. One of them, her hair scraped back into a sparse bun, began shouting, over and over, 'Stop it! Stop it now! Stop it! Stop it now!' staring at the water, ordering it to cease flowing and stand still.

Edging together along the low corridor, Betty's tottering gait dictating their speed, Alice and her companion finally reached Miss Swire's bedroom door. Pinned onto it, as a reminder that the past had been different, were a couple of photographs of the resident in her youth. The largest one showed her wielding a golf club and beaming happily at the camera, and in a smaller picture she was in an academic gown, distributing prizes at the school she had been headmistress of for almost quarter of a century. As Alice was examining it, at the same time trying to work out the best way to free herself, Betty pushed the door open with her forehead and, still hand in hand with her victim, began to walk into the room jerking her reluctant companion with her.

'Betty! Who've you got wi' you now?' an exasperated female voice asked, and as Alice stumbled into the room, she saw another care assistant, a stout, sandy blonde with a pitted complexion, standing beside the bed, tilting a spoon into the bloodless lips of its occupant, Miss Swire. The old schoolteacher herself registered nothing on the entrance of the uninvited pair, continuing to chew mechanically while looking beseechingly into her feeder's eyes, like a nestling begging a worm from its parent. Gently catching a drip that had begun to weave its way down from Miss Swire's puckered mouth, Una Reid shook her head fondly at Betty and asked Alice, in a nicotine-ravaged voice, if she had come to see Miss Swire.

'No,' Alice began. 'You. I was looking for you, if you're Una Reid?'

'Aha, I am, yes,' the woman croaked back, now patting the resident's bluish lips with a napkin, cleaning off a tidemark of tomato soup.

'Could I talk to you? I'm from Lothian & Borders Police, Detective Alice Rice. I'd like to ask you some questions about Gavin Brodie.'

'Aha,' Una replied, sounding slightly distracted. After offering a fork full of potato to Miss Swire, she added, 'It'll hae tae be in here, mind. We're short-staffed the day, an' I've another three ladies tae give their teas before seven o' clock.'

Moving towards an empty seat, and gesturing for Betty to sit on it, Alice said, 'As you'll know, Gavin Brodie was murdered on Saturday night, and I understand that you saw him on that date. You may, in fact, have been the last person to see him alive.'

'Is that right?' Una cut in, apparently unperturbed by the thought.

'Can you tell me what you did for him, on the Saturday?'

'Just the same as I always done. I gi'ed him his tea at aboot seven, then I gi'ed him a wee bed bath an' changed his PJs.'

'When exactly did you leave him?'

'Eight o' clock, mebbe, ten past eight, somethin' like that.'

'Which door did you leave by?'

'The front.'

'Did you check that the back door was locked before you left?'

'Naw, I never. I never done, that wasnae pairt o' ma job. Why would I?'

'How did Mr Brodie seem when you left him?'

'Like he always done. Moanin' awa' tae himsel'. He wis unhappy, cross . . . greetin' tae himsel'.'

'When you were with him, did anyone else come to see him or phone him?'

'Naw,' the assistant said, putting the fork back on the plate in recognition of defeat. Miss Swire's tightly closed teeth had barred its passage.

'Are you aware whether anyone else saw him after you left?'

'D'ye mean Mrs Brodie?'

'Anyone at all.'

'Well, she will hae, won't she, whenever she got in. She wis the wan who left a message tae tell me that I neednae come in, oan the Sunday morning like. That's how I wis able to see my friends in Aberdeen early.'

'One last thing, Mrs Reid. Can you tell me what you gave Mr Brodie for his tea on the Saturday night?'

'Aha.'

'Could you tell me what it was?'

'Why do youse need tae ken?' the woman asked, pulling the foil lid from a chocolate mousse pot and then licking it herself.

'Because we do.'

'Yes, but why?' The policewoman's answer had not been good enough.

'Because . . . because we just do,' Alice snapped, suddenly feeling impatient in the stifling, smelly heat, with

Betty's arthritic fingers gripping her own tightly. She was longing to get back into the fresh air, back into life and away from the place. And as if sensing her tension, Betty began gently stroking her captive's hand as if comforting a frightened bird.

'Aha, but why?' Una Reid repeated, unpersuaded, wafting a teaspoon of the mousse to and fro below Miss Swire's nose, as if the scent of chocolate might tempt her to open her mouth.

'Because we just do, alright? For the purposes of our investigation into the man's murder.'

'Okay doaky, doll. It wis Heinz's lentil soup. Just a wee pickle, all he'd ever take.' Una tried one final time to tempt the old lady to eat, and, defeated, put the dripping spoon into her own mouth.

As Alice moved towards the door, Betty began to move with her until the policewoman stopped and, looking into the old lady's eyes, gently tried to prize one of the gnarled fingers free from her own. Instantly the grip tightened once more and Betty began to shake with the effort of maintaining it. Seeing Alice's unsuccessful attempt and look of despair, Una Reid grinned at her, then clapped her red hands loudly and said 'BINGO!' Instantly, Betty released her hold, glanced at her wristwatch, then sped out of the door in the direction of the residents' lounge.

'Why didn't you do that earlier – when we came in?' Alice asked, mildly amused at the strategy and massaging her freed fingers.

'Because it wasnae 6.30, dear. The game doesnae start until 6.30.'

Once back home in her flat in Broughton Place for the night, Alice picked up her dog, Quill, from her neighbours. Mrs Foscetti and Miss Spinnell were a pair of octogenarian twins. The younger by a few minutes, Miss Spinnell, suffered from Alzheimer's, but was utterly devoted to the mongrel, and the pair of them were his day-time keepers.

Having first fed Quill, Alice set to work at speed, expecting Ian to return at any minute, putting his favourite food in the oven and running a bath. A birthday dip with him would have been perfect, had been her plan all along. But as time wore on and he failed to appear, she had it herself, the water now tepid, downing a couple of glasses of wine to keep her spirits up. Before she knew it half of the bottle had gone.

By the time she got out of the bath, all the dozens of candles she had lit, covering every free surface in the flat, were beginning to gutter, pools of hot wax dripping from them, deforming them and making them overflow their saucers. There were no spares left to replace them with, and the electric light seemed discordant, too unmagical in comparison.

She tried Ian on his mobile phone again, but as before, it had been switched off. Then, to cap it all, she noticed a strange smell, and she inhaled deeply, trying to identify it, uncertain what it could be. A loud bleeping began as the smoke alarm went off. Feeling slightly dizzy between the drink and tiredness, she walked slowly to the kitchen.

The pastry on the butcher's steak pie was burnt black, and the baked potatoes were no more than carbonised shells, crumbling when touched. She tossed the lot into the bin, thinking the evening could still be saved if she rushed to the nearby Indian takeaway for a banquet, but first of all the alarm would have to be silenced.

Standing on a chair she prodded the white plastic casing with a broom handle, trying to locate an 'off' button with it, but becoming impatient, she thumped it over-vigorously and part of the casing broke. It hung uselessly from the ceiling, showering her with a fine spray of black dust as it fell. But its innards continued to flash and shriek.

Hearing a loud knocking at the door, Alice leapt off the chair, believing it to be Ian, thinking that perhaps he had left without his keys that morning. Instead she was greeted by Mrs Foscetti, her sister peeping wide-eyed out of the nearby, half-closed door of their flat.

'We've had smoke coming into our house, and the alarm's gone off. Perhaps there's a fire here? Hadn't we all better evacuate the building, dear?' Mrs Foscetti asked, calmly.

'It's in my house, the fire . . . except it's not,' Alice said, coming out onto the landing and beginning to explain.

'In your house? Then for Heaven's sake, get Quill!' Miss Spinnell shouted, gesturing impatiently with her good hand for her neighbour to go back into the burning flat. Alice explained again that it was a false alarm, that they were not all at risk of imminent immolation, and apologised profusely. Then she turned, intending to go back in, snatch her wallet and rush off to the Taj Mahal.

'We've a window pole. That might do the trick and incapacitate the alarm,' said Mrs Foscetti, jabbing an imaginary pole at an imaginary ceiling.

'What's happened to your face?' Miss Spinnell asked, bemused, coming nearer and pointing at Alice, 'you look like a darkie!'

'Sshh' Mrs Foscetti said sharply, embarrassed both by her sister's use of the term, and her frankness in making such a personal comment.

70

'A blackie . . .' Miss Spinnell murmured to herself, 'inky . . . a coalface,' her voice petering out in thought.

Alice put her hand up to her cheek, and when she examined her fingers she found they were thickly covered in soot.

'Listen,' Miss Spinnell said mysteriously.

'To what?' her sister asked.

'The silence . . .'

The alarm had switched itself off.

Once in the flat again, disconsolate that everything was going so wrong and desperate for something to eat, Alice washed her face in the basin, producing black smears on it as she did so. And while she was trying to clean herself, Ian Melville walked in, a huge bunch of freesias in his hand.

'I'm so sorry . . .' she began, knowing before she had even started speaking that as she explained all the mishaps, the candles going out, the burnt food, the alarm going off and everything else, all of them would, even in combination, sound inadequate, an insufficient excuse for a presentless, celebrationless birthday. Even pleading the pressures of a murder investigation seemed too tired, too weak an explanation in her own ears, never mind his. If only he had been on sodding time though, she thought, but it seemed a churlish justification, better left unexpressed. He had red paint on the side of his face, and, as was often the case, on his hands too.

'So we've nothing to eat, eh . . . Sooty?'

'I think perhaps you mean Black Beauty . . .' she stopped, suddenly remembering that Black Beauty was a horse. She racked her brain to think of a suitable insult in return, but, drink-befuddled and exhausted, found all inspiration gone.

'Perhaps we should be flexible, change the plan, and just have a bath instead?' he said, smiling, his red fingers already hovering over the top buttons of her blouse. She nodded, only too pleased at the suggestion.

As she lay down in the warm water, letting it lap over her and beginning to relax, he disappeared, returning with a single candle. Just as he climbed in beside her, soap in hand, intoxicated by the thought of their evening together, the ring-tone of her phone shattered their peace.

'Leave it,' he said.

She looked at him and shook her head.

'Please, Alice, just this time. It is my birthday. Please, please, don't answer.'

'I have to.' It was pointless to explain. There would be nothing new to say, nothing that she had not said too many times before. By now he should understand.

DI Manson walked into his own front hall. He threw his overcoat over the banisters, his body aching, feeling work-soiled and drained. Glancing through the living-room door, he was dazzled by the blue and red lights blinking on the Christmas tree, then noticed a partly completed jigsaw on a tray on the coffee table. The radio was broadcasting a carol service from somewhere, and a woman's low voice, emanating from the kitchen, was accompanying the choir in 'Oh Come All Ye Faithful'. He entered the warm room, hoping that Margaret would be there and on her own, but instead he found one of her friends, singing to herself, busy removing his dinner from the oven.

'Where's Margaret?' he asked, feeling too tired to face any food.

'Upstairs with the girls.'

'What's she doing?'

'Never you mind, love. Just get that down you,' she answered, placing a plate of some green tagliatelle mixture in front of him. 'I'll keep you company, while you eat.'

He rose from the table, pushing the dish to one side, determined to see his wife and to rid his house of the coven that seemed to have taken up residence in it for the last few days. Suddenly, Margaret came racing into the room, his mobile clamped to her ear.

'It's Elaine,' she whispered. 'You left your phone in your coat. Here you are . . .'

'Ma'am,' he said, trying to force himself back into work-mode and summon some vitality from somewhere.

'Go to Saxe-Coburg Street now. Someone from Criminal Intelligence has just been in contact. There's been an incident there, a sort of break-in, I don't have all the details, except that it's an invalid's house. I'll tell you when I see you there, OK? Alice is already on her way. A constable's just picked her up.'

'Right,' he replied, moving towards the door.

'You don't have to go now, do you pet? What about your tea?' a concerned voice asked. But he did not feel the need to respond, because it was not Margaret speaking.

———

The man was chittering, trembling like a frightened dog, his whole body convulsed by continuous wave after wave of involuntary movement, as if it no longer belonged to him, but had been possessed by fear. Elaine Bell pulled up a seat opposite his wheelchair, looking into his anguished face, her eyes now level with his own.

'Can you tell us what happened, Mr Anderson?'

He said nothing, then his lower lip jutted out as if he was about to burst into tears, and he gave a low, vulpine moan. His carer leant over him and took one of his hands in hers, squeezing it gently between her fingers.

'Come on, pal, just tell them what you told me.'

The man nodded, lip still protruding, then began to speak, a slow babble of sounds issuing from his mouth, each word slurred and jostling with the next to form a single stream of incomprehensible noise.

Alice caught the DCI's eye and Elaine Bell shook her head, her expression one of bafflement. Eric Manson was staring at the man's mouth as if by looking at it for long enough, or hard enough, he might somehow acquire the art of lip reading. After speaking for a further thirty seconds or so, the man fell silent. His carer sighed and said, 'See? Just like what I told the constable earlier. What a bastard! You wouldn't believe it, would you?'

'Sorry. Sorry . . .' Elaine Bell replied. 'I'm afraid I didn't catch a single word he said. Could we try again?'

The invalid repeated his story, pausing every so often to look quizzically at the police officers, checking whether they could understand him. But again the noise that he made sounded entirely alien, reminiscent of a record playing at the wrong speed, far too slowly.

'Dreadful, eh?' the carer said, an expression of outrage on her face and her hands clenched pugnaciously on her broad hips.

'Diane, perhaps, just for the moment, you could translate for us, tell us what he said?' the DCI asked, rubbing her eyes with her fingers, desperate to find out what had happened and to be able to start the investigation.

'Well . . .' Diane began, 'Ron said that he was in his bed – he goes early like, I put him into his bed – he was in it, nearly asleep, and he heard a noise so he opened his eyes. He'd had a pill . . .'

'A sleeping pill, you'd given him a sleeping pill?'

'Aye. He opened his eyes and saw a man in his room, prowling about like. Picking up his things, even had a wee go in his wheelchair, using the joystick and everything. Well, the man comes over . . .'

A strange honking sound drowned out her voice, as the invalid joined in, gesticulating excitedly and jabbing the air with his right hand. Just at that moment the spin cycle on the washing machine started up, drowning their words with a high pitched whine.

'Unbelievable, eh?' Diane said, her eyes wide.

'What – what's unbelievable?' Elaine Bell asked, trying to control her impatience with the woman and the background noise.

'To do that – to do that to anybuddy.'

'To do what! You'll have to tell us, we can't understand him, remember,' the DCI snapped, her voice raised, ensuring she was audible over the loud whine, losing the battle for manners.

'Oh, aye. Right. The man came over and he'd a long knife in his hand.' Diane stopped speaking as the racket from the machine continued, now punctuated by an occasional clicking sound as a loose coin revolved in the drum.

'Then what? Then what?' Elaine Bell almost screamed.

'Then . . . well, I must have come in, I think, back into the flat. I'd left my bag behind in the kitchen so I came back for it. The key had gone from under the mat but the door was still open. I came in, picked it up, then I heard Ron shouting, shouting my name, shouting out what had happened to him. I was the one dialled 999.'

'Did you check the flat to make sure he'd gone?' Eric Manson enquired, looking all around the room, and then, with a sigh of irritation, turning off the switch for the washing machine.

'It'd no' quite finished,' Diane said, looking annoyed.

'Did you check . . .' the Inspector repeated, his hand still on the switch.

'Oh, aye. Looked a' ower the place, but the man had gone. Out the door, I suppose.'

'What did he look like?' Elaine Bell asked.

Immediately, Ron Anderson began to speak again, his head moving excitedly. Diane made no attempt to translate, so the DCI said, 'Well, what did he say?'

'He said it was dark, and he was half asleep, but it was a big fellow, heavy-made like.'

'Did the man say anything?' Alice asked.

Once again the invalid replied, his eyes darting from one to the other, as if expecting that they would understand the language of his eyes, if not his mouth.

'Diane? Translate for us, for Christ's sake!'

'He said . . . the man talked a lot – not really to him, though, more mutterin' to himself.'

'Anything else?'

'Ron said he stank. Reekin' like bath-time, or a baby or something.'

'It's him,' Alice said, 'it must be.'

'Who?' the DCI demanded.

'Norman Clerk. It must be him. Fat, arguing with himself, with the voice in his head. And when Tom and I saw him, in his flat, he smelt – I can smell it in here, now, too. Baby powder. It must be him.'

⎯

While Eric Manson searched Clerk's odiferous bedroom, she scurried around the rest of the flat, looking behind curtains, into cubby-holes, anywhere and everywhere that anyone could hide. In the bathroom, through her haste, she accidentally pulled down the shower curtain, exposing an array of tall cannabis plants in the old enamel bath, each flowerpot resting on a layer of damp newspaper. Spiders' webs hung from the bath taps and a chain dangled against the side, plugless and rusty. On the nearby cistern were the man's toiletries: a tin of Johnson's Baby Powder, a razor and dusty toothbrush. Four unopened packets of Risperdal lay beside them.

'There's a loft, I'm going into it,' Manson shouted, followed by the sound of a Ramsay ladder being unlatched and hauled down.

Alice returned to the kitchen, pulling open the doors of the units and peering inside a musty-smelling broom cupboard, double-checking the places she had already looked in her desperation. Suddenly she remembered that Clerk's brother lived on the bottom floor of the tenement. Maybe he was hiding down there.

'Sir – Sir, I'm going to check flat number three on the ground floor, Clerk's brother's place.'

There was no answer, but she could hear her colleague's heavy footfalls above her, see the plaster vibrate slightly as he clambered about on the rafters.

After racing down the three flights of stairs, she arrived out of breath in the entrance hall, pressed the bell marked 'R. Clerk' and waited for someone to answer it. Nothing happened, so she pressed again, harder this time, keeping her finger on it to produce a single continuous, insistent ring. Once more there was no response. In her impatience, she gave the scuffed grey door a slight push and it opened. In less than a second she had decided to go in, search warrant or no search warrant.

The place was in darkness, lit only by the faint orange glow of the streetlights outside. She padded about, going from room to room and giving each a hasty check. Finally, only one door remained, and from behind it came loud, intermittent snores which vibrated in the air and sounded like a chainsaw starting, revving up and then cutting out.

As she came in she was able to make out the vast bulk of Robert Clerk on a brass bedstead, his barrel-like torso rising and falling with each noisy breath and one pale foot protruding from below his duvet. The space under the bed was hidden by a thick, candlewick bedspread which lay in folds on the carpeted floor. Just as Alice was about to tiptoe away, one of the corners of the bedspread moved slightly, as if a mouse was trying to escape from beneath it.

Holding her breath, she waited and watched, and once again the material twitched. Her heart now racing, she stepped towards the bed, and as she did so, Robert Clerk let out a loud groan, startling her and stopping her in her tracks. Trying to keep calm, she stared at him, but he remained fast asleep.

Very carefully, she picked up one of the bottom edges of the bedspread and began to raise it. As she bent forward to look underneath the bed, a sweet smell hit her nostrils. Just as she realised what it was, a hand shot out, grabbing her hair, wrenching its roots and pulling her towards the ground. As she fell forward, Norman Clerk hooked his arm around her neck, pulling her face towards him, pressing her hard against his chest and suffocating her in the folds of his flesh.

She cried out but nothing came, her voice absorbed, muffled by his solid bulk. Keeping his grip with one arm despite her scrabbling hands trying to break it, he used his left hand to grind his knuckles back and forth in her eye-socket. The pain was excruciating, like a red-hot arrow piercing her eyeball. Its sharpness shocked her, revitalised her.

Suddenly, the thought that she might die by the hands of a creature such as him, an unwashed, pink Buddha-like thing, infuriated her. It seemed like a grotesque impertinence. Enraged at the very idea, and using every ounce of her remaining strength, she smashed her thigh up between his legs, her hard flesh hitting his soft flesh, feeling him instantly loosen his hold on her.

He groaned, recoiling from her, fell and doubled up, foetus-like, on the ground beside her, his hands now protecting his battered genitalia from any further attack. Aware once more of the sharp pain in her eye, her bruised scalp and with the disgusting scent of his rank, powdered flesh in her nostrils, she was sorely tempted to give him another kick for good measure. But the sound of a pro-longed, pig-like grunt distracted her, and as Eric Manson strode in she watched Robert Clerk's eyelids flutter as he snored on, oblivious to everything around him in his untroubled, drugged sleep.

—

The young psychiatrist who arrived from the Royal Edin-burgh had never had to carry out such an assessment before, but he was secretly pleased to be called upon to do it. Seeing his smooth, rosy cheeks and bright eyes, Elaine Bell's spirits rose too. This beginner should pose no problems.

'It's largely a formality. We just need you to speak to the man, check him out, make sure he's fit for interview. He was in Carstairs and he may have committed a murder, so there's a degree of urgency about the business as you'll appreciate.' She spoke conspiratorially to him as if he would, indeed, understand the need for urgency, looking him directly in the eye to emphasize the point. And the young man nodded, saying nothing by way of reply but seeming gratifyingly eager to please her.

The social worker who had picked the short straw and found himself allocated to assist Clerk as an 'appropriate adult', passed them in the corridor, making his way to the interview room in the company of a WPC. Recognising him, the DCI knew that their luck was holding, because the man was an unashamed time-server, his ideals lost long ago along with most of his hair. He was one of those raw-boned, denim-clad, northern Irishmen who had seen it all, tried to mend the world, failed, and finally discovered that their well of compassion was not quite bottomless after all. So, Pat could be relied upon. Usually he sat quietly in interviews, filling in the forms, no longer even attempting to hide his impatience, his desire to get back to the office to 'process' his remaining cases. His attitude was commendably simple: if they were fit to interview, they were fit to interview, and therefore his presence was a mere formality. This time, all he would be thinking about would be getting back to his bed.

After an hour had passed and Dr Tynan still remained closeted with their suspect, Elaine Bell listened at the door, then knocked loudly on it. She peered round it and said, breezily, but with a slight edge in her voice, 'Nearly finished in here?'

'It's up to you,' Clerk replied, brushing dust and fluff off the elbows of his pink pullover. 'I know I am.'

'Well,' the young man began, 'I'm finding it diff . . .' Then he thought better of speaking in front of his interviewee, smiled at him and left the room. Sounding slightly agitated, he said to the Chief Inspector, 'To do this properly, I really ought to see his records – from Carstairs, I mean.'

'Nonsense,' Elaine Bell replied, a fixed smile on her face. 'It's his fitness now that we have to be satisfied about. The records will provide his history, granted, but really it's his present state that concerns us. And it could delay everything significantly . . .'

'Yes,' Dr Tynan began, 'but I really ought to see them if . . .'

Elaine Bell interrupted him, speaking sternly. 'I had the advantage of exchanging a few words with Mr Clerk a little earlier. Then he seemed entirely lucid, rational, orientated in time and space; he did not appear to be remotely delusional, or confused. It's unlikely that anything's changed between now and then, wouldn't you agree?'

'Well, yes, I would, but it would still be better if . . .'

'Dr Tynan, I did explain to you when you first arrived that there is a degree of urgency in this case, didn't I? This man may have cut somebody's throat, so time is of the essence. So far you've had . . .' she looked at her watch, 'over one hour to satisfy yourself. Your colleague, Dr Lowell, who we know well, usually manages to wrap things up in forty minutes, sometimes less. Would another five minutes be sufficient?'

'Erm . . . yes,' Dr Tynan said, cowed and overawed by the woman's certainty, and sufficiently undermined by her manner to wonder if it had been reasonable, after all, to consider checking the records. Perhaps that was never normally done in these kinds of cases?

When Norman Clerk was introduced to the social worker and told that Pat would help him with the interview, make sure he understood what was going on, ensure that his interests were protected, he looked at his 'helper', held out his hand towards him and said, delightedly, 'All for me? You shouldn't have bothered.'

'My pleasure,' Pat said under his breath, shaking his head and returning his attention to his newspaper.

Once seated at the table in the interview room, Clerk busied himself straightening a stray paper clip, then used the jagged bit of wire to clean the dirt from beneath his fingernails. Eric Manson entered the room, his entry logged on the tape by Elaine Bell, sniffed the air and immediately opened a window.

'Too warm, officer?' Clerk asked, adding, 'me, too, thanks, I'm roasting . . . toasted.'

'Can you tell us what you were doing in Ron Anderson's flat in Saxe Coburg Street, earlier tonight?' Elaine Bell asked, gesturing for her Inspector to take the seat beside her.

'Looking around . . . I was just looking around it,' he replied airily, extending his fingers in front of his face as if he had just had a manicure, examining them, his tongue poking out as if in concentration.

'How did you get access to his premises?'

'With a key – with a key.'

'And how did you get the key?'

'From under the mat, dear Lilah, dear Lilah,' he sang, putting down the paper-clip and looking the Chief Inspector in the face for the first time.

'What were you doing with the knife in the man's bedroom?'

For a split-second Clerk was unable to disguise his surprise at the question, then he pursed his lips and said, 'Making a casserole. No, really . . . what was I doing with the knife? Nothing. I just picked it up. Indeed, I picked up quite a few things – a silver ashtray, a Chinese vase, a packet of chocolate buttons. No harm in picking things up and putting them down again, now is there?' He nodded several times, as if convinced by his own answer.

'And what were you doing concealed under your brother's bed when Sergeant Rice found you?' Eric Manson asked, leaning menacingly towards the man, annoyed by his flippant manner.

'Hiding,' he replied playfully, twiddling with his hair, then shuddering and removing a dead fly from it.

'Hiding from what?'

'From the intruder, of course! I heard noises, the sound of someone else in the flat, so I ducked for cover. Who wouldn't?'

'And you attacked her because?' Elaine Bell said, knowing already what his answer would be.

'Because . . . because . . . well, wouldn't you have done the same? An intruder comes into your flat – well, your brother's flat . . . he's an invalid, he can do nothing. Would you wait to be attacked? Indeed, I think not.'

⬤

'OK,' Elaine Bell said, leaning against the closed door of the now empty interview room. 'A good night's work. Bed now. But I'll want you back here first thing. Both of you. Is your eye alright, Alice?'

'Actually, it's bloody painful, but I can still see out of it.

It's just bruising, I think. In a couple of hours I'll look as if I've taken on Mike Tyson – and lost.'

'Fine. Clerk will be in court in the morning for battering you, Alice, and for entering Anderson's home. We'll oppose bail. With the search warrant we'll pull his flat to pieces. We'll take the cannabis plants and hopefully find something of Brodie's, a memento perhaps. That would give us enough to charge him with the man's murder. Eric, you go with Ally Livingstone to the Dean Bridge, everything's already tee'd up there for 11 am. See what you can find, eh?'

'Aye, aye, Ma'am.'

Returning to her room, the DCI moved a sheaf of papers towards the back of her desk, clearing a space for the cushion she intended to place there for her head. A single sheet fell off the pile and she picked it up. It was a note in Alistair Watt's cramped hand that she had not noticed before;

'Dave from the Lab phoned at 4 pm. We're to get the report on India Street tomorrow. Also Prof McConnachie's coming to see you, he thinks he'll be at St Leonard's at about 3 pm. Don't know what about. He wouldn't tell me over the phone.'

6

'It wis there, under they things . . . o'er there,' Ally Livingstone said, his voice echoing through the massive semi-circular arches of the Dean Bridge, as he pointed at a couple of leafless elderberry bushes.

Far below the path on which he stood, the Water of Leith flowed onwards on its journey towards the sea, its turbid waters tumbling over rocks, occasionally lapping lazily in the sandy shallows and depositing on the shore a froth of creamy foam like that left in an empty beer glass. The moisture-filled air seemed almost intoxicating, laden with the aroma of brewing, of hops and barley, a timeless scent and one characteristic of Auld Reekie.

Mid-river, a pair of police divers were on all fours, feeling their way along the bottom with their gloved hands. Near them, a colleague periodically immersed himself in a deeper pool, only to surface every so often with a hub-cap, a slime-covered milk-crate or other detritus consigned to the river by the litter louts of the capital.

Breaking the water again, his black wet-suit glinting like sealskin in the weak winter sun, the upright diver said, 'I think I've got something, Inspector.'

Amid the roar of the river his voice was lost. Realising that he had not been heard, he tried again, shouting this time: 'I've got something, Sir.'

'So what is it?' Eric Manson bellowed back, then cupped his hand over his mouth, sheltering his match from the icy breeze so that he could light his cigar. The diver, standing waist-deep in the water and shivering visibly in the cold, continued examining a muddy rectangular box clutched between his gloves.

'Eh . . .' the man said, pushing his mask onto this head to get a clearer view, 'seems to be . . .' He hesitated again, ducking the object back into the water to wash it. 'Em . . . I think it's a t . . . t . . . trinket box, boss. Yup, it's like a w . . . w . . . wee box for valuables.'

'Big deal,' Ally Livingstone thought, watching the diver wading heavy-legged towards the bank, and taking a deep draw on his cigarette. They were all supposed to be looking for the fucking wallet, weren't they? That was what this circus was supposed to be about. And, obviously, if they looked hard enough in the water, they would find it. He exhaled the smoke onto his linked hands, relishing the feel of warm breath on his chilled fingers, and allowed his mind to wander.

Their child would be a boy, he thought, a son. And the wee man would not be afraid of mice or snakes or any other creatures, including polismen. No, he'd handle them fearlessly, just like his dad.

Christ! A sudden thought struck him. It was freezing, the pale winter sun too weak to take the chill from the air, and with him having been banged up overnight, Armageddon would still be loose on the floor of the unheated Nissan. The snake would have become torpid, might even have died, and he had not had his tea, never mind any breakfast. And for sure, Frankie would not have been able to face lifting him out, the very idea likely to bring on a miscarriage.

As he was racking his brains, trying to think how to solve the problem, one of the divers in the shallows stood up, waving something above his head. The cold air had made his eyes water and Ally Livingstone screwed them up, trying to make out what had been found, and then gave a long, low whistle. The object was a long-bladed knife, and the sight of it held aloft made him shudder inwardly, banishing all thoughts of Armageddon, of Frankie, of the unborn baby even. And he cursed his stupidity. He should have said nothing as usual, no comment to everything, but it was too late for that now. Instead, he had brought them to this place as surely as a sniffer dog following a scent, but this time the hound had been following its own trail, tracking itself and condemning itself as it wagged its stupid tail. Now, he would not be holding Frankie's hand as she cried out while their son was born. No, at this rate, he would be lucky to know the child at all.

'So, Livingstone, what's with the knife?' the inspector asked, jerking his head in the direction of the water.

'Em . . . I'll have ma lawyer now, thanks. I dinnae ken nothin' about any knife.'

'What about the box, know anything about that?'

'Aha. I threw it in the river aifter I'd taken the jewellery from it, the necklace an' stuff an' the big pearly ring,' he answered, taking a draw on his cigarette and blowing a couple of smoke rings in the air.

'You never mentioned the jewellery or the box before.'

'Naw, and ye never asked us yesterday either, 'cause ye were in a dream most o' the time! How am I s'pose'd tae ken what ye want tae ken, eh, less ye ask us? Is that no' yer job? I found the jewellery box in the bushes an a', an' the computer, an old photy frame too . . . empty,' Ally retorted crossly, jangling the loose change in his pocket.

'Now, you tell us. What did you do with the computer?'

'Eh, I took it to ma work, checked over the case, put the rubbish from it, like, in the bin, sold the computer to one of the Parky boys.'

'And the drugs, medicines, morphine and so on?'

'Eh?'

'Don't "eh" me! What did you do with the drugs?'

'I found a bag o' bottles – that what ye mean?'

'Funny, isn't it, the way you know about pretty well everything – everything except the knife.'

'They wis empty, and it's no' funny tae me. Expect I'll get the blame fer a' the shoppin' trolleys an' a'? Oh, aye, that wis Ally, ye'll a' say – he's the wan spends his days chuckin' stuff in the river – knives, forks, spoons, prams, the lot. It's his hobby.'

Alistair Watt stifled a yawn and looked around the room, surveying the assembly of pale, weary faces in it. Beside him, Alice was leaning back on her chair, her eyes closed, arms crossed over her chest. Black bruising encircled her left eye-socket and she, too, looked exhausted.

'A domestic? Or too much of the sauce followed by a collision with a door, perhaps?'

'Clerk attacked me, since you ask.'

'What did you do to him?'

'Not nearly enough . . .' she began, but stopped abruptly as Elaine Bell took her place at the front of the room and the murmur of quiet chatter died away. Eric Manson, his lips blue with cold, shuffled towards the only remaining vacant chair.

'Good news. I've just heard that Clerk was refused bail . . .' the DCI began.

A spontaneous ripple of applause filled the air, reaching a crescendo when, acknowledging it, she took a bow and pointed at all of them as a conductor might at an orchestra.

'But . . .' she continued, 'I also heard that he's appealing the decision. So we may have only a few days before he's back out again. Eric, how did you get on?'

'The stuff was just where Livingstone said it would be. And we've got the weapon, I reckon. One of the divers fished a knife, looked like a kitchen knife, out of the river.'

'D'you think he's involved in any of this?'

'Livingstone? No, no way. I was watching him. He looked horrified when he saw the blade, started gibbering away. I think he was telling the truth, saying that he found the stuff, I mean. It's given him the fright of his life. Serves the bastard right.'

'OK. Alice, how did you get on with the carer woman, Una . . . Una Reid?'

'She told me what Brodie last ate and I phoned the lab with the information, for what it's worth. Oh, and she didn't leave him until eight, eight-ten or so.'

'Ma'am,' DC Littlewood said, 'you're sure Clerk done Brodie, that he's our man, aren't you, eh?'

She nodded, a half-smile playing about her lips, and he, emboldened by her apparent good humour, continued. 'Me too. Looks like he preys on the disabled as easy meat, you could say. Can't be chance, can it? A knife, a disabled person. Each time.'

'Easy meat?' the DCI said, repeating his phrase with an expression of extreme distaste on her face.

'Em . . . the vulnerable, then,' the Constable said, blushing.

'If it was him, why did he chuck away the jewellery box and so on that he'd filched? Did he do that with the old woman's stuff?' Alice asked.

'No, I checked that out earlier this morning,' the DCI replied. 'He didn't, but don't forget that over fifteen years have passed since his last crime. M.o.'s change – maybe just a little bit here and there, but they do change – perhaps he liked the old lady's stuff, wanted to keep it, but not Brodie's. He took what he wanted and threw away the rest. Who knows? Let's leave that for his defence.'

DC Gallagher marched confidently into the room, but when he saw his boss's face darken at his lateness, he said immediately, 'Sorry, I'm late Ma'am. I was on the phone. The crime scene manager wanted to speak to you. I took the message.'

'And?' she said, crossly.

'And they've found a book there, in Clerk's flat. It's got a bookplate on it which says "Ex Libris Gavin Brodie" or something like that.'

'Yes!' Elaine Bell said triumphantly, raising her fist in the air. 'We've got the creepy bastard now.'

━

Tonight would be spent in her own bed, Elaine Bell thought, seeing and smelling the freshly-ironed sheets as if they were in front of her. And, another big bonus, now she would have time to prepare herself for the confrontation with the Super, assemble all the evidence she needed and consider the best strategy to make him rewrite that travesty of an appraisal. She would have to give him wriggle-room to change or rephrase his expressed views without it resembling a retreat. The slightest hint of such a thing would make him more recalcitrant, more uncompromising and, possibly, if cornered, positively belligerent.

Their meeting would take all her tact, all her diplomacy, virtues she was well aware that the good fairy had left out at her christening. And if these failed, then she would simply appeal over his head to his superiors, or perhaps try the grievance route. Of course, resort to either would result in gossip about her predicament. An appeal of any sort, however legitimate, would leave her damaged or tarnished in some intangible way. She would be marked out as another troublesome woman, hand-bagging her way to the top over the bodies of better candidates, all men. And that would be a victory for the Tyrannosaurus, although a different sort of one. No, somehow he would just have to be persuaded to change his mind.

It took four hours to compile, then distil, the evidence that she needed for her campaign, and it could all be contained in one large brown envelope. Looking at it, it seemed strange that her future could depend on such an unimpressive package. Stage two was to arrange the meeting, ideally for some time after lunch, when his belly would be full and his mood benign. Her phone rang and she picked it up, her thoughts still centred on the confrontation to come.

'Chief Inspector Bell.'

'Just thought you'd like to know, Ma'am,' Alistair Watt said, 'we've had Mr Anderson in and he's just positively identified the video clip of Clerk as the man in his flat. He thinks he may have recognised him from the day centre in Raeburn Place, he sometimes goes there too. That's where Robert Clerk goes as well.'

'Alright,' she replied, sounding unexcited by the news. 'There was no doubt about that anyway, was there? Clerk didn't deny being in the man's flat, even admitted to picking up the man's things, including the knife, didn't he?'

'Well, yes, but . . .'

'Probably picks his victims from the place. It would make perfect sense wouldn't it? I'd bet money that Gavin Brodie also attended that day centre.'

Seeing Professor McConnachie standing waiting in her doorway, she glanced at her watch and quickly terminated the conversation, waving the pathologist in. He sat down opposite her, his battered old leather briefcase perched on the edge of his fleshless knees.

'And how are you this cold afternoon?' he began, fumbling inside it and taking a couple of sheets of paper from its ink-stained interior.

'I am fine, just fine,' she replied, feeling well-disposed towards him, content with the way the investigation seemed to be going.

'Well, we've got the toxicology report back, and I thought I'd bring it myself. I was due to see one of your people anyway.'

'Anything interesting?' she asked, picking it up and beginning to read the first paragraph.

'Yes.'

'Yes?' she repeated interrogatively, her head on one side, waiting for him to explain.

'That Brodie man seems to have been very unpopular. He was poisoned as well as having his throat cut.'

'Bloody Hell!'

'It was, I agree, a rather unexpected finding . . .'

'Are you telling me,' she interrupted him, 'that the cut to the throat wasn't the cause of death? Because if so, we may have wasted the first few, crucial days of this investigation . . .'

And, glowering at him, she added with real anger in her voice, 'If only these reports weren't always so bloody late!'

'What I'm telling you, actually, Elaine, is that this is a complex, difficult picture,' Professor McConnachie replied emolliently, trying to calm her down and ensure that she took in his news, digested its import properly.

'Then he did die in consequence of the cut?' she chipped in, unwilling to proceed at his sedate pace.

'Yes, yes. Brodie was undoubtedly alive when his throat was cut and he did die in consequence of it. He exsanguinated, bled to death, if you like. We know that, you saw the evidence of it splattered all over the place, running down his bedroom wall. But the toxicology here's . . . well, anything but straightforward. At the P.M. I had difficulty getting blood, so as you know I submitted liver and heart samples too. They've been analysed, and the tissues contain significant concentrations of two drugs – morphine and nortriptyline – at a toxic or near-toxic level. A level, possibly, probably, suggestive of an overdose.'

'What do you mean "possibly, probably"? We need beyond reasonable doubt, remember,' she said sharply. 'And which is it? "Possibly" or "probably"? And neither's good enough, as you'll appreciate.'

'Yes,' the Professor said, trying to remain unriled despite her combative tone. 'I do appreciate that, but we can't give you a more categorical result because of post-mortem redistribution. It's likely there's been some degree of post-mortem diffusion from the gastro-intestinal tract into the liver lobes lying closest to the stomach and into the cardiac tissues.'

'So?'

'So that makes it difficult to estimate ante-mortem drug concentrations, and the ingested dose, from the post-mortem measurements.'

'So what is it, exactly, that are you telling me? I told you, I need, as a minimum, to understand.'

The Professor sighed, 'From the toxicological results it looks possible . . .' He corrected himself, '*Probable*, that at some interval, perhaps a couple of hours before his throat was cut, Mr Brodie ingested a toxic or near-toxic dose of morphine, in some form, plus an anti-depressant, one of the tricyclics called nortriptyline – both medications he took for his condition.'

'So we'll need to check it all out, won't we? Find out if he could have taken the stuff himself . . . or if it had to be fed to him – if it could even be fed to him – and then he's bloody killed by something else anyway. I wonder where that leaves us?'

'I really don't know,' the Professor said, his head bent as he fished in the interior of his bag once more.

'Could he have taken it himself, accidentally or otherwise?'

'As I said, I don't know. I had a look at his medical records this morning, but you can't tell from them.'

He rose to go, handing her another sheet of paper. 'One other thing – and I'm just the messenger, remember – here's the lab report.'

As soon as she lowered her head to read it, he took his opportunity to escape, casually ambling out of the open doorway, humming under his breath as if without a care in the world, but feeling the need for a good strong cup of coffee.

Although he was seated at his desk in the murder suite, Inspector Eric Manson's mind was on his wife, rather than his work. Under his left hand lay a sheaf of papers that he was supposed to look at, fresh from the photocopier and still warm to the touch, but they remained unread. Tom Littlewood was scurrying about the room distributing the copies, the DCI's barked orders ringing in his ears. The milk in Manson's coffee had begun to form a skin, and he gave his cup an absent-minded stir, then removed the spoon from it but did not pick up his drink. Even his mid-afternoon snack, a white pudding, had been allowed to grow cold within its paper bag.

This could not be happening to him, he thought morosely. Not to him. To others, obviously, but to him? No. It was not that Margaret was plain – on the contrary, taking into account her age and so on, she had fared really quite well – but she had no interest in other men, surely? Years and years ago she must have ceased to look at them in that way. But maybe they continued to look at her in that way? Impossible! She had 'happily married woman' stamped all over her, every inch of her, she was positively matronly. She would never give anyone the glad eye, or make a spectacle of herself. Well, not that he had witnessed, anyway, although on reflection, she wouldn't do it if he was watching her, now, would she? But it was ridiculous! Margaret must be . . . was, above suspicion.

On the other hand, perhaps that was part of the problem? Complacency. It could make the clearly visible, invisible, and prevent you from seeing what was right in front of your nose. And maybe he had taken her for granted. A bit. But not Margaret. Sweet Jesus!

He groaned, looked round to see if anyone had heard the sound, and then cleared his throat noisily to disguise it. The possibility, and that was all it was, must be faced, would have to be taken seriously. The evidence had to be considered and a conclusion reached. 'Feeling' or 'intuition' or other nonsense of that sort could not be relied upon. He would not be cuckood . . . cuckolded, or whatever the hell it was called.

His mobile rang and he snatched it up, annoyed at the intrusion into his thoughts.

'Yes,' he said sharply.

'Eric, Eric, love, it's me . . .' the words were meant to be soothing, but the characteristic discordant squawk, instantly identifying the caller, had the opposite effect. The female journalist at the other end, unaware of the Inspector's irritation, added in a rasping tone, 'What've you got for me today, darling?'

Had Manson been standing beside her he would almost certainly have softened, as he usually did, on seeing her blonde good looks and inhaling her expensive scent. And he would have imparted information to her, whether confidential or not, before he had even realised what he was doing. But the ugliness of that disembodied voice still ringing in his ear had a very different effect, one unlikely to make him compliant. The assumption implicit in her question positively annoyed him.

'Em . . . I'm in the office the now, Marie, and nothin's doin'. I gave you your wee titbit about the Brodie murder yesterday, and it's all I've got.'

'Come on, Eric, sweetheart. You're the man. You can do better than that.'

Again, if he had seen the words spoken by her full lips he would have found them flirtatious, heard some magical double-entendre, but when she was not there in the flesh they were open to a very different interpretation.

To his preoccupied, troubled mind they had a nagging or goading sound. Did the woman imagine that he was her pet or something?

'Em . . . I've got to go, Marie. Somethin' urgent's just . . . eh, breaking.'

So saying, he shoved his mobile back into his pocket, regretting instantly his use of the word 'urgent'. It was bound to make her reporter's ears prick up, and she would re-double her efforts. Never mind, she had been fobbed off for the present and reminded of her place.

Anyway, he thought, crossly, what had he ever got from her apart from a few come-ons ending in brush-offs? She was like some kind of mirage in the desert, shimmering and beautiful from afar, but turning out on closer inspection to be a mere illusion. No more than a puff of hot air. Not that, as a married man, he would have ever been led astray by her, obviously, even if he had had the chance, but to date she had not offered him the chance. The chance to refuse. Oh, no, she appeared to believe, he fumed, that he could be led by the nose endlessly like . . . like . . . a circus pony or a bull or something, never actually receiving a reward but still traipsing endlessly after her. A reward he would decline when, and if, she offered it. Even though it was long overdue.

He opened his desk drawer, intending to remove a couple of biscuits from the packet inside it, and noticed under his digestives a framed photograph of his wife. He picked it up, tipping off stale crumbs as he did so, and studied it. There she was, smiling at him, wearing a large navy boater and her favourite cream dress, the one with navy embroidery on the collars. Her 'going away' outfit. He had taken the picture on the first day of their honeymoon. Tucked into the frame was a more recent image, snapped less than a year ago. Staring at it, he became anxious once more. It reminded him that she had worn well for fifty-five, a little on the matronly side nowadays maybe, but she could still be described as 'attractive'. And if he thought so, after over thirty years of marriage, then other men might well do so too. Christ Almighty!

But, he comforted himself, it was all right, everything was all right, because she would not be interested in the unscrupulous swine anyway. On the other hand, if that were true, then why had she taken to dressing so much more snappily of late? Her neckline had plunged lower than ever before, even he had noticed that, and her clothes were more clinging, more . . . He paused, trying to think of the appropriate word. 'Sexy'. Christ, that was it. They were more sexy, she was looking sexier. And why, in heaven's name, would she be doing that? Unless there was another man.

While he had been daydreaming, thinking about his wife, the DCI had come into the room to talk to him. And, now she was standing beside him, watching in disbelief as he frittered away valuable time, staring fixedly out of the window, his jaw loose, his mouth hanging open. She had already taken in the fact that the papers in front of him remained unread. A second earlier she had swept her hand across his line of vision, but, in his absorption, he had seen nothing.

'Eric!' she said, impatient to get his attention.

'Ma'am,' he answered automatically, coming to and becoming aware once more of his surroundings.

'So, what do you think?'

'Mmm . . .' Having no idea what she was talking about, he played for time, quickly deciding to try and bounce the question back to her.

'I'm just not sure what to think, really. What do you think, Ma'am?'

'You haven't read it, have you?'

'I've made a start, but not very thoroughly, no . . .'

'Well, to speed things up a bit – the toxicology report suggests that Brodie may have been poisoned before he had his throat slit, doesn't it?'

'Shit! Poisoned . . . you're joking.'

'I knew you hadn't read it. Perhaps you'd like me to read it to you?'

'No, Ma'am.'

'Have you looked at the lab report?'

'Not as such'

'Well, if you had you would know that Clerk's prints are on the handles of Brodie's wheelchair in India Street. And there's some other, so far unidentified, DNA in the house – which is, perhaps, not surprising really.'

Eric Manson cocked his head to one side, unsure quite what to think, but keen to look thoughtful.

'Anyway, I've spoken to the fiscal and he agrees that with the prints and the book we've got more than enough now to charge Clerk with Gavin Brodie's murder. We'll interview him first thing tomorrow. But, in the meanwhile, I need to find out more about the poisoning, overdose or whatever. McConnachie's quite clear that it wasn't the cause of death, but we still need to know, in case his defence makes something out of it, as I'm sure they'll try. And we don't want him to get off, do we?'

'So . . .'

'So, I'm leaving it to you and Alice to find out what was going on, to dig about the place. I want an explanation, so just read the bloody reports, will you?'

He nodded, but said nothing.

'Begin by seeing the man's doctor, Colin Paxton. It may be Brodie took the stuff himself, that he was suicidal and there's an innocent explanation for all of it. And if so, good, that'll be an end of it. So, we need to find out if he could have done that, if there was enough in the bottles for the overdose – you get the picture. And Eric . . .' she added unnecessarily, peeved that she still did not appear to have his full attention, 'you'll catch flies if you keep your maw open like that.'

Picking up the phone on her desk Alice immediately recognised Mrs Foscetti's bird-like warble. 'Alice, dear, Ian was supposed to collect Quill by six o'clock but he's not been. And it's nearly eight, and we're supposed to be going out.'

But before Alice had said a word, begun to apologise, she heard a loud scuffling noise at the other end of the line, and then, in the background, Miss Spinnell's irritated tones, followed by a brief, heated exchange between the sisters.

'What *are* you doing, Annabelle?' Miss Spinnell hissed. 'It's only the spiritualists, a Blue Lodge meeting.'

'But I thought you wanted to go to it! You used to go, before I came.'

'Yes, but I've found you haven't I? It is you, isn't it? I only joined to speak to you, when I thought you were dead. I wasn't looking for company, for any old soul you know. Goodness me, you're not the only one to have friends, dear! Tell Ali . . . Alice . . . that we'll keep the dog, all night, if necessary. He can sleep on my bed . . . someone seems to have taken his.'

Reaching the entrance to Broughton Place, Alice looked up at the windows of the flat to see if any lights were on, but it was in darkness. Rather than spend time at home alone she carried on to the bottom of Broughton Street, over the roundabout at Mansefield Place and down towards Canonmills and Inverleith Row. As she walked, she kept her eyes peeled in case Ian was scurrying home, coming in the opposite direction, eager to get into the warmth and call it a day.

As she passed the terrace in the Colonies, drops of rain began to fall, getting bigger every second, until what had started as a light shower became an icy downpour. Soon streams were cascading off the pavements and setting the gutters awash with mud-coloured water. Everyone but her seemed to have had some kind of early warning of the deluge and had taken shelter. Opposite Reid Terrace, the usually sluggish Water of Leith was being transformed, its mild babbling turning into the roar of a gathering torrent.

Crossing the low bridge by the turn-off to Arboretum Avenue, she put her head down and began to run, heading for St Bernard's Row. Suddenly the sky was lit by a flash of lightning and in seconds the boom of thunder followed it. Turning into Henderson Row and wondering if she would be struck by the next bolt, she tried the handle of the studio door, rattling it to no effect until she noticed the large padlock on the high latch.

Now soaked to the skin, she turned to leave, but saw a young woman, whom she recognised as a studio-mate of Ian's, standing in a doorway opposite the dilapidated building. Desperate to get out of the ceaseless rain, she ran across the road and stood beside her, shivering, cursing herself for losing every umbrella she had ever possessed.

'Ian's not still in there is he?' she said through chattering teeth, hoping against hope.

The woman, taking a final draw from her cigarette, said, 'No, the place's deserted. Everyone went hours ago. There's a power-cut, and it'll not be put right until tomorrow morning.' Then she snatched up the rucksack at her feet and plunged out on to the pavement, clattering along it with an uncoordinated pigeon-toed gait, her bag swinging from side to side with each heavy footstep like Quasimodo's hump.

Watching her as she disappeared, Alice wondered if, for once, Ian had taken a different route home and was now sitting in the light, enjoying the warmth of their flat. That was it – he, too, must have gone home by the Henderson Row route for a change. But what a night to choose.

With her hair and clothes drenched, water streaming down her face, she trudged back eastwards, keeping herself going with the thought of the hot bath and drink that would be waiting for her at the other end. It was his turn to do make the supper, so there would be some food, too, with luck. But the stone stairs up to their flat were as dry as ever, the odd puff of dust rising under her feet as she climbed, and no light was visible in the glass panel above their front door. Neither Ian nor Quill were there to welcome her in her dripping state, and the flat was cold. Where on earth was he?

An hour later, and having found something to eat, she tried to read the paper but found that she could not concentrate, flitting from one world disaster to the next, unmoved by them all. When she phoned him again she got his messaging service once more. Why had he switched his phone off? What was he playing at? If he had been in an accident surely she would have heard by now?

Perhaps he had just gone to the pub, was there still and had lost all track of time, having a few jars too many.

He could have bloody contacted her though, she thought crossly. Then, hearing the sound of his footsteps on the stair, she rose to greet him, running to the door to open it. But she got there only to hear a bout of consumptive coughing, and the footsteps carrying on up the stairs to the next landing. Nothing more than the signature noises of another of their neighbours, Jim the Vicar, on his way to bed.

Just before midnight, Ian woke her, trying to slide silently under the covers beside her, and she said sleepily, 'Where on earth have you been?'

'In my studio,' he answered, snuggling up against her curved back, 'finishing things off for the exhibition.'

7

Wednesday

Sipping her coffee in the interview room, waiting for the others to arrive, Alice tried to mull things over, work out what was going on. Nothing had been said between them that morning. She had left the flat at a godless hour, with him sleeping like a baby as she crept out of the door. She must not jump to conclusions, she thought, but it was proving difficult not to. He had said that he had been in his studio, and his exact words had been, 'finishing off things for the exhibition.' Well, he could have been nowhere else if that was genuinely what he had been doing, because all his work was there plus all the equipment he needed to complete it. But, but . . . she could not get away from it, he had not been in his studio when she had called there.

And he could not just have popped out for something, returning later, because that woman had said that there had been a power cut, with no electric light available until the next day. Could he have worked in the place by torchlight, by candlelight? A preposterous idea. There would be insufficient illumination for anything and the place would be as cold as the grave, too cold to hold a paintbrush steady. So he must have lied to her, but why?

Another thought struck her, and it filled her heart with fear. If this time he had not been where he had said he had been, then it was perfectly possible that on other occasions the same thing had happened. On his birth-day, for example, when through her inefficiency she had managed to cover most of the surfaces in their flat in candle-wax, burn the food and set off the fire alarm.

No, no, she could relax. It was all right, because then he had paint on his fingers, bright red paint which had coloured their bathwater. But thinking about it again, that might mean nothing. The paint could have got onto his hands at 10.30 in the morning. Because without trust, anything was possible, and the very ground beneath her feet no longer felt solid.

'Did you say something, Alice?' Elaine Bell said, putting down her papers and a mug of tea on the table.

'No, Ma'am. Why?' She had not noticed her boss entering the room.

'Because your lips were moving. Like a lunatic,' the DCI answered dismissively, glancing down at the front page of her newspaper.

Alice nodded and stared out of the window, as blind to the view as if the panes had been painted over, and in seconds her mind had returned to Ian. Maybe he had had enough of her, no longer loved her but was unable to summon up the courage to break the bad news? Yes, that could well be it. Because, gradually, by degrees and almost unconsciously, their lives had become linked, entwined together, and such ties, without love, would feel suffocating, terrifying. How could she have been so stupid? They had both been sleepwalking towards some kind of unacknowledged state of permanence, and he must suddenly have woken up, or been woken up, from it. Perhaps that was it? Perhaps, not only did he no longer love her, but he had also found somebody else, or been found by somebody else.

And his birthday had been worse than a fiasco. But she had had to leave him then, not wanting to, with her body longing for his. But that was the deal, part of the bloody job. And he knew that. He should be able to understand.

'Is the tape machine ready?' Elaine Bell asked, her hand hovering over the phone ready to contact the cells.

'Not yet,' Alice said, rising to attend to it as if in a dream, still preoccupied, trying to work out what to do. Tonight she would sort things out. No, it would have to be tomorrow. He was spending the night with his mother. On Thursday night she would find out exactly where she stood. Ask him a single straightforward question, allowing him no rope with which to hang himself, because the thought that he might lie to her again made her feel physically sick. And maybe, just maybe, everything would be alright, there would be a perfectly innocent explanation for it all.

On his own in his cell, sitting waiting for an escort to take him upstairs for the interview, Norman Clerk patted his mouth with the tips of his fingers, taking off the little grains of sugar from his breakfast, then licking his lips to clean the rest away. Frosties always needed more sugar, whatever the packet said. Sugar Puffs, of course, too. And they were supposed to have honey on them. A likely story.

He was bored, unable to make out the turnkeys' hushed conversation, keen for something, almost anything, to happen. Idly, he rapped his knuckles on the wall of the cell. Immediately, a response came rat-tat-tatting back and so, delighted, he tried again. This time he tried a longer sequence of knocks, though completely meaningless to him. A thundering reply followed and so he banged excitedly again, one long tap, two short, and one long again.

'Fuckin' stop that!' his neighbour shouted, tired of the game before it had even begun.

'Keep your hair on,' he whispered, unwilling to get into conversation with the raging beast caged next to him.

He wandered over to the lavatory, examining his distorted reflection in the metal bowl, sticking his tongue out and flattening his nose. Not a good day: his sparse, grey locks looked matted, almost untidy, and his ears seemed to have grown overnight.

'Think you look good?' the voice in his head asked, sounding louder and more distinct than last night.

Hearing the crunching noise made by a couple of pairs of tackety boots clumping along the corridor, he rushed to his door, standing on his tip-toes to look out of the window. He watched as a drunk man, his arms hanging loosely at his sides, was hauled into the cell opposite him. Once the drunk was inside he heard one of the turnkeys say, 'D'you think we should get the doctor?'

'Yes,' Clerk bawled back, 'you should!' and laughed uproariously to himself as he saw their annoyed expressions. Then he added, hoping to vex them further, 'Well, you did ask.'

Still chortling, he returned to his bench, intent now on combing his hair with his fingers, but heard the lock in his own door turn and looked, expectantly, at the two men detailed to escort him.

Recognising Eric Manson as he entered the interview room, Clerk sighed inwardly. He had wanted this to be an all-female affair, that would have been cosier and more relaxing all round. His ribs were still smarting from the end of the man's boot, the 'tap' administered as he lay on the floor of his brother's flat to persuade him to get to his feet. Following behind the detective was a man he recognised

107

but could not place, a face from his past perhaps, a shabby creature with an over-large suit concertina-ed in wrinkles about his ankles. The fellow deposited his briefcase on the table and clicked its locks open, exposing a pigskin interior. All he could see inside was a packet of oatcakes.

'Your solicitor,' the inspector said, and he and the two women retreated, talking in hushed tones, leaving the pair of them alone.

'I'm here, Mr Clerk,' the man began, 'to make sure that no questions are asked about your entry into Mr Anderson's flat and the assault. You've been charged with both of them now, so they're out of bounds for the officers, so to speak.' Then he held out his hand for his client to shake. But Norman Clerk simply rolled his tongue along his cheek, making no attempt to respond, sitting still where he was and looking the solicitor up and down. The voice in his head had just murmured a caution, warning him that this man was not what he seemed to be at all. Oh yes, he was pretending to be on his side, a friend, an ally, but in reality he had a very different agenda. So far, no damage had been done by him, but actually touching him might be risky and was best avoided. This man must not be made angry, must be kept calm at all costs. He was dangerous.

Obeying the voice's advice and now feeling frightened, Norman Clerk smiled graciously at the stranger but said nothing.

'OK?' the solicitor asked.

'Yes,' he replied in a cheerful voice, looking straight out of the window, trying to evade the man's attention.

'I'm from Campbell & Martin SSC. My name's Mr Nicholl. My firm represented you the first time . . . before, but I was just a trainee then. Now I'm a partner. Starting yesterday, I'm in charge of our Court Department. But you probably won't remember me.'

'Oh, yes I do, I certainly do,' Clerk lied, trying to imbue his voice with the same warm tone, to get across to the man that he would never dream of forgetting him, that the pleasure of their first encounter was etched forever on his memory. For what seemed like an eternity the lawyer droned on, but his client heard little of it, distracted by continuous mutterings from the voice in his head, a whispered commentary which undermined all the professional advice he was being given out loud.

The sound of the door opening and closing warned him that they were no longer alone, and three familiar figures came in, taking their seats opposite him. He continued to look straight ahead, not focusing on them, deliberately registering nothing.

After some kind of formal recitation, the DCI turned her attention to him and said, 'Mr Clerk, you told us that you did not know Gavin Brodie, that you hadn't ever come across him or met him. Is that still your position?'

'Yes,' was all that he could manage. He glanced at the solicitor to see if the answer was satisfactory, and was relieved to be given a nod of encouragement. So far, he was keeping him happy.

'So you've never seen the man or been to his house. No connection between the two of you whatsoever?'

'Yes. No . . . no connection.'

'Then can you explain,' the DCI asked, looking hard at him, 'how it is that a book belonging to Gavin Brodie was found in your flat, amongst your own books?' She held it up in front of him.

'Yes,' he said, his tone almost expressionless once

more. That answer seemed to be alright too. The solicitor did not appear displeased and nodded once more.

'Then could you tell us?' the policewoman asked tartly.

'Don't turn your head,' the voice inside him ordered. 'Whatever you do, don't look at her.'

Continuing to look dead ahead, as if she had said nothing, he replied, 'I collect books and things. Maybe it was one I got from the Oxfam shop or something.'

'Perhaps, for the tape, we should know the title of the book. It's *Not a Penny More, Not a Penny Less* by Jeffrey Archer,' Eric Manson said.

Catching sight of the cover out of the corner of his eye, Clerk recognised it and said, 'Indeed it is. That is one of mine. My brother Robert gave it to me for my birthday.'

'Your brother, the man who had the stroke? The one who can't move or speak?' asked Alice Rice.

'Yes, good old Bob, he got it for me before . . . before his stroke.'

'That's funny,' the DCI observed. 'Brodie's murdered and his things turn up in your flat.'

'Funny . . .' Norman Clerk repeated, keeping his eye on the solicitor and noting, with concern, that he now looked very annoyed, his brow furrowing. His frown deepened and then suddenly he struck out, swatting a fly on his elbow. As he did so, Clerk ducked.

'I'm so sorry,' Mr Nicholl said, appalled at his client's reaction.

'Not at all . . . er, my mistake,' Clerk replied, bobbing up from below the table. His head had begun to hurt and he felt frazzled, unsure how to placate the solicitor and keep himself safe. How could you survive when enemies pretended to be friends, friends pretended to be enemies?

The lawyer, satisfied that none of the police officers had strayed onto either of the prohibited subjects, was now deep in thought, wondering whether to opt for a fixed price Chinese meal for lunch or to go for the all-day breakfast. As a result he did not notice his client's increasing pallor or the beads of sweat gathering on his forehead.

'You've never been to Gavin Brodie's flat in India Street, you say?' the DCI continued.

'Indeed not. Like I said, I don't know the man.'

'Don't use the word "I" again. It's too dangerous,' the voice in his head hissed.

'Then can you tell us how your fingerprints got onto the wheelchair in his flat?'

'No,' began Clerk, '. . . can't do that. Don't know why. I can't . . .' He stopped, putting his hands to his cheeks, a look of acute distress contorting his fleshy features. His lengthy hesitation made the Chief Inspector look at him, and she noticed, for the first time, his pale face and clammy-looking skin.

'You alright?' she asked, quite kindly. 'You look a little peely-wally.'

Only his mother used the expression 'Peely-wally', and hearing what sounded like genuine concern in the woman's voice, he weakened, was almost tempted to tell her the truth. He wanted to say, 'No, I feel awful, terrified of something – something I've done or not done. Maybe I have killed a man, skinned a cat, raped a woman. Any of these things, all of them . . . but who knows?'

Instead, remembering in the nick of time that he must not say the word 'I', he nodded his head mutely, stealing another glance at the solicitor and catching, to his relief, a wide smile from him. 'Well done,' the voice said, congratulating him on fooling all the people all the time, reminding him that they were blind and would never see. He alone saw it all, understood it all.

———

Outside in the main hall after the interview had finished, the DCI asked Mr Nicholl what the likely course of the case would be, given the psychiatrist's opinion that the prisoner had been fit to interview. Was it likely to proceed as normal or what?

'Oh, no,' the solicitor replied, collecting his dark blue Crombie from the coat-stand. 'Early days, but I doubt it very much. Of course, we haven't consulted with Counsel yet but I expect there's a very good chance that we'll be going for a plea in bar of trial.'

'So, surprise me, what's it likely to be this time?' she asked, already sure of the answer.

'Insanity, of course. I spoke to our consulting partner before I left this morning, and he reckons it'll be the ticket. I'm seeing two eminent shrinks next week, and we'll get them to examine him too. Both treated him in Carstairs, so they'll know him well already.'

'The very ones who decided he was safe to let out, I expect,' she remarked dryly. The solicitor, not having heard what she said, nodded politely, keen to get away and sample some dim sum.

———

'I'm already running twenty-five minutes late,' Doctor Colin Paxton thought, 'and now it's bloody Mrs Gurney, and she'll ensure that I get no break at all. Well, we'll see about that. And what in heaven's name are the receptionists thinking about, letting her past their defences again? What else are they being paid for?'

Clutching a bulging carrier in each hand, the widow lowered her massive behind onto the chair, very, very slowly, as if her buttocks were made of glass and likely to shatter on contact. Once she had made a safe landing she put both of her bags on the floor. Immediately, the room filled with the scent of eucalyptus.

'It's ma back,' she sighed, bending forwards towards the doctor and rubbing her spine with one hand as if to ease the pain. It was her usual opening gambit.

'Yes,' he answered impassively.

'Is there anything you can give me for it?'

She must, he mused, know the answer to that one. Week after week she re-appeared with exactly the same complaint, all consultants long ago having given up on her. Every week she wanted him to adjust the dosage of her medication or, occasionally, alter it altogether, but whatever he did always had exactly the same result. No effect whatsoever. Maybe she was lonely, needed company, was desperate for someone to talk to? Fat chance. Her pupils were like pinpricks, and her manner radiated hostility, the pursuit of some kind of undeclared vendetta or battle of wills. No. She did not like him, simply wanted to ensure that her symptoms were recorded with a view to being signed off again.

'Well,' he said evenly, 'we upped your co codamol last week, didn't we? So perhaps we should give it a proper chance, see if it works?'

'Yes, but it's shifted, the pain's shifted.'

Just as he was about to give his usual reply at this stage in their combat, 'shifting' being one of the pain's recurring characteristics, his telephone rang.

'Yes?' he answered. 'Ah, Mr Tyler,' he added quickly, recognising the strong South African drawl of the surgeon.

'Mr Tyler! Mr Tyler!' Mrs Gurney broke in excitedly, 'he's one of the ones I've seen. Tell him about my back, Doctor, see what he says.'

Unable to think straight because of the competing voices, Paxton waved at the woman to try to quieten her down, simultaneously attempting to record the results of a bladder capacity test for a patient no longer even under his care. As he put the receiver down, Mrs Gurney said, petulantly, 'You could at least have asked him . . .'

'No,' Doctor Paxton replied, looking at his watch, 'I could not. You've seen Mr Taylor and Mr Titler, both ortho-paedic surgeons, not Mr Tyler, the urological specialist.'

'He might be able to help me though,' she replied reproachfully, beetling her thick brows.

'No. Incontinence is not your problem, not bladder incontinence anyway. Now, was there anything else?'

Thwarted once more, she decided on one final gambit: 'Yes, there is. My ears need skooshing. I cannae hear a thing.'

Thinking of his coffee, and clutching for a lifeline, he said, 'Have you been softening the wax – putting almond oil in?'

'Eh?' she said, cupping her ear.

After he had shouted the question once more, she shook her head, finally conceding defeat.

'Fine,' he said calmly. 'You'll need to do that for a few days before your ears can be syringed.' Checkmate.

'OK, doc. See you next week, or maybe earlier.' And from her lips it sounded like a threat.

—

Alice, accompanied by Eric Manson, scanned the wait-ing room looking for a safe seat. Most of the chairs were occupied by pallid, handkerchief-wielding adults, each exhaling lungfuls of germs, in dire need of medical help to cure them of their recurring bouts of flu. The warm air would be thick with seasonal viruses and possibly, God forbid, even swine flu or whatever latest deadly pandemic was going the rounds.

Taking the first available seat he saw, Manson sat down next to a feverish-looking young man who was wiping his nose, rheumy-eyed.

'How about over here?' Alice whispered to her colleague, gesturing towards a possible sanctuary, a small recess with a couple of old people seated together in it, the old man's stick resting between his bandy legs. Thinking that this was bound to be a safer bet, she manoeuvred her way through the sneezing patients to a chair beside the old couple. With luck they would be attending for geriatric, non-contagious problems such as dry skin, varicose veins or ingrowing toenails. Looking puzzled and slightly irritated, the Inspector followed, sitting down beside her and immediately picking up a dog-eared copy of *Hello*.

However, no sooner had he sat down than a harassed mother, with three children in tow, parked herself on the remaining chair in the recess. Sighing, she set the two larger infants down at her feet and began jiggling the baby up and down on her lap. The toddlers, both as pale as chalk, soon started investigating, then sucking, the nearby collection of coloured building blocks. The baby, meantime, a torrent of mucus pouring from its nose, seemed determined to clamber from its mother's lap onto Alice. Feeling no urge to cuddle it, she leant away, keeping her eyes fixed firmly on her magazine. Other people's children held no allure for her, even when healthy.

Initially the mother kept a tight grip on the child, physically restraining it and pointing at pictures in a book

115

to entertain it. Every so often she put a hand to its red forehead until, unexpectedly, she turned to Alice and said, 'Could you keep him for a second or two, just while I go to the toilet? I don't like taking him in there with me.'

Despite her fear of catching flu or something far worse from the baby, Alice answered faintly that she would. She was ashamed to voice her terror of infection, and too cowardly to refuse such an apparently reasonable request.

Once on her lap, the baby looked up into her face for a few seconds, registered mild alarm, and then began bawling inconsolably at an ear-splitting volume. She tried everything she could think of to quieten him, jiggling him up and down, putting her arms around him, making comic faces, all to no avail. Everyone in the room now seemed to be staring in their direction.

'You've had children, Sir, what should I do?' she whispered in desperation.

His eyes never leaving the picture of a pouting Angelina Jolie, Manson said, 'Try Incy Wincy Spider or something . . .'

'I don't know it.'

'Then try "Round and round the garden".'

'I don't know that either.'

'Oh, for Heaven's sake!' he replied, his ears now hurting from the constant screeching. Flinging down the magazine, he scooped the startled child from her lap.

'Incy Wincy Spider climbed up the water spout, down came the rain . . .' he sang.

Suddenly the baby sneezed loudly, showering him with a fine spray of green snot, and simultaneously made a strange parping noise below.

Fortunately, at that point, the mother returned and a nurse's voice announced, 'Eric . . . Eric Manson?' Hearing his name, the Inspector dropped the baby like a hot brick onto its mother's knee and he and Alice rose simultaneously, following the nurse down the corridor to the doctor's consulting room.

Still finishing off the notes for his last patient, Doctor Paxton signalled for them to come in. This appointment would require his full concentration, he thought. It was not the sort of thing he was used to, and if possible he hoped it would not be repeated. Turning from his computer he said, 'And how can I help you, officers?'

'We need information about a patient of yours, Gavin Brodie.'

'Yes, that's what I had understood from the call. But what exactly do you need to know? A copy of his records was sent to the pathologists, and I provided someone from St Leonard's with a list of the drugs he was taking.'

A nurse knocked on the door, waited and then came in with a cup of steaming coffee.

'Would you mind if I had it?' the doctor asked, 'I'm already behind schedule.'

'No problem, on you go,' Eric Manson replied, eying the drink longingly and then looking around the room, his eye caught by a large, full-colour illustration of the inner ear or, possibly, some reproductive organ.

'The prescriptions for Nortriptylene and Oramorph . . . what quantity of each drug was contained in each bottle?' Alice asked.

'You mean if it was full? I don't know, not off the top of my head. The pharmacy would, though. I could get the information from them for you,' he said, sitting back in his chair and taking a sip from his cup, then putting it back carefully in its saucer.

His telephone rang and, apologising silently, he picked

it up. 'I can't speak, love . . . no, really. A patient. I'll call you later . . . yes, promise.'

'Sorry,' he said, turning his attention back to his visitors.

'When did he last get a new supply of each drug?' Alice asked.

'Both were new on the Friday, the Friday before he died. He'll have hardly used any by the Saturday night. We could calculate the exact amount left – obviously I know his daily dosage. So once we know what the bottles contained we could work out what was left for the junkies or whatever . . .' So saying, he made an expansive gesture with his right hand and sent his coffee cup flying.

'Bother! Sorry, sorry,' he said quickly, taking some paper tissues from the box on his desk and starting to mop the spillage up.

'Would Mr Brodie have been able to open either of the bottles if he wanted to?' Eric Manson enquired, watching the doctor beadily as he dabbed ineffectually at a sodden sheet of paper.

'No, I don't think he would have had the necessary co-ordination. But I must admit I'm not sure about it, he might have managed.'

'Would he have understood what was in any of his bottles, would he have known that it was his medicine or whatever?'

'Well,' he paused in his cleaning, clearly applying his mind to the question, 'I doubt it. But maybe? He was pretty far gone, but you just never know with those patients, do you?'

'Well, we certainly don't, doctor, that's why we came to you,' Eric Manson said truculently, annoyed at the man's inability to provide them with any black or white answers, any certainties.

Smelling the unmistakeable delicious aroma of chips, Alice looked round the murder suite in search of the source, ignoring for a moment the remaining soggy ham-salad sandwich in its triangular box on her desk. She had made a bad choice, but perhaps whoever had been to the chippy might be interested in a swap.

Thomas Riddell, the Family Liaison Officer, who was making one of his rare visits to the office, was glued to his computer screen and appeared to be making do with soup from a plastic cup. No luck there, then. At the other end of the room, Alistair Watt was leaning against his desk, carefully picking out lumps of apple from his fruit salad and throwing them in the bin.

'Eleven sodding bits out of twenty,' he complained, scowling in disgust at the pink, watery mess that remained.

Alone among the company, DI Manson was not having his lunch. He was standing with his back to them all, staring out onto Arthur's Seat, and his sausage roll was getting cold on the window sill.

'So, how did you and Eric get on this morning?' Elaine Bell asked Alice, wiping grease from her mouth with a paper napkin. 'Could Brodie have taken the stuff himself – tried to commit suicide or not?'

'No,' Alice replied, noticing that, unfortunately, it was her boss who had the chips, 'probably not. But Dr Paxton wasn't all that helpful. He left it all slightly open. It doesn't sound as if it would have been impossible for him to take the stuff himself, just unlikely.'

'Then let's assume, for the moment,' the DCI said, 'that he couldn't take the stuff himself then, where does that leave us?'

'Someone must have given it to him, or forced him to drink it, I suppose. Probably someone in the family, or close to him at any rate. Maybe it was accidental, an accidental overdose by someone? Clerk's never done that kind of thing, drug people I mean. Why would he, anyway? So perhaps someone close to Brodie thought they'd help him out or something? Fed him the stuff, knowing he wanted it, that he wanted to die but couldn't manage it himself.'

'Oh, I don't think so,' Thomas Riddell broke in, in his usual ponderous manner, tipping his cup to drain the last drop. 'I've met all the family, got to know them, relate to them, and that wouldn't be my impression. None of them would do that. Anyway, the children were together on the Saturday night and . . .'

'And why not them, exactly?' Eric Manson said, turning round and facing Riddell. 'Who else would do it?'

'Well, certainly not Heather,' replied the Liaison Officer, taken aback by the fierce tone of his superior.

'I think you mean Mrs Brodie,' the Inspector corrected him, his mind temporarily back on his work. Bloody Liaison Officers! What a breed they were, more like social workers than policemen. Supposed to be the force's eyes and ears in the family, but before you know it, they'd been turned, become the family's eyes and ears within the force. And this great big lummox was no different. He was probably under the woman's spell already, with her baby-blue eyes and refined ways. He would be a sucker for someone like that.

'Mrs Brodie's very upset – about her husband, I mean. And the two children obviously really loved their father. They were close, I'd say an unusually close family unit. The kids were together on the night as I said. The young lad seems very angry, acting up, taking out his grief issues against his mother. Ella has Katy, so she's better able to channel . . .'

'What *are* you on about now?' Eric Manson butted in, 'and who the fuck is "Katy"?'

'She's Ella's daughter.'

'And the father?'

'He's not on the scene. But the rest of them, like I said, they're a close family unit . . .'

'Quite,' Elaine Bell said, cutting off Riddell mid-stream. 'And that's exactly why we'll check them out.'

'Sure, but the man's throat was cut,' Riddell said, bemused. 'That's what killed him . . . isn't it?'

'Yes. That's right,' the DCI replied, speaking unnaturally slowly as if he might find it difficult to follow, 'that's correct. But we still need to know, don't we? Because, otherwise, some smart-arse Counsel will use it to confuse the jury – if it ever gets that far. And Clerk's still denying having anything to do with Brodie, don't forget. No confession from him. So, I'm taking no chances. We'll talk to the family again, check them out, and that Una Reid woman, too. Apart from anything else, they may have a different view as to whether Brodie could have taken the stuff himself. And if he could have, then we may be off this particular hook.'

'D'you want me to speak to Hea . . . Mrs Brodie?' Thomas Riddell said, rising from his chair as if already on his way.

'No,' the DCI said, gesturing for him to sit down again. 'Alice can do that this time, can't you, Alice?'

Without waiting for a reply, she continued, 'And Eric, you can check out the old woman, Brodie's mother, for us. And Alice, find out if he ever attended the Raeburn

Place Day Centre. I reckon that's where Clerk spotted his victims. Anything else, anyone?'

DC Littlewood entered the room, both arms laden with carrier bags and dropped them noisily onto his desk.

'Sandy and me are having people in tonight,' he said by way of explanation.

'Sssh!' Elaine Bell said. 'We're trying to think in here.'

'Sorry, ma'am. One thing, though . . .'

'Later,' she replied impatiently, adding, 'What do you think about it all, Eric?'

The Inspector did not turn round, so she repeated the question, speaking more loudly.

'I think,' he said slowly, 'I think that Clerk is scum, S.C.U.M., complete and utter scum. That's what I think.'

'Thanks. That's very helpful,' Elaine Bell said sarcastically, rubbing her hands over her eyes as if wearied by his response.

'Ma'am . . .' the DC tried again.

'Yes?'

'It was just to pass on a message. While you were talking to the ACC, the lab phoned to say that the eliminatory sample that the woman, Una Reid, gave matches stuff taken at the scene. And the rest of the family's samples do too.'

'And?' Her bored tone suggested that she expected nothing from this quarter.

'And . . . that was it. They're still trying to find a match for the other stuff. No luck so far.'

'Mmm. Well, it would have been odder if the family hadn't left traces of themselves about the place, wouldn't it? Alice, you'd best speak to the children too. I'm not sure that our Inspector's up to it today.'

8

As Alice Rice walked into the hallway of the flat in Brunts-field Place the next morning, she noticed droplets of fresh blood on the light grey carpet, and on the kitchen floor, a trail·of tiny red splashes led to the sink. Mrs Brodie herself appeared quite at home in her sister's flat, either unaware of the spatters of blood or unconcerned by them. She sat with her legs crossed, dressed in a towelling robe, her wet hair clinging to her unmade-up face, the magazine that she had been reading open on the table before her. In one hand she clutched a wad of paper hankies as if she might, at some stage, need to stem the flow of tears, but her eyes were not red-rimmed, and when she began speaking her voice sounded normal, unaffected by emotion.

Leaning over to get her cup of tea from the nearby kitchen unit, she inadvertently, knocked over one of the countless plastic containers that littered every available surface in the room. Rows of yoghurt pots lined the windowsills too, most of them empty, a few containing a single, parched, yellowing seedling.

'One of Pippa's many hobbies,' she said, almost apologetically, picking up the container and adding, 'my sister, Pippa Mitchelson. This is her flat. I'm staying with her.'

Glancing at the spilt soil on the lino, Alice noticed a red pool below the woman's bare foot, and watched as two dark streams of blood trickled down her ankle and dripped off onto the floor. The other leg, too, appeared to have countless little nicks on it. As she puzzled whether she should say something and, if so, what, Heather Brodie caught her eye. Seeing her uneasy expression she looked down at her legs and said, reassuringly, 'Oh, don't worry, sergeant, I've come prepared.' She began to dab her legs with a couple of the hankies, adding, 'I ran out of cream. I was shaving them when you rang the doorbell, so I finished the job in a hurry, botched it and ended up in a bloodbath. You know how it is . . .'

Alice nodded, and waited until the woman had staunched the blood before saying, 'Mrs Brodie, we're still trying to work out everyone's movements on the Saturday night, trying to prepare an exact timetable. So we need to know a little more from you. You said that you left India Street at about 6 pm?'

'Yeah,' the woman replied, concentrating on the cuts, depositing a heavily blood-soaked paper hankie onto the kitchen table and bending to hold another in place.

'Why isn't it Tom finding out these things? Mr Riddell, he's the one who was allocated to us. I thought he was supposed to deal with me, to liaise with us,' she said, adding, slightly querulously, 'we've got to know him, too. He's a friend.'

'He's busy at the moment, I'm afraid,' Alice said. 'If you could just remind me where you went that evening?'

'To Pippa's, my sister's. Well, not here to her flat, but out with her. We'd planned to spend the evening out together, like I told you.'

'So where did the pair of you go?'

'Em . . . to the shops, window shopping, in the St James Centre. Next, John Lewis – those sorts of places – then we had supper together.'

'Where did you eat?'

'The Norseman on Lothian Road – smoresbrod or whatever it is called. Great thick slices of over-priced bread. She likes it, but we hadn't booked it or anything.'

'And then?'

A caterwauling of faint, breathless miaows started up, and Alice watched as a long-haired tortoiseshell cat slunk through the door, weaving its way towards Heather Brodie and winding itself between her legs, its fluffy tail waving snakelike behind it.

'Who's this?' the policewoman asked.

'Fanta, Pippa's companion. She's come to see her kittens. She's a rescue cat, used to be called 'Cade', as in 'Cavalcade', but that was meaningless, so Pippa changed her name. The new one fits her better, I think, but she doesn't come when called.'

'Where are the kittens?'

'In that corner, up on the unit, behind the microwave. They were born there, two pure white and one black. I'm getting one of the white ones.'

Restraining herself from getting up and going to see them, giving them a stroke even, Alice watched as the cat leapt up and disappeared behind the microwave, contented purring soon replacing the anguished high-pitched mews. With luck she would see them on the way out.

'After the Norseman, where did you go?'

'Further down the same road, to the theatre, to see *A Woman of No Importance*.'

'Who was in it – taking the leading roles?'

Looking for the first time slightly vexed, as if the question was pointless, she replied, 'Since you ask, it had Martin Jarvis in it. That's why I wanted to see it.'

'You're a fan of his? Was he good?'

'Yes, I like him. I think he's a superb actor and he was wonderful as Lord Illingworth.'

'Then what?'

'Then,' she said slowly, her voice tailing off as if she was re-living the moment in her head, 'then I walked home on my own. It took a while, you'll appreciate. I didn't look at my watch, but I'd have got back at about eleven or maybe half past, I think.'

'Thank you very much, Mrs Brodie. You said, last time, that you'd planned to spend the night with your sister but you changed your mind. Why, what made you change your mind?'

'Oh,' Heather Brodie said, standing up and tossing the blood-stained collection of hankies in the bin, 'who knows? I can't really remember. A voice in my head told me to go home and, for once, I listened to it, obeyed it. That's the best I can do.'

A young woman entered the kitchen with a toddler balanced on her hip, and, as they arrived, the child opened her eyes, rubbed them and said in a sleepy voice, 'Aunty Pippa – where's Aunty Pippa?'

'No,' said Heather Brodie, opening her arms wide to receive the child, 'there's only Granny here today, Katy, I'm afraid.'

'Mum!' her daughter said in mock reproach, lifting the child and trying unsuccessfully to pass her into the outstretched arms. But the little girl clung onto her mother more tightly, turning her head away from her grandmother.

'Well, it's true, darling,' Mrs Brodie answered, frowning. 'We both know she prefers her aunt.'

'Only because she has more to do with her. She sees her nearly every afternoon when I'm at Uni. Sometimes

I think Katy prefers her to me, she cries when it's time to come home with me. But I don't take it amiss . . . do I?' She lowered the toddler onto the ground and then went over to her mother and kissed her.

'Is Harry coming?'

'Yes. He's just parking the car.'

'So, sergeant,' said Heather Brodie, turning her attention back to the policewoman, 'here they are. I gather you'd like to talk to them too?'

As she was speaking, Harry Brodie slouched into the kitchen. He was wearing a dark blue hoodie and carrying a copy of *The Hungry Caterpillar*. When he saw the child, he immediately went towards her, smiling broadly, and put the book on her lap.

'Harry, darling . . .' His mother got up to kiss the boy.

'Mother,' he replied coldly, accepting the kiss but making no attempt to return it. He then deliberately avoided meeting her gaze, concentrating his attention exclusively on the others, as if snubbing her.

'No kiss for me?' she said good naturedly, offering him her cheek.

'Yes. No kiss for you,' he spat back, now looking her straight in the eye, ignoring the presence of a stranger. The woman paled but said nothing.

'I would like to talk to them,' Alice said, resuming their previous conversation, 'but separately from you and from each other, please. But I've a few more things to clear up with you first.'

'Very well,' Heather Brodie replied, signalling to her children that they should leave the room. They chattered to each other as they went out, with the child stumbling after them.

'Boys!' she said, as if to explain her son's behaviour.

'Could you tell me a little about your husband. For example, could he take his own medication, measure it out, lift the bottle and so on?' Alice asked.

'I always gave it to him,' Heather Brodie replied, sitting down and pulling the loose sides of her robe together.

'No one else? The children, his mother?'

'My mother-in-law? You must be joking. She found it "too distressing" to have anything much to do with him. For which read "Too busy". She had far better things to do with her time – bridge, NADFAS, the Conservatives.'

'Could he have taken it himself?'

'He could lift things sometimes, but things got spilt.'

'So he could have taken his own medicine?'

'Yes, certainly – drunk it from the bottle, say, but not measured it out or anything like that. Why?'

'We need to get an impression of . . . of his abilities shortly before he died. Did he know what was in his medicine bottles, what they contained?'

'He must have done. He was given the stuff in them every day, more than once a day.'

'One other thing. Did your husband ever attend a day centre?'

'A few times. He had to,' Heather Brodie said, sounding defensive, 'but only if everything else had failed. I did need some time to myself, just occasionally, anyone would have. He was getting worse, you know.'

'Which one did he go to?'

'The one in Stockbridge, on Raeburn Place. Frankly, it was a pretty good hell-hole, but it served its purpose.'

'Finally, Mrs Brodie, and I'm sorry to ask, but did he ever express a wish to die? Did he want to die?'

'Yes,' she replied quietly, 'he wanted to die. He spoke about little else, but after a while I stopped listening.'

Several times while she was talking to the policewoman, Ella Brodie's fair hair fell across her eyes, but each time she flicked it away again with a languid toss of her head, a few loose strands always remaining. Seated on the sofa, she was trying not only to answer the questions put to her but also to keep her fractious child content, holding up framed photos of another toddler and showing them to her.

'Is that Katy?' Alice asked, looking first at the image and then at the little girl.

'No, me. They're all of me. We look identical at the same age.'

'Is that one not Harry?' Alice asked, pointing to one of a child with short hair, sticking out its tongue and brandishing a bow and arrow at the photographer.

'Nope. None of them are, I'm afraid. I'm Aunty's favourite, you see. But it evens out. Granny adores Harry.'

'Well, down to business, I suppose,' Alice said, getting out her notebook. 'Where were you last Saturday night?'

'On the Saturday night I was with Harry in his flat. We went to Smith's first, then home. All night,' she said, slightly petulantly. 'I stayed the night there – as I've already told Mr Riddell more than once.'

Forgetting that he was supposed to wait until his sister's interview had finished, her brother wandered into the room, his eyes fixed on the screen of his DS. Ella shook her head, exasperated at his absentmindedness. Catching sight of her, he said, irritably, 'What?'

'You were supposed to wait, dimwit, remember?'

'Whatever,' he replied, making no attempt to move from the armchair where he had sat down.

'Where were you on the Sunday night, Harry?' Alice asked.

'Pub, then home,' he replied, never looking up, his thumbs continuing to move feverishly over the controls on his little black box.

'All night?'

'Yeah. With her.'

'Could either of you tell me,' Alice asked, 'whether your father would be able to take his own medicine from the bottle? Was he capable of lifting the stuff to his lips and drinking it?'

'Nah . . .' the boy replied, 'he'd drop it or something.'

'Yes, probably not,' his sister confirmed, now opening a glossy magazine and showing it to her silent but fidgety child. 'As Harry says, he'd drop it or miss his lips or something.'

'Who usually gave him his medicine?'

'Mum. It was always Mum,' Ella Brodie replied, the boy remaining silent, apparently unaware in his absorption in his Nintendo that a further question had been asked.

—

Following Heather Brodie out of the kitchen, Alice walked towards the front door, and as she stepped over a new patch of blood-soaked carpet their eyes met. 'Fanta,' the woman said, a little smile playing on her lips, 'it's Fanta this time. Looks like she killed Cock Robin. She did it, detective, she's the guilty party, I can assure you. Look, you can still see a few feathers . . . oh, and a leg.'

As Alice was returning to her car, trying to digest the information she had received, her phone went.

'How did you get on with the widow?' It was Eric Manson's voice.

'Fine. She was easy, talkative, seemed to say much what she had said before,' she replied, searching in her pocket for her car key.

'And the kids?'

'They said exactly what Thomas said they would say, nothing new. They don't think their father could have taken the stuff.'

'Are you coming back now, then? I'm just off to see the old woman Brodie, somewhere in the wilds of East Lothian. You might even know the place. I could wait for you, pet.' He sounded as if he wanted the company.

'I'd planned to speak to Heather Brodie's sister, Sir. I imagine she'll say the same as before, but I think I'd better double-check it. She's a part-time reception teacher at Hamilton Stewarts, over Cramond way.'

'OK. Fine. See you back in the office in a couple of hours.'

—

Alice turned the car into the winding drive of the private school, and every so often its shock-absorbers squeaked in protest as they rocked over the sleeping policemen which broke the otherwise flawless surface. The car park seemed to be the exclusive preserve of shiny black SUVs with tinted windows, BMWs and Range Rovers, and the small police vehicle seemed like an unloved interloper amongst them, further marked out by its caked-on dirt and missing hub cap.

Following signs to the junior school across an immaculate gravelled area, Alice reached a pair of double doors guarded by a security lock. She searched in vain for a bell or an intercom, and just as her patience was running out, a heavily pregnant woman smiled indulgently at her as if she was a forgetful fellow-mum, punched in the code and allowed her to follow her in.

Inside was a large, glass-roofed atrium with classrooms leading off it on all four sides. In one corner, an anxious-looking schoolmistress stood poised over a CD player, and arranged around the walls were rows of empty chairs, as if awaiting the audience for a performance.

As the strains of 'Colonel Bogie' started up, Alice made for the nearest seat and suddenly pairs of children filed in, hands clasped and raised high for the Grand March. Within a couple of minutes a reel had begun, and through her feet she could feel the wooden floor begin to vibrate as fifty or more little children bounced up and down on it, the tartan sashes over their shoulders loosening and flapping free. Among them, like giants, moved members of staff. The tallest of these bore a strong resemblance to Heather Brodie – a paler, subdued version of her, like a poor prototype for the more glamorous younger sister.

When first spotted by Alice, the woman was dancing a Dashing White Sergeant, and dangling from the tips of her thin fingers were her partners, both little girls, neither of whom reached much above her bony knees. Her head was held erect, gaze directed straight ahead, and the foot-work of her *pas de basques* was impeccable, high-stepping in time to the beat. She appeared determined to ignore the fact that all around her the children were skidding and spinning, not dancing, little boys and girls colliding, bouncing off each other, then falling in dizzy heaps to the floor and giggling.

As her threesome drew parallel to another, a school-master with his own diminutive partners now jigging opposite her, she flashed him a token smile and then her mouth resumed its tight, trap-like set. After a further pairing, she looked short-sightedly around the hall, and when she saw Alice she bestowed on her a discreet nod of acknowledgement.

The sound of the final chord was the cue for her to disentangle herself from her tiny partners, one of them continuing to pirouette alone. The teacher set off resolutely towards the policewoman, and on reaching her extended her over-large hand and said, in a thin, quavery voice, 'I'm Miss Michelson. The Head told me that you needed to speak to me, I assume it's about poor Gavin's murder. Sorry to have kept you waiting, we're practising for a country-dance festival in Perth tomorrow.'

Then she sat down, legs to one side, ankles clamped together and hands folded in her lap. Alice followed the sequence of questions that she had asked earlier, and listened intently to the schoolmistress's answers as she recounted the evening's events. As she spoke, all the while she clasped and then unclasped her fingers. And the responses she gave accorded with those given by Heather Brodie in almost every detail, providing perfect corroboration of her account. She named precisely the same shops, precisely the same eating-place, dropping in precisely the same asides as she did so.

While she was in mid-flow, a little girl with anxious, wide saucer-eyes plumped herself down on the seat next to Alice's, swinging her legs to and fro, then leant over towards her and said, 'Guess what?'

'What?' Alice whispered, distracted by the child.

'Boys' poo is *gold*. It's *gold* – they do *gold* poo.'

'Really? How d'you know?'

'Rhuari told me. He said I could buy . . .'

'Helena!' Miss Michelson said, interrupting the girl and tapping her gently on the knee with her left hand.

'Off you go. It's playtime now and I need to speak to this lady.'

Instantly, and apparently taking no offence at her peremptory dismissal, Helena slid from her seat and ran off to join a crowd of children who were milling around a tea trolley, chattering and jostling while they waited for their piece of cake.

'They're all obsessed,' the schoolmistress said fondly, shaking her head, her eyes continuing to follow the girl.

'After The Norseman?' Alice asked, nudging her onwards, reminding her where she had got up to in the story.

'After that . . .' the woman replied, her washed-out blue eyes finally moving from the child and onto Alice's face, 'we went to the theatre to see *A Woman of No Importance*. It had Martin Jarvis in it. We both love him. We had no booking at The Norseman so we took pot luck.'

'Really?' Alice said, thinking to herself how unconvincing it all was. The sisters' versions tallied unnaturally well, the very expressions they used were identical. Everything matched, and all just too closely. They sounded more like echoes of one another than two independent voices, and that effect could not have not been achieved by accident or coincidence, but as a result of planning. They had conferred together, exchanging and agreeing all the details. Something was going on.

'What,' Alice began, conscious as she asked the question that it might push this highly-strung woman beyond her limits, is *A Woman of No Importance* about?'

A new-born baby rabbit finding itself staring into the eyes of a stoat could not have looked more petrified. But Miss Mitchelson drew on her reserves, managed to control herself and said, in a cracked voice, 'You know . . .

I simply cannot remember. I slept through large chunks of it. I haven't been sleeping well lately for some reason. Martin Jarvis took the part of Lord Illingworth, I know that much. Otherwise it's completely slipped my mind. Perhaps, thinking about it, the trauma of Gavin's death . . . has blanked it out, somehow. But Heather could tell you, I'm sure of that. You could always ask her, if you really need to know.'

—

The theatre's website was of little use, as the play's run had come to an end, so Alice, deciding to try her luck with a human being, phoned the theatre instead. When the receptionist answered the call she was still trying to get her head around number nine of the 'Ten Ways To Titillate Your Lover' in her magazine. It must surely be for Olympic athletes only, she thought, turning the page upside-down in wonderment. Finally wresting her attention away from the article, she answered her caller, parroting, 'Martin Jarvis, on Saturday?'

'Yes, he was in a starring role in your recent production of *A Woman of No Importance*, is that right?'

'Martin Jarvis was in *A Woman of No Importance*?'

'Yes, was he? On Saturday last?'

'Sorry, I'm temporary here,' she replied, then, turning away from the receiver, shouted, 'What you sayin'? He what?' In the background, Alice could just make out the voice of a man bellowing at the receptionist.

Her voice returned. 'He was, but he got sick, like, so for the last few performances it was his understudy. What's that?' she bawled at her colleague before returning to the line. 'Simon,' she said, 'Simon . . . something or other took over for him.'

'On the Saturday, for the Saturday performances?'

'Yer. Yer. On the last performance on the Friday and all Saturday.'

'Are you certain about that? someone told me he was playing the part last Saturday.'

'We certain?' the receptionist shouted to her informant, and after a short pause she came back and continued, 'He wasn't even in Edinburgh on the Saturday. He'd gone home.'

———

Dusk was beginning to fall as Detective Inspector Manson drove down Haddington's High Street, drawing furiously on his cigar, inhaling and re-inhaling its smoke endlessly, his car windows sealed against the cold. Chains of sparkling Christmas lights were hung between the elegant Georgian buildings on either side of the street, lighting it and the people below as they scurried from shop to shop, parcel-laden, racing against closing time. Just as he passed the Victorian statue of a rampant goat, he was forced to swerve in order to dodge a mud-spattered Land Rover, which, accustomed to the local car etiquette, had reversed from its parking place into the main thoroughfare as if it had right of way.

'I'll get you later, you fucker,' shouted Manson, his words lost behind the glass.

Hand still pressed hard on his horn, he turned right into the Sidegate, past the entrance to St Marys, heading south across the Tyne on the Waterloo Bridge and then hugging the Lennoxlove Wall for a mile or two. To his jaded eyes, the countryside before him looked dead, bare-leaved and black-earthed, no crops yet through with their promise of life to come. The vast expanse of East

Lothian sky was tinged with crimson from the sun's dying rays, and, suddenly and unexpectedly, he felt unutterably miserable, intimidated by the oppressive, unnatural silence, and made desolate by the empty, alien landscape. He speeded up on the deserted road, determined to finish his task as quickly as possible and return to the city with its bright lights, its warmth and its people. Return to Margaret.

As he passed the turn-off to Samuelston, a pheasant dashed out of the verge, straight under his wheels. Immediately he jammed on his brakes, trying to avoid it, but he heard, and felt, the thump as he hit it square on. A few stray feathers floated upwards, one brushing his windscreen. In his rear-view mirror he watched the wounded bird, lying in the middle of the road, a single wing flapping piteously, its body getting smaller all the time. He knew he could not go back to finish it off. It would die soon anyway, he told himself. The next person's wheels would have to do the deed for him. Correction. For it.

—

For over a minute Manson stood outside the front door of the old manse, summoning up all his strength, all his energy, preparing to knock and begin the wearisome business of interrogation once more. But it was no good, his mind remained constantly plagued by uninvited thoughts, the host of jagged fears which now ran amok in it. And all the while, his eyes roamed over the moonlit garden, taking in the two herbaceous borders, trimmed evenly for the winter, and the perfectly circular pond set between them, its margin now fringed with ice. Beyond lay an avenue of pollarded Whitebeams leading to a rose bed, the plants there throwing their sharp shadows onto the hard ground.

A drystane dyke, with not a stone out of place, marked the boundary of the garden, and in the distance lay the pale undulations of the Lammermuir Hills, their gentle curves sculpted by the passage of time.

This old woman must have some staff, gardeners in abundance, to keep the place up so well, he decided, pulling himself up to his full height in preparation for meeting a County lady and, in all likelihood, a bit of a Grand Dame.

Just as he raised his hand to knock, a Honda Civic crawled up the short driveway and drew to a halt behind his own car. Inside it, three immaculately-clad old ladies began to unbend their stiff limbs to begin the long process of disembarking from the vehicle, one of them, apparently, fankled up with her own stick. The driver, the fittest, was the first to get her swollen feet onto the ground, and with her head now down, handbag swinging on her wrist, she made unsteadily for the door. The policeman stood to one side, allowing her unimpeded access to the porch. Once there, and seemingly oblivious to the man's presence, she proceeded to ring the doorbell. Having done so, she bestowed a gracious smile on him while pulling the ends of her coat collar close together against the cold air.

When Erica Brodie opened the front door her eyes lit immediately on her friend. She said, excitedly, 'Well done, Beatrice! In you come. I've got the tea on. Did you manage to pick up Honor and Marigold as we discussed?'

'Of course,' Beatrice replied, starting to remove one arm of her dark-blue husky jacket and edging towards a row of coat hooks in the outer hall.

Having seen to Beatrice, Mrs Brodie noticed the stranger standing to the side of the doorway and said, sounding slightly irritated, 'I am sorry, I didn't notice you there. Can I help you?'

'Well, I'd like to speak to you . . .' the inspector began, but was cut short in imperious tones.

'Could you possibly come back tomorrow? We're just about to play a four at Bridge . . .'

As she was still speaking, the two remaining elderly ladies shuffled past Manson, beaming at him benignly as they did so, and starting to ease off their jackets with arthritic fingers.

'No,' Eric Manson answered, more forcefully than he had intended, but feeling the need to regain control of the situation. This was a police matter after all, it had priority over any social engagement.

'No? No?' Mrs Brodie repeated coldly, taken aback by the man's persistence. Whatever charity he was collecting for had just lost its donation. Unless it was the lifeboats, then she would just have to grit her teeth and pay up. Those brave men battling the waves in their sou'westers deserved every penny they got.

'I'm sorry,' the man tried again, 'I should have told you immediately. I'm from Lothian & Borders Police, and I need to speak to you now. It's about your son, Gavin Brodie. We need to find . . .'

He stopped speaking, noticing a trio of powdery faces clustered behind the woman's shoulder like benevolent barn owls, each fixing him with unblinking, curious eyes, nodding, eager for him to continue.

Sensing their presence behind her, Erica Brodie turned to face her bridge partners and said, with distinct testiness, 'Beatrice, perhaps you could show Honor and Marigold to the drawing room, and then close the door. I've laid the tea things out and the fire is lit. Just help yourselves. I need to speak to . . . er . . . this gentleman, on a private matter.'

Obediently the old ladies turned away. To the sound of a stick clacking on bare floorboards, they began their stately progress down a narrow corridor as directed.

'What about Gavin?' Erica Brodie asked, her brows furrowed and her gnarled thumbs flicking in and out of her clenched fists.

'It might be better if I could talk to you inside, in the warmth, where there's a seat for you. This may take a little time,' Eric Manson said firmly, conscious of her great age, moving towards the woman as if to follow her inside. But she remained immobile, blocking the doorway, so that their bodies came closer together than either would have chosen. Manson leant back on his heels slightly and Erica Brodie began to speak.

'No, thank you. I would prefer that things remained private. Marigold will eavesdrop if she possibly can, and my legs are quite steady, I can assure you.'

So he questioned her where they stood, his exhaled breath snowy white in the cold, marvelling as she spoke at her composure. Occasionally the slightest change in her voice betrayed her distress, together with the incessant movement of her thumbs, and when once, instinctively, he moved towards her again, arm outstretched to comfort her, she responded by backing away from him, as if his touch might weaken her.

'So, you think it unlikely that he could take his medicine without help?' he continued.

'Very unlikely,' she replied in her plummy voice. 'In fact, I'd go so far as to say completely impossible. He could do almost nothing for himself . . . just like his father before him.' She added, in a tired tone, 'Is that it?'

'Almost. I'm sorry to ask you – but did your son want to die?'

'Of course he did. Just as I do. Now, is that it?'

'Yes,' he said, impressed by her fortitude, recognising someone of the old school and finding himself strangely touched by her. She was like a little, fluffed-up robin red-breast, bold and unafraid, prepared to take on anyone within her own territory.

She turned to go in, but then stopped and asked him, 'And Heather, the "grieving" widow – how is she coping?'

'I'm not sure,' he answered truthfully, surprised by her new, unmistakeably sarcastic tone.

'Well, I'm sure everyone's rallied round. Particularly her new man.'

'Her new man?' he asked, puzzled. 'How do you mean, her new man? Who is her new man?'

'I don't know his name, or his address. Still, I'm doing better than you chaps. At least I'm aware of his existence.'

'Why are you telling me this?'

'I thought,' she replied serenely, 'that you might want to know.'

'How do you know about him? Have you seen them together, or did she tell you about it or what?'

'It is not, Inspector,' the woman said, with a look of exaggerated disbelief, 'the sort of thing my daughter-in-law would be likely to tell me, now is it? Nor have I caught her with the other man.'

'So, then, how do you know?'

'Because, antediluvian remnant that I am, I still have all my senses. In the last few months her hair has miracu-lously turned back from grey to auburn, she's wearing new clothes, the bathroom is filled with different potions, scents, lotions. If she had a scarlet letter 'A' for adulteress

141

tattooed on her cheek it couldn't have been much clearer . . .' she hesitated, 'to a woman.'

'So you're sure, quite sure, about this new man?' Manson asked numbly, apparently still talking about Heather Brodie, but in his mind, in fact, drifting back to Margaret. Talking about Margaret. If this old woman had any doubts about her daughter-in-law, could even change her mind, then he would be alright. They would be alright. He and Margaret.

'Absolutely. I'm not in the habit of spreading false rumours – even about Heather,' she replied bitterly, limping through her front door and thereby informing her uninvited caller that he was dismissed.

———

Chugging back to the office along the old A1, Manson turned the wipers off, their noisy swishing too intrusive and distracting for him to bear. Then the undimmed headlights of an approaching car caught the raindrops on his windscreen, nearly blinding him, and he hastily switched them back on again.

In his dark mood, the village of Tranent seemed like the end of the earth, metal shutters barricading its tawdry shops, dirty water stagnant in its gutters and the only pedestrians about being drunks, shambling from doorway to doorway on its sodden, litter-strewn pavements. The place was no more than a fucking midden, he said to himself, as he accelerated along its main street, ignoring the speed limit and swinging wildly round a bend in his haste to leave.

The 'Honest Toun' appeared little better, the firth beyond Fisherrow not sparkling as it sometimes did, but looking like thick brown soup under a grey, lifeless sky.

The two solid colours merged on the horizon. Even the bungalows lining the Milton Road seemed squat and misshapen. And now, thanks to Heather Brodie and her shenanigans, he would get home later than ever. The woman would have to be challenged by him, in person, in her den – well, her sister's den. He would have to be the one to confront her with the old woman's suspicions. Not a hint of any affair from Thomas Riddell, of course – the inefficient git! And it was exactly the sort of thing he should have been burrowing about to discover. What else was he for?

Out of habit, he lit another cigar, but after the first drag he felt slightly sick, persevering only in order to calm his frayed nerves, comforted by its familiar orange glow in the darkness. As he reached the traffic lights by the King's Theatre he rolled down his window and chucked the stub out, the ashtray inside already overflowing with his dog ends.

—

Sitting at her dining room table, Pippa Mitchelson felt distinctly uneasy as she began to wrap a pink teddy bear in Christmas paper, the prickly feeling at the back of her neck telling her that every movement was under the unblinking scrutiny of the morose man seated opposite her. All her attempts to engage him in conversation had failed, and now, with every second that passed, she felt more awkward and anxious, intimidated by his fixed gaze and silent, oppressive presence. Realising that if she wrote on the gift tag she would have to use her spectacles, she dithered, unwilling to put them on in front of him. Maybe she should just wait until he had gone before she put pen to paper? And soon, please God, Heather would return and the man's attention would shift away from her and on to her sister. That was who he had come to see, after all, that was what he had said. So it must be true.

Self-consciously, and with shaking fingers, she tied a bow in the red ribbon round the present and then peered, short-sightedly, about the table in search of the kitchen scissors to snip its end off. They were out of her reach, and the paper would unwrap itself if she let go of it, so, momentarily, she stopped as she tried to figure out what to do next. While she was still thinking, the policeman wordlessly handed the pair to her as if he had read her mind. And this confirmation that she was being watched, observed by him, made her yet more uneasy, so that when, after a brief silence, the next track of Rutter's carols started up she almost jumped in the air with fright.

The song, 'Shepherd's Pipe' was one of which she was particularly fond, but hearing it now as if through this stranger's ears, this worldly if not actually world-weary man, it suddenly sounded unbearably sentimental, stickily twee. She felt an overpowering urge to turn it off, but could not summon the courage to make such a decisive move. Instead, she sat through it, increasingly embarrassed by its sweetness, offering another prayer that Heather would appear soon and remove this unwanted limelight from her.

Eric Manson, his mind freewheeling for once, found himself oddly moved by the sight of the childless spinster, spending her time wrapping presents for other people's offspring. A crib, with cotton-wool snow on the roof of the stable and a plastic baby Jesus in the manger, had been placed on the sideboard, and beside it a Christmas tree stood with white tinsel and fairy lights wound around its evergreen branches. All arranged, no doubt, by those trembling, oversized hands, and for her own lonely pleasure.

Glancing surreptitiously at the woman's face, he was struck by her quiet dignity, her resolve in going on with her life as if everything was normal, as if everything remained the same when, in fact, chaos had begun to encroach, its cold waters now lapping around her feet. Listening to the music, he wondered what it could be, it was pretty and melodic for sure. Perhaps he would manage to get a glimpse of the cover before he left. Buy a copy of the CD and put it in Margaret's stocking. Margaret . . . but before he became lost in thoughts of his wife once more, the telephone rang and the shy schoolteacher rose to answer it.

'So you're stuck,' he heard her say, her voice sounding strained. 'Don't worry, love. Yes, I'll pick you up. At Waverly in two hours. Yes, I'll be there.'

Putting down the receiver, she turned to him and said wearily; 'That was Heather. She missed the train she was supposed to catch. So she'll not be back for another couple of hours, I'm afraid. I have to go out myself in about fifteen minutes. I'm babysitting for Ella while she goes to her art class, and I can't let her down. Probably best that you come back tomorrow morning?'

⚊

Elaine Bell, feeling tense after an afternoon preparing for her appraisal meeting with the Super, strolled into the murder suite. Her labours had renewed her sense of the enormity of the injustice the man was trying to commit, to perpetrate against her. Her record was exemplary, all her appraisals bar his proved it, she deserved the promotion, and if she had to go into battle to achieve her due then she bloody well would. Bring it on. The sooner the better.

'So, Alice, how did it go?'

The sergeant looked up as the DCI came in and pushed her report to one side, accidentally knocking an all but empty coke can to the floor.

'Very interesting. I learnt a lot. For one thing . . .'

At that moment Eric Manson returned, bringing with him the stench of stale cigar smoke, and came over to join them. Seeing the can rolling around the floor he said, petulantly, 'That was mine.'

'It's empty,' Alice replied.

'Not quite.'

'Never mind that,' Elaine Bell said irritably, moving quickly away from her Inspector, overpowered by the miasma clinging to him. 'How have you both got on?'

'Mrs Brodie doesn't think that her son was capable of taking the stuff herself. So he must have been given it, fed it or whatever,' Eric Manson said, his arms now tightly crossed against his chest.

'And young Mrs Brodie, Heather Brodie. What did she say? She should really be the one to know, I suppose? She tended to him, saw him every day after all.'

'Yes, and she thinks he could have done it by glugging it straight from the bottle. The children don't, though, but apparently she was the one to give it to him. Not them or old Mrs Brodie. She said that he wanted to die . . . he told them so every day.'

'Good. That may be our answer then, if there was enough in the bottles, that he took it himself for some reason. Knowingly or unknowingly. Anything else, Eric?'

'Aha. The old woman thinks that her daughter-in-law is carrying on with someone. She doesn't know who, but she's adamant that the bitch is having an affair.'

'The "bitch"?' Elaine Bell said, her surprised tone allowing the inspector to reconsider his choice of words.

'Mrs Brodie. Heather Brodie.'

'Maybe that explains it, then,' Alice said slowly, thinking out loud, 'what's going on. Because Heather Brodie's been lying to us, got her sister to cover for her too. She wasn't at the theatre on Saturday evening. The actor she claimed to have seen, Martin Jarvis, wasn't performing on the night she supposedly saw the play. And she was a great fan of his, she told me, so I don't think she can put it down to some sort of mistaken identity. Perhaps she was with this man or something. Maybe that's why she was lying.'

'She's been lying? Bloody Hell, the stupid, stupid cow! Do we know who he is, yet?' Elaine Bell demanded.

Eric Manson shook his head. 'I went there this evening, to Pippa Mitchelson's house, to ask her, find out who he is, but she's stuck in Perth. Won't be back until after ten.'

'Well, we'll have to find out what she was actually doing and who she was with. Neither of you have seen Una Reid again, eh? She might be able to help us out. She'll have seen Heather Brodie and the rest of them at close quarters . . . unguarded. She'll know if the woman was up to something and, quite probably, who with too. And, Eric, I don't want Mrs Brodie to know that we're interested in her. Not yet.' She paused, thinking, 'On the other hand, I'm not sure how much all of this matters. We've got Clerk, he's inside and we've plenty of evidence against him, haven't we? Brodie died at his hands, McConnachie was crystal clear about that. Thank God. In a way this is all just a sideshow really.'

Aware that her contribution would be unwelcome, Alice said tentatively, 'I don't think it is, Ma'am – a sideshow, I mean. Apart from anything else, I'm not sure the evidence we've got is that good, the evidence against Clerk.'

'What on earth d'you mean?' Elaine Bell said, frowning angrily.

'Well, Gavin Brodie did go to the Raeburn Place Day Centre. We know that.'

'Yes, yes, I know that too. And your point is?' the DCI spluttered, interrupting her. 'That's probably how Clerk chooses his victims – finds disabled people, chats to them, learns where they live, works out their security and so on. He meets them through Robert, and I bet he came across Brodie that way.'

'Possibly,' Alice replied, 'but it may also leave a big question-mark over the significance of the fingerprint evidence.'

'What on earth are you going on about?'

'Well, a wheelchair's not like a fridge or a washing machine is it? It moves about the place with its owner, or at least he moves about with it. So, Brodie and his wheelchair go to the day-centre that Clerk goes to as well. All he needs to do is claim that he sometimes helped push people about or some such thing, then the prints are worthless or near worthless. And maybe it's true, maybe he's not our man. He left traces of himself all over his first victim's flat. Ron Anderson's too. He doesn't take trouble. So, why just one set of prints in Brodie's place, on the wheelchair?'

'And the book?' Elaine Bell said, hotly. 'That's a bit more difficult for him – for you – to explain away, I think you'd agree.'

'Mmm,' Alice said, hesitating, conscious that her next piece of information would cause further consternation, 'not really. I asked Mrs Brodie if her husband had disposed of that Jeffrey Archer, and she said she wasn't sure but that it was quite likely. Apparently, as he got worse and worse, they had to bring in aids to help with him, rails, commodes, hoists and so on. Extra space was needed. They had a clear out to make room for all the equipment. She said that he loved "airport reading", as she called it, had a huge collection of paperbacks. She sold the bookshelves and got rid of the A-M section in one of the charity shops in Stockbridge. Archer was one of his favourites, along with Dan Brown. Their system wasn't perfectly alphabetical, she said, but not bad. The book was an odd thing for Clerk to keep, too, having thrown away a wallet, jewellery and all that.'

'And the remarkably similar M.O.?'

'Cutting the throats of invalids? It's a remarkable coincidence if Brodie happened to overdose himself on the very night that someone else had chosen to kill him, don't you think? I'd say it's much more likely that one individual did both, even if we don't yet know why. I know we've charged Clerk, but as things currently stand I don't think we'll get a conviction. Not with what we've got at present, will we, Ma'am?'

'Alright, alright, you've made your point. Find out who the merry widow's having it away with, eh? Don't ask her, go and see that carer woman at the Abbey Park Lodge. Let's see what Mrs Brodie was actually up to. But, for Christ's sake, don't let her know we're onto her.'

9

Bustling angrily from the room, like a hen forcibly deprived of a tasty scrap, the DCI was now thinking hard, trying to work out in her own mind how she could best describe the latest development to the ACC, ensuring that it did not sound like a setback. Her colleagues, both weary after a long day's work, remained seated, each now reluctant, although for different reasons, to go home. Alice was dreading a confrontation with Ian and its result, and Manson, though too fearful to risk a confrontation with Margaret, was unable to bear the uncertainty of the status quo.

'Alice?'

'Yes, Sir.'

He hesitated, trying to work out the best way, the most innocuous way, of introducing the subject, alerting no one. That Margaret should no longer love him was bad enough, but he was not, yet, the butt of office jokes, the object of ill-concealed sniggers, or worse still, sympathy.

'I wondered,' he continued 'you know how Mrs Brodie, the old one, told me that Heather was, how should I put it . . . on the pull? That she had a "fancy" man,' he added with distaste. Usually, his manner on discussing this kind of thing would be bantering, lewd and jocular, so Alice looked at him, her attention caught by his uncharacteristic diffidence, but he did not follow it up, sinking into silence. She rose, stretched, and lifted her coat from the back of her chair. Infidelity was not a subject she wanted to discuss with him now.

'If she was unfaithful, how would you know?' he enquired, after a long pause.

'How d'you mean, Sir? How would you know? You've just told us that the old lady told you that Mrs Brodie was unfaithful.'

'Yes,' he hesitated again. 'Yes, I did . . . but it's only an inference drawn by her, by a mother-in-law, you understand. She doesn't actually know, she hasn't seen the man, or caught them together or anything. What I'm thinking is, is she – is she right? In the inference she's drawing, I mean. About her daughter-in-law. You're a woman, Alice, aren't you?'

'To the best of my knowledge. Of course, I haven't been subject to any tests,' she replied acidly.

'Exactly. So, as a woman, what would make you draw the inference that another woman, a married woman, was having an affair?'

'A number of things, I suppose,' Alice said, her interest briefly kindled, finding herself entering the discussion almost against her will. 'I suppose she might dress better, take more care with her appearance generally – her underwear in particular. Her mood, her behaviour might be different too, depending on things like her attitude to the adultery . . .'

'Like what?' the Inspector shot back, sounding anxious, then rephrasing the question in an attempt to sound less concerned. 'Um . . . what d'you have in mind?'

'It all depends. If the woman was in love, too, then she might be radiant, feel she's walking on air, be unusually happy. On the other hand she could be tortured, as well, racked with guilt, unsure how to resolve things and more irritable as a result. She might be kinder to everyone, feeling benign, content with the world and her place in it, or she might appear to lose interest in things that had previously held her attention – things like their home, old hobbies shared with her husband . . . I don't know, Sir. Perhaps you're asking the wrong person!'

'Oh, I didn't mean to suggest . . .' he began, briefly apologetic before adding, dismissively, 'you're not married anyway,' as if sexual fidelity outside wedlock had no significance.

'True,' she answered, putting on her coat and starting to walk towards the door. She wanted no more of this discussion. It was far too close to the bone.

'If she had started cooking dishes she particularly knew that her husband liked, fancy ones – ones she hadn't cooked for years, then that could be indicative of her adultery, of a guilty conscience, you think?'

'It could be.' Alice shrugged her shoulders. 'She might be compensating in some way, her new "interest" making her kinder, making her even pity her husband . . .' Jesus, did Ian pity her?

'Pity!' he snorted, then nodded sagely to himself, muttering, 'Pity . . . yes, I can see that.'

'Or it might just mean that she loved him. Really loved him,' she added quickly, a sudden doubt assailing her. How could she have been so slow in the uptake? It was obvious that his interest in the topic of adultery went far deeper than was required for the job. Glancing at his tired face, at his slumped posture, she knew what was worrying him, and felt nothing but sympathy for him. He must be on the rack, too. They were sparring partners of old, and more often than not his jabs irritated or annoyed her, but she took no pleasure seeing her old adversary like this. Off-balance, dancing on the canvas no more, supporting himself on the ropes and unable to conceal his injuries. She only hoped that her own had been better hidden.

—

Alice sat in the kitchen of their flat, a second glass of white wine by her hand. She had already consumed one to give her courage, stiffen her spine. Beside her on the floor Quill lay peacefully asleep, snoring gently, sated after his second dinner.

Throughout the entire journey home she had been rehearsing in her head what she would say, imagining Ian's likely responses, sometimes scaring herself half to death. Now she could feel butterflies fluttering about in her stomach, she was anticipating the worst and trying to prepare herself to deal with it, or, at the very least, accept it. She looked down at the newspaper again but her eyes glided over the print, taking in nothing. Soon she found herself in the business section, where she finally gave up.

Restlessly, she rose and wandered over to the fridge, then moved away from it and went to look out of the window, watching for his familiar figure tramping homewards on the pavement below. Rain had fallen on the cobbles, making them glisten in the orange lamplight and shine in the headlights of each passing car. She let her nose rest against the cold glass pane, seeing her breath mist it up. Still unable to settle, she returned for no good reason to her seat at the kitchen table. A pile of old newspapers at one end of it caught her eye, and, for the first time, she noticed a sheet of A4 paper resting on top of them. It was a note from Ian.

'Darling Alice,

Have caught the train to London. The owner of a Gallery saw my website and is very interested in my work. Am taking five of the wishbone lithographs with me for him to see in the flesh. Back late on Saturday.

Love
Ian.'

After she had read it she covered her face with her hands, her heart sinking, more anxious and even more unsettled. Why had he not phoned her to tell her about the trip in person? What was, could possibly be, so urgent that he had to leave her without saying anything. He hadn't even said where he was staying. And, over a month ago, he had come home annoyed that he had cleaned the stone for the wishbone lithographs, had discovered that he had none left and now could produce no more. He was such a bad liar, and she forgot so little.

Her first reaction was to call him on his mobile, but he might lie again, and what would she say then? She did not want to listen to his disembodied voice making things up, conjuring some paper-thin untruths from the air while sweating at the other end of the line. No. This had to be done face to face. She had to look into his eyes, see him again, if the 'him' whom she had believed she knew and loved still existed.

Thinking about what she had lost, tears came to her eyes and rolled unchecked down her cheeks until she could taste the salt on her lips. She had to be a detective at work, but not, surely, at bloody home, too.

Her phone went and her DCI's name and number came up, but this time she let it ring. Getting no reply, her caller did not bother to wait for the messaging service. Instead, Elaine Bell took another sip of her claret, placed her knife and fork neatly on her plate and looked round, hoping to attract a waiter's attention and get her bill. But all of them were busy attending to the other diners, one scurrying into the kitchens, empty plates balanced on both forearms.

Her eye was caught by the sight of a large, red-faced man who had his arm around a woman. She was giggling loudly, and he, playfully, put his hand over her mouth, allowing his fingers to caress her full lips. The DCI, now even more painfully self-conscious than usual about her lone and unloved status, rose and went to pay at the till, eager to get back to her office. The Super, she thought, ruefully looking at him, might already have retired on the job and have plenty of time for play, but she had not.

Friday

At 9.30 that morning, the manageress of Abbey Park Lodge was deep in thought, trying to work out what to do next about the latest staff spat. One of her nursing auxiliaries, Agnes Cauld, a large West Indian lady with a fiery temper and a foul mouth, had just stormed out of her office. Her parting shot had been ' . . . and don't think I'll not be taking this no further, because I bloody well will!'

So all the tea and sympathy she had lavished on the woman had failed to pacify her. And the Irish woman, another auxiliary who had visited her earlier, had been no more amenable to her blandishments, muttering darkly about racism and sizeism in the workplace and uttering the dreaded words, 'Grievance' and 'Legal Advice'.

Perhaps, she wondered, the time had come to involve Julia from HR? No, all that would happen then was that she would be subjected to an earful of jargon about grievance procedures, appeal procedures, protocols and the like, and neither of them, Julia included, would have the faintest idea how to implement any of them. In fact, it was sheer gobbledygook, no more than a lot of meaningless incantations or spells. If only she had stayed within the NHS, then she could have availed herself of a proper, grown-up legal department instead of this tin-pot operation. Now, before you could say 'Hobnob', she would find herself on a witness list for an industrial tribunal!

She took a sip of her hot water, delicately removing a stray lemon pip from her mouth, consciously trying to re-hydrate herself and enter a calm place. A beach, maybe, with turquoise waters and palm fronds overhanging the lazy surf . . . No! No, no. First she must sort out this business. The nature of the complaint must be recorded, that was surely the first step, and fortunately the accounts given by the two troublemakers had not really differed. It must all be written down now, while her recollection remained fresh. She held her pen ready.

Agnes had been moving an elderly patient from her bed to a nearby chair, assisted by her Irish colleague, Detta O'Hare. Allegedly, at some stage in the manoeuvre Detta had lost her grip, and Agnes had ended up bearing the patient's whole twelve-stone weight. Consequently, Agnes had screamed, 'Detta, you fuckin' leprechaun, get a hold of her again!'

Detta, apparently deeply insulted, had simply crossed her arms and said 'How now . . .' seeing no need to complete her sentence.

Really, she thought to herself, putting down her Parker, the residents might have some excuse for occasional name-calling – dementia, loss of inhibition and so on – but what excuse was there for the staff? None whatsoever, the besoms! Oh, the complexity of it all, and still they had not managed to identify the prankster in the laundry responsible for putting raisins, which looked uncannily like rat droppings, in the freshly ironed underwear.

Her head now in a spin, the manageress was glad to hear the knock on the door and her own confident voice say, 'Come in.'

Seeing the well-coiffured individual behind the desk, her gold-plated Parker lying centrally on a spotless pad of paper, Alice Rice was quite unaware of the inner turmoil in the manageress's breast. However disturbed the woman was by events in her professional life she managed to convey an aura of perfect calm and tranquillity, the epitome of grace under pressure. Only her torn and bleeding fingernails would have alerted the shrewd observer to the difference between her inner and outer states.

In her reassuring mellow contralto, a voice that had clinched many a job interview for her, she explained to the policewoman that she had heard that Una was helping Dr Coates at this moment in time. As she, herself, was on her way to the Bluebell wing, she could take her there if that would be helpful?

As they passed through one of the many hallways, frenzied screaming broke the stale air of the place, and instantly attendants appeared from all directions, homing in on one room. After a strange thumping sound was heard emanating from it, the cries slowly died away like ripples on a pond, and the unnatural calm returned.

'Old Mr Morris . . . we should have a vacancy there soon,' the manageress said with a knowing look, gliding onwards through the next set of double doors. As she followed her, Alice suddenly felt that breathing the lifeless air of the place was dangerous, as deadly to its inmates as to a butterfly gasping in a killing jar. No one was safe in it. Her neighbour, Miss Spinnell, must never end up in a place like this, nor her feisty twin. It was no more than a waiting room for death, a place to store the elderly and infirm like unwanted luggage until the grim reaper finally turned his attention to them, or to what was left of them. And so the problem of the old would be solved.

'Ah, Mr Braid,' the manageress said, stopping in her stately progress to talk to a small overall-clad man who was pinning up a notice on a board.

'Perhaps you'd be good enough to take this lady,' she gestured to Alice, 'to room 143. I've just remembered that I promised I'd look in on Sandra.'

'No problem,' he replied. As Alice fell into step beside him, he cupped her elbow as if she was another infirm resident, introducing himself in a sing-song voice as he did so. Resisting the impulse to shake him off, she walked beside him until, thankfully, they reached their destination and he went back to his notice-board. A black and white picture of a laughing woman, on her knees and surrounded by Border terriers, was pinned to the open door.

Inside a gaunt female figure was propped up, stiff and motionless as a log, her dead weight supported by the sides of a high-backed armchair. Her skin seemed shiny and unnaturally taut, and her head was tilted towards the window, which gave an unimpeded view of a tiny courtyard walled in brick, its pitted tarmac covered with recycling bins. Beside her, raising a spoonful of soup to her closed lips, sat Una Reid, coaxing her patient in her gravelly, twenty-a-day voice to 'take a wee sip, just a wee sip for Una'.

As the policewoman came in, the patient's eyes never so much as flickered. Though fixed on the drab outlook, they did not appear to be taking anything in. As if unaware of the presence of the spoon, never mind of anyone else in the room, she raised her hand and, uninhibitedly, felt along the edge of her tongue with her fingers. Then she let her arm drop back to her side, slamming into the spoon on the way down and spilling soup all over herself. Una wiped the woman's bosom with a paper hankie, cleaning the broth from it, but the patient showed no sign of being aware that she was being cleaned or even that she was being touched. Suddenly her arm went up again and she fingered the sides of her tongue once more. Then, like a wounded animal, she let out a pathetic moan and slowly closed her unseeing eyes as if she was dying.

'Mebbe she'll sleep now,' Una said, returning the spoon to the bowl and looking fondly at her.

'Has she had enough?' Alice asked, noting that the broth appeared virtually untouched.

'No. But I'll not get any more into her. She's got Huntington's, ken. Doesn't know anyone or anything any more, not even that she needs to eat. I'm fighting a losing battle wi' her,' Una answered, sounding upset and surreptitiously wiping the corner of her eye with her finger.

'You knew her – she's a friend of yours?' Alice asked gently.

'Oh, aye. I worked wi' her for years.'

'Whereabouts?'

'Here, in this place,' she replied, as if it was obvious. 'Doctor Coates was one of the resident doctors here when I first came and . . .' she stopped momentarily to wipe away another tear, 'and it was a very different place when she was in charge, I can tell you that.'

'Was Mr Brodie in this sort of condition, unable to do anything for himself?'

'No. He could dae a wee bit, lift a spoon and the like. He wis no' as far gone as what she is.'

'Could he take his own medicine, straight from the bottle, say?'

'No' really,' she replied, putting the bowl on the trolley, where it joined an uneaten slice of buttered bread and an untouched glass of water.

'Why not?'

'He'd take anythin', like, if you gave it him, but he didnae know anythin' any more. So, he wouldnae have known whit wis in the bottle. Could have been juice, water, wine. He'd no' ken that it wis his medicine, like.'

A moan interrupted their conversation and they both shifted their attention back to the doctor. Her eyes were now wide open, staring straight ahead, a look of utter dread contorting her features as if a vision of hell was unfolding before her. She whimpered, turned her face into the chair and groaned once more. Instantly, Una sprang up and put an arm around her, murmuring, 'It's all right, Doctor, dinnae you worry, darlin'. You'll be all right, I'm here beside you.' Slowly the fear receded from the bloodshot eyes, and, for a second, intelligence shone in them as they rested briefly on the nurse. Then, like a comforted child, the doctor allowed her heavy head to flop onto Una's shoulder and rest there.

A few seconds later, the nurse's phone went and, using her free hand, she got it from her pocket, nodded several times in response to the voice at the other end, and then began, ever so slowly, to slide her body free of its burden, tenderly resting the patient's head against the side of the chair. The call ended with her saying, 'OK, OK. I'll tidy up the place before I go. Make sure it's neat and tidy for everybody.'

'A visitor?' Alice asked.

'No,' Una replied, picking up the tray and moving towards the door, 'she doesnae get any visitors nowadays. She's got a daughter, like, but she cannae face comin' any more. See, she's got a fifty-fifty chance of developin' the disease herself, and she cannae bear tae look at her own future. The Doctor doesnae recognise her anyway, an' twice she's scratched her face wi' her nails, bit her oan the nose once. She can be a wee bit violent sometimes, but she's aye quiet as a lamb wi' me.'

'Can I ask you about Mrs Brodie?' Alice asked, following Una out of the room.

'Aha.'

'How did she cope with her husband's illness? How did she manage?'

'She jist got oan wi' it. She hud tae. She couldnae dae much else, noo could she?'

'Did she have any support, anyone to help her? The children?'

'They'd both gone, left home, like. The boy's at college and so's the girl, an' she's got her own wee wan noo.'

'Was there anyone else to support her? Did she . . . was she seeing anybody else?'

'How d'you mean? You mean the Doctor or somethin'?'

'No. I meant socially.'

'Aye. Me an' a'. She wis seeing him "socially" as you cry it. Havin' it away wi' him as I'd say . . . her "toy boy".'

How d'you know?'

'I've eyes in ma heid like everybody else. and I wisnae born yesterday neither. Onyway, he was aye sendin' her flooers, big bunches o' red roses usually. I seen the cairds. You couldnae miss it – she and him, Dr Paxton, were eyeing each other up. I'd bet ma life oan it. If I had wan.'

<hr />

'That settles it. We'll just go and see her again, that Brodie creature,' Eric Manson said, switching off his computer and not bothering to hide his dislike of the woman. 'Let her know that we know that she's a sodding liar. That she's been two-timing her sick husband with the poor bugger's own doctor, and that he's a lot younger than her too.'

'Fine, Sir. Of course. But if we do do that, she'll know we're onto her, won't she? And, apart from her lying to us, we don't have much on her yet, do we? We don't even know that she was with him, and if he is involved, in some way, then there's a question-mark over all the information we've got from him – the drugs stuff, his opinion about Brodie's condition and the rest. And maybe he wasn't with her – for all we know he may have an alibi for the Saturday night. Having an affair in itself is not a crime, after all.'

'No? Right. What we'll do is speak to him, eh? See where he says he was, get a DNA sample from him, make like it's routine. If they're both lying, then chances are . . .'

He stopped mid-sentence as Elaine Bell came over to his desk. She looked grey with exhaustion, her clothes rumpled from another night spent in the office.

'So, what did the Reid woman have to say?' she asked Alice.

162

'Heather Brodie's lover seems to be her husband's doctor, Colin Paxton.'

'His doctor! Bloody Hell! Are you quite sure? Were they together on the Saturday? He'd know all about drugs, quantities and so on, and he'd be able to get prescriptions if he wanted. This puts everything in a very different light. We'll need to go over the India Street house again – thank God it's still ours. But we'll have to scour it for completely different things this time. You can do that, Alice. Look over all of Heather Brodie's stuff this time. Anything that ties her and lover boy together would be useful, letters, cards, whatever. I'll get permission to have their phones checked. Eric . . .'

He was sitting with one hand covering his eyes, and did not respond.

'*Eric!*' she repeated, shaking her head in disbelief.

'Ma'am.'

'Go and see Paxton, but do not – I repeat DO NOT – scare him off, OK? Ask him politely where he was on the Saturday night. Just accept whatever he says and then check it out. Got that?'

'Aha. Loud and clear.'

⟞

As soon as Alice entered the hallway of the India Street house, she was hit by its chilled air, the raw coldness of it. The place was now dank, unheated, unloved and unlived in. Silent. Her breath was as visible as steam from a kettle, and she crossed her arms, hunching her shoulders and trying to husband her body heat. The murdered man's bedroom door was open and she glanced into it, a musky smell instantly assailing her nostrils. Her attention was caught by the trails of blood spattered across the faded wallpaper, now looking more like black ink than blood.

A cursory inspection of the kitchen suggested that it would reveal nothing, so she pushed open the door to the drawing-room, and entering it was surprised how shabby it now seemed. Without the presence of the normal occupants of the house, breathing in and breathing out, moving around, attending to the myriad, small, inconsequential affairs that make up a life, the room's tiredness could not be hidden. There was nothing to distract the eye from the frayed patches on the carpet, the cracks in the glass of the cabinet or the odd broken ornament on the mantlepiece. A thick layer of dust coated the antique wooden furniture, masking its lustre and turning it grey, and the panes in the sole window were dirty, providing only the subdued light of perpetual dusk. Everywhere needed redecoration and a good clean.

A writing desk was tucked away in one corner, its sun-bleached walnut veneer beginning to part from the wood beneath, and Alice sat down at it. First she pulled out all of the miniature drawers on the desktop. Only a magnifying glass, a thimble and a couple of half-empty needle cases were revealed. The first of the larger, lower drawers seemed to be filled with the paraphernalia of Christmas: decorated paper, tinsel, hundreds of old cards and baubles for the tree, many cracked or discoloured. The middle drawer contained about forty brown envelopes, some with their contents listed on the outside: 'Harry's and Ella's school reports – 1995-1998, 1999-2003, 2004-2007', 'Ella's art project (Roman)', and 'Letters from mum'.

In case something had been misfiled and partly out of curiosity, Alice gave them all a quick check. From her cursory scrutiny of the reports a vague picture of both of the Brodie children emerged, and it largely accorded with the impression she had formed from her brief meeting with them in their aunt's house. The boy, Harry, seemed to be intelligent, slightly nervous and immature, excelling in drama and English. Many of his teachers seemed concerned by his lack of focus, some remarking on his inability to handle pressure, particularly at exam time. Almost all of them commented that his head was always in the clouds, and criticised his absent-mindedness. Ella, in contrast, seemed to have sailed through school, collecting prizes and positions of responsibility from her earliest childhood. Great things seem to be expected of her, her last head teacher remarking on her high hopes for the girl's future.

Putting the last report cards away, her mind drifted onto Ian as it had done periodically throughout the day. Only by making a conscious effort could she stop thoughts of him intruding whenever they liked, wrecking her concentration and making everything else seem unimportant, whirling round and round in her head but resolving nothing. Deliberately banishing him from her mind again, she turned back to the drawer and picked out one of the letters from the 'Mum' envelope, but it was in an impossible hand. Only 'My darling' on the first line could be deciphered, the rest of the writing, including the signature, being completely illegible. After wasting a further five minutes trying to read the most recent one, dated 2008, she gave them up as a bad job and bundled them all back into their envelope.

When she hauled out the bottom drawer, Alice's spirits sank. It was weighed down with files, each one bulging, the contents overflowing into a ghastly sump of miscellaneous papers. Anticipating hours of probably pointless drudgery ahead, she gave a deep sigh and then picked up the first document in the 'TAX' file. Methodically, she ploughed through them all, before passing onto 'BANK', then five other equally dull folders. 'HEALTH' briefly caught her attention, documenting as it did the course of Gavin Brodie's hopeless decline and the mass of quack remedies that they had invested in before accepting the inevitable. Wondrous crystals, exotic fruit essences, animal serums and the frozen scrotums of bulls, all promised cures. Each advert had been cut out and kept, each marked with 'cheque for £50 sent' or some equally poignant note.

Three hours later, and conscious that her eyes were no longer focusing properly, she opened the second last folder. It was marked 'INSURANCE'. Inside, as anticipated, were a mass of certificates of car, house and household contents and travel insurance. Like the rest of the files, they revealed that the woman's grip on the family's administrative matters seemed to be slipping. Her filing was becoming progressively less accurate, many of the dates were higgledy piggledy, with papers eventually being added in no particular order at all.

At the very back of the folder, stapled onto the cover, was another certificate, a term life insurance policy in Gavin Brodie's name. Amongst the details listed on it were the extra premium charged for an unspecified 'Underlying Medical Condition', the sum assured, the date on which the policy was taken out and the date of expiry. Alice put it to one side, relieved to have found something to show for all the tedium, something concrete and, surely to God, significant.

The final file, untitled and with a dark blue cover, was the thinnest. It seemed unpromising, and held a only small sheaf of papers. Picking out a five-page document from it she saw that it was headed 'Court of Session, Scotland. Petition for Interdict against Agnes Hart'.

Hart's address in Henderson Row was given. The aim of the document seemed to be to get the Court to prohibit her from coming anywhere near Gavin Brodie or any members of his family, his house or his possessions. Reading the numbered paragraphs that made up the petition, a picture began to emerge, and it was a disturbing one. It catalogued a campaign of harassment and intimidation waged by an obsessive woman as she worked out a grudge against Gavin Brodie and his nearest and dearest. Dog excrement had been put through the India Street letterbox, cars scratched, obscene notes attached to the front door, his children shouted at and his mother had received a gob of Hart's saliva on her cheek. The list of hate-filled deeds perpetrated by the woman covered two full pages. Agnes Hart, whoever she was, had plainly loathed the dead man, and judging from the description of her behaviour, she was both unbalanced and highly effective in her campaign of revenge. Another document among the papers, headed 'Extract Decree', revealed that the Court had granted Gavin Brodie's request that Agnes Hart's behaviour be restrained on 5th July 2008.

Late that same evening, Eric Manson tiptoed past his open sitting-room door, straining for a minute or two to decipher the high-pitched, excitable chatter coming from it before retreating into the kitchen. He had heard more than enough. Not least the sudden change into whispers. All Margaret's friends seemed to be there, divorcees to a woman, of course, apart from sour Helen whose interests, he felt sure, lay in another direction altogether. They would be offering advice, laughing among themselves in their venal way, eager to enlist another member into their unholy club. Nowadays, however late it was, when he got home it was never just the two of them, with Margaret waiting eagerly for his return. No, the harpies had positively taken the place over.

Nosing inside the fridge, he saw with alarm that a raspberry mousse appeared to have been made for him. Half-heartedly he dipped a finger into it, licked it, and as he did so the telephone rang. Picking up the receiver and, still in work mode, he said gruffly 'DI Eric Manson, here'. Instantly, and with an ominous click, the phone went dead.

It must have been Him, the Other Man, the Bastard, now intruding into his home! His own home! He threw down the instrument as if it had been contaminated and, had the house been empty, would have howled out loud in his anguish like a wolf. Instead, he sat at the table with his head in his hands, hiding from the world, and sighed involuntarily.

Covering his eyes, he repeated to himself over and over that this should not be happening to him, him of all people. And not now, in the middle of a murder investigation, when all his time, all his thoughts, had to be devoted to the job of tracking down that poor, sick bugger's killer. What the fuck had he ever done to deserve this? But he could not talk to Margaret, or have it out with her, because he did not know where to begin, or where it would all end. Heavens above, she might actually admit to playing away, and what would he do then? The awful nightmare would have become reality. And Margaret would no longer be Margaret, and who, no, what, would he be without her?

'You alright, Eric?' It was sour Helen's voice, so he rubbed his hands up and down over his face as if to refresh himself, and replied as brightly as he was able, 'Yes, just fine, thanks, love. Rarely better'. Then Margaret herself swept in, and seeing him, asked tenderly, 'Tired, pet?' Catching her eye and forgetting what he had just said, he nodded mutely and watched, speechless, as she took his supper out of the oven for him, laid it before him and departed to return to the gaggle of women. A dish of beef olives, prettily garnished with a handful of freshly chopped parsley.

His phone went again. He threw down his fork and shouted down the mobile, 'If that's you, again, you fuckin', fuckin', fuckin' . . .'

'Sir! Sir, it's me, Alice. I was just calling to let you know what I have found out, in case you wanted to speak to the DCI.' The man sounded possessed.

'OK. Right. Get on with it.'

'It's not really what we were expecting, but it may be significant,' she continued, slightly breathlessly, still taken aback by the unexpected tirade. 'There's a life insurance policy in Gavin Brodie's name. His widow was to get a payout on his death, as long as he died prior to the 10th of February next year. Are you alright, Sir?'

'Aye. Fine. How much?'

'Two hundred thousand pounds. I didn't think people like him would be able to get that kind of insurance. But it looks as if you can if you're prepared to pay an extra whack each month. Maybe they exclude death from the disease or something, I don't know . . .'

'Right,' he said, cutting her off and sounding uninterested.

'And there were some court documents, too.'

'Yeah. Well, tell the boss tomorrow, eh? We're already well on the way with things. Paxton gave me a right load of porkies as far as I can see. Said he was at his health club until late, but nobody there seems to have seen him, his usual day's Wednesday anyway. Said he went on to the pub, then home. Lying fucker. The pub was closed all day as they had a pipe burst in the night, it didn't open again until the Tuesday. I've already spoken to the boss. We're going to bring him into the station, first thing tomorrow morning, straight from his morning surgery. Marked police car, blue light and everything. That'll make the toy boy sweat.'

10

'So, Doctor,' Elaine Bell began, feeling tense already, knowing that the man might be a difficult interviewee with his university degrees and the ease, the self confidence, which came from his position in the community. But some bloody pillar of it he was – pillock, more like – and she would get the better of him. The lying toad. Fortunately, he looked rattled now, his dark eyes looking anxiously into hers, sweat shining on his upper lip, and all before she had even begun. The ride in the marked police car seemed to have done the trick.

'I understand from the Inspector that on last Saturday night you were at your health club, Triton, until about 10 pm or so, is that correct?' Let him assent, and hang himself here and now. A firm 'yes' would leave him no room for pleas of error or forgetfulness later.

As she had hoped, he did say yes, glancing nervously at Eric Manson's well-built figure as he was doing so. In American cop programmes they beat people up, but not here, surely? If only he had watched *The Bill* or *Taggart*, anything, then he would have had an idea.

'And after that you went on to the Geordie in Rose Street?'

He nodded, adding quietly, 'Yes, that's where I went.'

'Sure about that?'

171

He nodded once more, crossing his legs and fingering the cleft in his chin.

'Funny, then, that nobody at Triton, your club, saw you?'

'Not really, Chief Inspector,' he replied. His voice sounded hoarse, so he cleared his throat and repeated, 'Not really funny. It's a big place, lots of machines, a swimming pool, showers. Not a difficult place to hide . . . if you wanted to.'

'OK, I follow that. Maybe the Geordie was the same. Lots of people, busy, jolly Christmas crowd, that sort of thing?' Please God, another 'yes'.

'Exactly. That's exactly what it was like. Still, I'm surprised that no one could remember me being there, if that's what you're going to suggest to me. Not even Brian?'

'Brian?' she replied, inviting him to enlighten her.

'Brian. Irish Brian. He's one of the barmen. I could have sworn he served me with at least one pint. He'll probably remember me.'

'That would be a bloody miracle,' Eric Manson growled, looking hard at the doctor.

'It would be a little . . . odd,' the DCI said, in a slightly perplexed tone, 'since the Geordie was closed on Saturday night. There'd been a flood, you see. So, "Irish Brian", and everyone else, now that I think about it, would be elsewhere.'

'So, "Doctor",' Eric Manson said, raising crooked fingers on either hand to put inverted commas around the man's title, and leaning closer towards him, 'where the fuck were you?'

All the remaining colour drained from Colin Paxton's face and he said, in an apologetic tone, 'I'm sorry, sorry,

I think I'm about to be sick.' No sooner had he said the words than he bent forward and threw up onto the table, copiously, splashing himself and the nearby Inspector.

'Bloody Hell!' Manson shouted, leaping to his feet, his chair tumbling to the ground behind him.

Later, in a different interview room, the same group reassembled. Paxton seemed somehow smaller, dressed in borrowed clothes, his head bowed and licking his lips incessantly as if he had just crossed a desert.

The DCI looked quizzically at him, inviting him to begin but saying nothing herself.

'I wasn't at the club . . . or the pub. I was seeing Heather,' the doctor said, head bowed.

'That'll be Heather Brodie, your patient's wife, eh?' Eric Manson said, as if helpfully clarifying matters.

'Yes,' the man replied, in a low voice, closing his eyes briefly as if unable to face them.

'So, tell us,' Elaine Bell said, 'what exactly did happen on Saturday night?'

Slowly, the story of the evening at *Il Gattopardo* and in his flat emerged, he having to be prodded occasionally to ensure that his narrative did not dry up. When he had finished Eric Manson leant across and snarled, 'So, you're knockin' off a sick man's wife, right? No, sorry, correction, a dying man's wife . . . then, after that . . .'

'Eric! That's enough,' the DCI reprimanded him, alarmed by the fury in his voice and the ferocious expression on his face.

'Why didn't you accompany Heather Brodie home?' she asked the doctor.

'I would have . . . I would have liked to, but I'd have

had to stop before India Street anyway, and there's always the risk . . .'

'The risk?'

'That we'd be seen. It would be awful for Heather, and if the GMC caught just a whiff of it I'd be struck off . . .'

'For knocking off a dying man's wife? Surely not?' Eric Manson sneered.

'That's why you lied?' Elaine Bell asked, ignoring her colleague's aside.

'Of course, I had to. Why else would I?'

'What do you think, Alice?' the DCI asked, after they had congregated once more in the murder suite, leaving their interviewee in his room to stew in his own juice, pacing up and down, uncertain what would happen to him next.

'About Paxton?'

'Of course.'

'I think he's telling the truth this time. He's petrified. I don't think he was lying.'

'But do you think he was involved? In the killing?' the DCI asked.

Before Alice had time to answer, she added, 'What I don't understand is, why? Why would Heather Brodie or Paxton, alone or together, bother to kill Gavin Brodie? If they wanted him out of the way, he was on his way out already. They would hardly have had to wait. And they weren't really waiting anyway, they were already getting on with their lives together. He couldn't have lasted more than . . . what, a couple of months or something? He was wasting away in front of their very eyes. Why would they take the risk?'

'I don't know, but something I came across yesterday might explain it,' Alice replied. 'In Heather Brodie's desk I found some insurance policy documents. If Brodie survived beyond early February next year, which is a month or so away, then she would not get a payout of two hundred thousand pounds. If he died before then, she would.'

'He had to die before then for there to be a payout? Why didn't you tell me this last night?' Elaine Bell demanded crossly. 'It might have been useful to have known that this morning, don't you think? For questioning Paxton, if nothing else.'

'Er . . . I think I thought . . .' she racked her brain, wondering why she had failed to pass on the news.

'Oh, never mind,' the DCI interrupted in a tired voice, 'We've got him for a bit longer, I suppose. But we'll still need a lot more evidence, motive or no motive It's all circumstantial so far.'

'I don't know, we've a fair amount against them both now, haven't we?' Eric Manson commented, wrinkling his nose in disgust as he wiped a spot of something from the shoulder of his jacket with a paper hankie.

'No, we haven't, Sir,' Alice said bluntly, too exhausted from lack of sleep to bother how her intervention might sound. 'Surely any prints or DNA in the house can be easily explained away? He'll not have been on the database, but if the unidentified stuff is his, prints or DNA, it was in the kitchen and the bedroom wasn't it? He'll account for it on the basis of his role as the man's doctor. And there was nothing on the knife or anything else, thanks to the river and the rain. We've no witnesses. All we've got so far, surely, is opportunity, means and now, possibly, motive. Nothing concrete. And what did they do? Poison him and then cut his throat, but why both? And why would they take stuff, then throw it away?'

'Well, if it was them,' the DCI answered, ruffling her hair distractedly with her hands, 'they'd take the stuff just to make it look like an outside job. But I've no idea at the moment why they'd do both.'

'Have we heard from the pharmacy whether there was enough in the bottles for the overdose?'

'Yup. There was enough – well, enough if we can rely on Paxton's prescription records. Which, of course, is rather a big if now.'

'Presumably,' Alice said, 'we should discount, for the present, at least, Heather Brodie and Paxton's evidence about the victim's ability to take the stuff himself?'

'Yes, I agree. We'll go with the old lady and what's her name Reid's version, the children's too, that he couldn't do it himself, and he no longer knew what was in the bottles.'

'One other thing, Ma'am,' Alice said, tentatively, keen to avoid provoking another outburst, 'amongst the stuff in Heather Brodie's desk there were papers, court papers. He had to raise an action to stop some madwoman pursuing him, scratching his car, yelling at Harry and Ella, breaking his windows. It all happened quite recently. Just last year in fact. Should I check the woman out? I've done a bit of digging with her neighbours, and apparently she works at the Abbey Park Lodge.'

'Mmm, does she now,' Elaine Bell responded, her interest engaged immediately, falling silent as she thought things through. A few trails seemed to have led back to that place. And, remembering the Dyce enquiry and her failure to follow up a possible lead, she nodded.

'On you go. We'll leave Paxton to sweat in here for a bit longer. In the meanwhile, we'll re-do her closest neighbours, and make a start on his. Maybe someone will be able to say whether he left the place with her, when, or have seen the pair of them go into India Street together, anything. Anything to show that he's still lying. Because if he is, with a bit more pressure, I reckon he'll break.'

'And if he doesn't, then that leaves her, the Brodie woman,' Eric Manson said, adding grimly, 'and she'll be the only one left in the picture.'

—

'That's it then, Detta,' the manageress of the Abbey Park Lodge said, airily, 'there'll be no more raisins sprinkled in the clean underwear, eh?'

'Em . . . like I told you, I just spilt them there . . . the sultanas, like.'

'Raisins, sultanas, whatever . . . they all look like rodent droppings, don't they? And once could be accidental, twice carelessness even, but six times? No, I don't think so. However, I . . . no, we, will manage to forget all about this little incident, I'm sure, and you'll not be going to the lawyers, to the Industrial Tribunal either. Is that right, dear, you'll give up your claim now, eh?'

Victory, the manageress thought, as she looked into the little Irishwoman's resentful eyes, was almost in her grasp. It was true, as the manuals said, that management sometimes resembled a game of chess, but, fortunately, every so often one's opponent turned out to be not a Russian Grandmaster but, as in this case, an ass. And yes, she would admit it, hers was an unorthodox approach, certainly not one recommended or sanctioned by those manuals, but innovation and flexibility were surely the hallmarks of the competent manager? This morning, fortune had favoured the brave, and Julia from H R.'s timid advice could now be consigned to the wastepaper bin of industrial relations. And, as 'brown cow' did not always, inevitably, follow 'How, now,' Agnes, too, might get nowhere with her complaint.

Detta O'Hare, her head lowered as if in church, nodded mulishly, and then turned to leave the manageress's office, hitting her elbow on the door frame in her haste to escape.

A few minutes later, and feeling reinvigorated by the routing of the woman, the manageress found herself informing the police sergeant that no Agnes Hart worked in their premises.

'No.' She shook her head, replacing the cap on her gold Parker pen with a single assured movement, 'I'm afraid I can't help you there. No one with that name works here. As I'm sure you'll appreciate, I am familiar with the names of all my staff.'

'You're quite sure about that?' Alice enquired, 'because this is where a neighbour told us she works.'

'Yes.'

'Any other Agneses employed here?' Alice asked doubtfully, with little expectation of a useful reply.

'Two. Agnes Cauld and Agnes Leckie. They're both on bed-making duty in the Drumsheugh Wing, or at least they should be. If they're not there, then try the lifts, they may be cleaning them out.'

—

As Alice entered the first room after the fire doors, Agnes Cauld's large posterior greeted her as the nurse bent over a resident's bed, smoothing the covers for him. Unaware of the policewoman's presence, she began to swing it playfully from side to side, singing as she did so, all to the evident delight of the hairless old fellow below her who

began excitedly clapping out a calypso rhythm, determined to keep his jolly nurse's company for as long as
possible. Amused, Alice watched them for a few seconds,
then cleared her throat loudly to alert them to her arrival.

'Oh, hello,' she said, turning round to face the policewoman and smiling broadly, her bright smile remaining
undimmed as Alice asked her name and about the likely
whereabouts of her namesake.

'Agnes? Easy. Agnes will be smokin' . . .'

Then she added in singsong voice, 'A-smokin' or
a-shakin'. Agnes is always a-smokin' or a-shakin'.
A-shakin' or a-smokin'.'

The designated staff smoking area for the home
amounted to no more than a corner of tarmac in the yard,
minimal shelter being afforded by a ragged piece of corrugated iron over the triangular piece of ground. Standing in
the corner, her head sunk low into her shoulders to prevent
it from touching the edge of the roof, was the woman Alice
was looking for. She was absorbed in her own thoughts,
inhaling deeply from her cigarette, then watching the
stream of smoke as she exhaled it forcefully through pale
and pursed lips. On either side of her were piles of bloated
rubbish bags, overspills from the nearby dustbins, and the
air was rank with the stink of rotten cabbage and bad fish.
By her feet were dozens of small blue polythene bags, most
of which appeared balloon-like, inflated to near-bursting
point with some kind of self-generated noxious gas. But
she appeared oblivious to it all, to the awful odour, to the
light rain falling all around her, and to the approach of
the stranger, because all her attention was focused on one
thing and one thing alone, her cigarette.

The woman was unusually short and almost spherical
in shape, her elasticated tracksuit bottoms encircling the

179

globe of her waist and clinging to it, cruelly outlining her vast, protuberant belly. Beneath it, and in its shade, her little feet were shod in scuffed white trainers, both of which had their pink laces undone. A pair of raisin eyes peered out from behind her fleshy cheeks, and her mouth, when not occupied in exhaling smoke, moved incessantly as if she was talking to herself.

'Agnes Leckie?' Alice asked, approaching the woman, trying to work out the wind-direction, to ensure that she would not be downwind of the rubbish pile.

'Aye,' answered Agnes, looking at the stranger with little curiosity, her trembling hand raised to her mouth, ready for another draw. 'Who are you?'

If Alice had said that she was from the refuse department the woman could not have shown less interest in her answer, and when asked if she had ever used 'Hart' as a surname, she nodded, showing no curiosity whatsoever as to how this police officer could know such a thing or why she would wish to meet her.

'And you knew Gavin Brodie, didn't you?' the Sergeant continued, 'when you were still called Hart, I mean. I need to speak to you about him.'

'Gavin Brodie? Oh aye, fire away,' she replied, wrinkling her adipose features in disgust, 'I've no' forgotten him . . . No' likely tae forget him.'

'Before I ask you about him,' Alice said, 'can you tell me where you were on Saturday night, last Saturday night?'

'This is like oan the telly, eh! Me 'n' Gareth went to see his friend. Then I went back to ma ain flat. Whit's all o' this tae dae wi' Gavin Brodie?'

'On your own – were you at home on your own?'

'Aye,' she said rubbing her stomach round and round as if to polish it, 'well, almost oan ma ain. After the wee wan's born me 'n' Gareth will move in tegither. I've taken his name already, "Leckie" for the wee wan's sake. Like I said, whit's all o' this tae dae wi' Gavin Brodie?'

'You know who I'm talking about? The Gavin Brodie who lived in India Street?'

'Aye, there's only the wan fer me,' she said, drawing deeply on her cigarette. 'I ken him, but what's a' this tae dae wi' me? He's the wan you should be interested in – wrecked ma business, broke up ma marriage, made me ill. That wis a crime! You wouldnae believe it, but when I wis at college I used to be petite, I wis only seven stone. I could fit, nae bother, into a size eight. I'm oan a diet now, no crisps or chocolate, like, jist fags.'

'How did he wreck everything for you?'

'Because it wis his job tae keep me right, see? He kept the accounts for ma business. I'd a wee sandwich shop oan Henderson Row, below ma flat. Thanks tae him, all ma tax wis wrong, he got it a' wrong, an' the next thing the taxman wis aifter me. I got letter aifter letter, but I couldnae pay 'cause I didnae have the money. So the tax people made me bankrupt an' then I lost the lease of the shop, then my man dumped me because he wis stressed to bits.'

She stopped speaking, dropped her cigarette butt onto the tarmac and ground it up with the heel of her trainer, then added, 'Still, he got his come-uppance, didn't he?'

'His "come-uppance"?' Alice repeated, her voice sounding nasal, a sudden whiff of bad eggs making her clamp her nostrils between her fingers. But Agnes Leckie did not respond, too busy attempting to prise another fag from the foil-covering within the packet.

'How do you mean, "got his come-uppance"? Who did he get his "come-uppance" from?' Alice said more

181

loudly, moving towards the care assistant, eager to inhale the cigarette smoke now drifting about her head. The little woman took another draw, threw away her match and said, smugly, 'God, hersel'. By givin' him that disease.'

'Have you been back, recently, to India Street, or anywhere near Gavin Brodie?

'Me? Em . . . em, naw.'

'Sure about that?'

'I never done, naw, I never done that. I'd be put inside if I'd done that.' Agnes sounded agitated, and she began scratching a rough, inflamed area on her forehead.

'Aggie . . . Aggie,' cried an anxious voice in the distance, and a little later Una Reid's solid figure appeared, running towards the shelter with a newspaper held over her head, to protect it from the persistent rain.

'You'll hae tae make the last three beds . . .' she began breathlessly on her arrival, 'I done the rest of the Drumsheugh wans but I cannae dae it all mysel'. I'm supposed to be helpin' the residents wi' their breakfasts now.'

Agnes Leckie glanced at the newcomer, nodding her head several times in response, but she made no move to leave the shelter. Instead, she returned her gaze to Alice as if expecting the interview to continue.

'Come oan, Aggie!' Una Reid said excitedly. 'Mrs Drayton kens that you're here. She saw you leavin' the dining hall, an' she's been watchin' you ever since frae her office.'

'Mrs Hart – er, Ms Leckie, stay here, please. There are a few other things I need to know,' Alice began, but she was quickly interrupted by Agnes Leckie who, as if she hadn't spoken, squealed in a high voice, 'Mrs Drayton? She's no' seen me, has she, Mum?'

'Aye. Mrs Drayton, the manageress. So get a move oan, eh, Aggie.'

'I never went nowhere . . . nowhere near Gavin Brodie,' Agnes said, her face now scarlet and tears rolling down her fat cheeks.

'That's right, pet, you never,' her mother replied quietly. 'But dinnae worry, I'll tell the lady fer you. Off you go.'

'I would rather speak to Agnes . . . directly,' Alice said.

Ignoring the policewoman's words, Una Reid started shooing her daughter away with her hands and then replied firmly, 'Naw, you can speak tae me instead. Agnes's already oan a final warnin', she'll lose her job if she disnae go. But you can speak tae me . . . again.'

'You sure, Mum? It'll be alright then, I'd best go, eh?' Agnes Leckie said, zipping up her tracksuit top, preparing herself to brave the downpour, huge drops of rain smashing onto the tarmac and soaking her trainers.

'Aye. Off you go. Dinnae you worry yourself, pet. I'll deal wi' her,' Una Reid answered, jerking her head in Alice's direction.

Agnes lurched out from under the corrugated iron roof and squelched across the yard, her rounded arms flapping loosely at her sides.

'Right,' said Una Reid, watching her go, then finally giving Alice her full attention. 'She's away. You can speak tae me an' I'll tell you anythin' you need tae ken. So . . . why are you botherin' Aggie – my daughter, Agnes?'

'I wasn't "bothering" her,' Alice corrected her, annoyed at not being able to speak to a possible suspect, 'I was questioning her. We're investigating Gavin Brodie's death, as you well know.'

'Aye. So whit dae you want wi' her?' Una Reid demanded, unabashed.

'You didn't tell me about Agnes, your daughter, and Gavin Brodie – the connection between them. You never mentioned Agnes's troubles, the interdict that had to be taken against her to stop her harassing him, harassing his whole family.'

'Naw, I didnae,' the woman replied, then she paused as if thinking and said slowly, 'I dinnae think it mattered. It wis history. You never asked me, neither.'

'I didn't know about it when I last spoke to you – that she had a grudge, to put it mildly, against the man.'

Una Reid gazed unblinkingly into the policewoman's eyes before answering, and then said, 'Aye, she does. And nae wonder! Who could blame her? Aggie went bust, lost her husband, an' she blamed Gavin Brodie fer everythin' . . . everythin'. And she wis right. So dae I. Her business wis goin' OK up until the bother wi' the tax people, and her man couldnae take it when things started going wrong. He just walked away, walked oot on her. Aggie stopped lookin' aifter hersel'. She's bi-polar, see. It's been diagnosed now, but not before she wis sectioned for it, mind, put intae the Royal. She blamed him fer everythin' that happened. I done and a'.'

'Has she ever been back to India Street, anywhere near Gavin Brodie, as far as you know?'

'You're jokin' aren't ye? Ye must be. No, Never. She's shit-scared, terrified. But you're no interested in that, are you? The court case and a' that. No, you're wonderin' if she killed the man, aren't you? Aggie? Jeez!' she sighed. 'Just to let you know,' she added, hotly, 'it's ridiculous. you seen her for yourself. Are her prints all over things or somethin'? Course they're fuckin' not! Oh, and youse'll have them, you know. Before she went into the Royal she wis in an' oot the jail. Shoplifting, malicious mischief, drink and everythin'.'

'OK, but we . . .' Alice began, pausing momentarily to

move further into the shelter in an attempt to avoid more drips going down her collar.

'Aggie!' the woman continued, fired up with anger at the thought, 'Aggie can hardly get oot her bed in the mornin' the now. She's so drugged she can hardly think.'

'Did you realise, when you got the job with the Brodies, who you were going to work for?' Alice persisted.

'No' at first, it was a' done through here, through the Abbey Park. Aifter the first few days I realised.'

'And then, once you did realise, how did you feel about the man who had ruined your daughter's life, seeing him every day?'

'What d'you think I felt? I just about quit at first. But then, well, I needed the money. They're private payers, like, good payers, too. And I didnae kill him, if that's what you're getting' oan aboot the noo. Naw, I didnae need to. I watched him being punished day in and day out, that was reward enough for me. Why'd I bring his suffering to an end? I enjoyed seein' it . . . got paid by him to watch it an' a'.'

—

'Alice?' It was Ian.

'Yes,' she answered, her voice dull, but her heart suddenly thumping against her ribs as if trying to escape its cage. Simply at the sound of his voice at the other end of a phone.

'I'm back. Have you had lunch yet? Could you spare half an hour or so, so I can see you. I've something to tell you.'

'No, I haven't had lunch. Whereabouts were you thinking?'

'Say, that café in Stockbridge, in twenty minutes or so.'

185

She arrived first and took a table in the window, watching the people passing on the street outside, trying to calm herself by breathing in and out more deeply. Every time the door opened she looked up, and eventually, five minutes late, he walked in. Seeing her he came over and tried to kiss her cheek, but instinctively she turned her head away.

'What's the matter?' he asked, sitting beside her, looking anxiously into her face.

Where to begin? It was, of course, the very question that she had been anticipating, but all the answers that she had envisaged herself giving fell away, and she heard herself muttering 'Nothing,' like a sulky schoolgirl. After a second, she spurred herself on and tried again. 'Well, no, not nothing actually. Something. Why did you tell me on Wednesday night that you'd been at your studio when you weren't? I went there at about 10.45 and looked round about it for a bit and you were nowhere to be seen. I saw Susie and she told me that there had been a power cut, and the place was out of action until the next day . . .'

'I know, I know, that's what . . .' he began, frantically waving the bemused waitress away as you might a troublesome wasp.

'And London. I don't even believe you were there. You told me before that you'd cleaned the stone you used for the wishbone lithographs . . . you told me at the time you did it. No address, no call, no text. What's going on?'

It had all fallen out in a breathless rush, but as she had promised herself, nothing had been kept back, no accidental traps were left for the unwary. She had shown her complete hand, including, by the tone of her voice, her annoyance, her hurt at his deceit. Hearing her words, he looked taken aback, but said not a thing. Seconds passed in silence between them, feeling like hours.

'Well?' she heard herself say, her tone more like a magistrate than a lover.

'I . . . I . . . I was intending to tell you . . .' he began, but stopped again, moving towards her and holding out his hand for her to take. 'I was intending to tell you . . .'

'What?' she said, sounding horribly shrill in her own ears, wanting the worst to be over and forcing herself to add, 'tell me what? That it's finished? That we're finished and that it is all over? Fine. OK. I understand that, but what I'd like to know . . .' She ground to a halt, but it was all right, she had somehow got it out, so that all that was left for him to do was to nod his head. He would not have to say a thing. But as he listened to her, the expression on his face had changed, and he looked distraught, hurt, like a dog who had received an unexpected blow.

'No! No! Alice . . . that's not what I wanted to say. Not what I wanted to tell you,' he said.

'Well, what is it then?'

'Not that, not anything like that. Christ Almighty! How could you even think such a thing?'

'What can I get you?' a waiter asked, pad at the ready, looking expectantly at them for their order.

'Not now, nothing,' Ian answered, then added for politeness' sake, 'later. We'll order later, thank you.'

'What is it then, tell me,' Alice said once the man had gone, already feeling a wave of relief rushing over her at his passionate denial, able to muster a weak joke: 'You're not pregnant, are you?'

He took her hand in his and looked into her eyes. 'That's not so far off the mark . . . On Tuesday last . . .' he swallowed, but continued speaking, 'I discovered that

187

I'm a father. I've got a three-year-old son. I knew nothing about him, I promise you. Nothing, I promise you. His mother, Paula, never let me know that she was pregnant. I lived with her for a little while on and off when I was in St Bernard's Row, but it was never serious for either of us.'

'Why is she telling you about the boy now?'

'She isn't. She didn't. It wasn't her. She didn't tell me, it was her sister. Paula died in a car accident about two months ago . . .'

'So, why didn't you tell me that, about the boy? Why lie?'

He sighed. 'I don't know, I'm sorry. I was ashamed, having a child, and having done nothing for it – for him. Like some kind of deadbeat. I did go to London, I promise, but it was to meet his grandparents, talk to them. Before that, on the Wednesday night, I went to the sister's house, that's where I was. I saw him for a little while before he went to bed, I talked to her.'

'So what are you going to do?' she asked, still trying to digest the news.

'I don't know. Get to know him, first of all, I suppose.'

'What's his name?'

'Hamish. Hamish John Melville.'

—

'No, Pippa, I'll do it,' Heather Brodie said, making no effort to disguise her impatience at her sister's ineffectuality, 'I know how it works. It's got its own idiosyncrasies . . .' So saying, she almost barged her sister out of the way, turned the key in the lock and simultaneously pushed the door with her right shoulder. Her forceful tactic worked, and the pair of them walked into Harry Brodie's flat, a dark and dingy basement in Raeburn

Mews. Heather Brodie was feeling annoyed. She had not wanted company on this occasion, particularly on this occasion, and was finding her extended stay with her sister rather a trial.

Pippa was far too neat, too quiet, too set in her ways, and seemed to have nothing better to do than mope about re-arranging her immaculate possessions on a daily basis. And she seemed to have sunk into a decline, ever since that interview with the police. But how many times would she have to repeat 'It went fine,' and explain that they had been believed, reassure her that the police would never discover their lies. How much more bloody reassurance could she give? And, for that matter, how much more silent resentment could she endure? And today Pippa had taken to shadowing her. Had she no life of her own? No friends? Were they not living in each other's pockets enough already?

The cursory inspection Heather Brodie made of the place revealed the expected mess: unwashed clothes strewn on unhoovered carpets, dirty dishes stacked beside the sink, and books and papers scattered throughout as if a strong wind had blown them there.

She was quite accustomed to the sights and smells of her son's quarters, since every fortnight or so for the past year she had gone there and cleaned them out. Today, however, the squalor of the place struck her with new force. In the company of her sister, she suddenly saw it through her eyes and imagined the thoughts that were likely to be passing through her mind. And Pippa, of course, only had dealings with six- to eight-year-olds, and then only during school hours, so she had, could have, no real experience of a normal nineteen-year-old boy and his habits.

And Harry was certainly entirely normal, the state

of his flat testified to that, although it would, no doubt, be considered an abhorrence, an abomination, by his spinster aunt. And, actually, for the record, no amount of discipline, chastisement or reward would have turned him into a tidy boy, she thought crossly to herself, so it had nothing to do with his upbringing or lack of it, and everything to do with his . . . his character and his heredity. Gavin had been an untidy creature, too, always was.

'This is disgusting,' Pippa said, stooping to pick up a greasy frying pan from the top of the television set in the boy's bedroom.

'But quite normal – for students,' her sister replied, evenly.

'Ella doesn't keep her flat like this. It's always immaculate.' The riposte was immediate.

'Ella, Ella, Ella! Ella can do no bloody wrong, though, can she, Pippa?' Heather Brodie said, unable to stop her annoyance bubbling to the surface and exploding as it did every so often. 'She's always been your favourite. I know that, Gavin knew that, Harry knows that. Ella too. You don't even try to hide it. Ever since she was born she's been perfect as far as you're concerned, hasn't she?' The injustice of it rankled. Only a childless woman would be so blatant in her partiality.

'Yes, perfect,' the spinster replied defiantly, bending over Harry's unmade bed, lifting the duvet up and emitting a horrified gasp as she did so.

'What is it now?' Heather Brodie asked.

'What on earth is *that*?' Pippa Mitchelson replied, sounding appalled and holding up a copy of *Nuts* magazine between her thumb and forefinger, an open centrefold showing a naked girl smiling and cupping her breasts in her hands.

'They all do it, read it, I mean,' Heather Brodie said in as matter-of-fact tone as she could muster, taking the magazine from her sister and adding, 'though not Ella, obviously.' As she took it a scrap of lined paper fell out and floated down to the floor. In a trice Pippa Mitchelson picked it up, her face breaking into a smile as she said excitedly, 'It's a poem, Heather. I'll read it out, shall I?'

Without waiting for an answer, she cleared her throat and then began chanting out loud in a sing-song voice:

> 'In the olden days,
> In the golden days,
> You held my hand in yours
> And led me to the sea,
> You did that for me.
>
> But in the new days,
> Such black and blue days,
> I held your hand in mine
> To lead you to the sea,
> May the Lord forgive me.'

'It doesn't scan very well,' she said dismissively. 'D'you think he wrote it? It seems to be in his handwriting.'

'Yes, yes,' Heather Brodie answered, impatient to get on with the job in hand, 'he'll have written it. He likes poetry. He's written his own since he was a very little boy. And it scanned perfectly well, Pippa, I thought. He's good at rhythm, always has been. His English teacher even told me.'

'No,' Pippa said, looking at it again, 'let me see. First line six, no seven, syllables. Second line the same. Third line, nine syllables . . .'

'Oh, for heaven's sake, Pippa!' Heather Brodie remonstrated angrily, 'I don't care how many syllables. We haven't got time to analyse the poem. We're supposed to be tidying up his flat. Couldn't you just finish making the bed?'

'Very well,' her sister answered huffily, pulling the rest of the duvet back inch by inch as if afraid she might expose a severed body part. On the other side of the room Heather Brodie opened the curtains, letting daylight flood onto the disordered interior. She lifted a baseball bat from the carpet, disentangling three wire coat-hangers which had become attached to it and each other, and walked towards the door, intending to put it in the hallway. As she was doing so the telephone rang. She dropped everything immediately and picked it up, curious, but also determined that Pippa would not be the one to answer it.

'Harry Brodie's flat,' she said, tension making her sound slightly hostile.

'Oh, is that you, Mrs Brodie?' a surprised voice asked, and Heather Brodie immediately recognised the high-pitched tones of Vicky MacSween. The girl was a friend of both of her children and Harry's current girlfriend.

'Yes, Vicky, it's me,' she said, and hearing the impatience in her own tone, added, in an attempt to make herself sound less intimidating, 'Can I help you?'

'Is Harry there?' Obviously not, Heather Brodie thought, otherwise he would be answering the phone instead of me, but she simply said, 'No, Vicky, I'm afraid he's not. Would you like me to leave a message for him?'

'Is Ella there?' Biting her tongue, her mother said, 'No, sorry. She's not here either. You could try their mobiles?'

'Mmm . . . I will.' A long silence followed.

'So, Vicky, would you like me to leave a message in case they've switched them off, or what?'

'OK. Yes, thanks. Could you tell Harry that I'll see him tonight at about 8 pm at my place, and could you tell Ella that I've still got her jacket from last week. She left it in my flat on Saturday evening before we went on to the pub. I meant to give it to her before she left in the morning, but I'll just give it to Harry when I see him tonight.'

'Ella left it with you last Saturday? OK. And you'll give the jacket to Harry. Righto. Anything else?'

'Nope.'

Now deep in thought, Heather Brodie put the phone down and began picking up some of the sheets of A4 paper scattered all over the floor. As she was doing so her sister stooped to help her, but after she had gathered a few of them she came to a sudden halt.

'They're all mixed up – look,' she said, holding up one of the sheets. 'This one looks like English Literature, and this one . . .' she added, pulling out another from the sheaf, 'looks like a language paper or something, and this one,' she tried to extract another sheet without losing her grip on the rest, 'must be Russian studies.'

'And?' Heather Brodie said, still bent double, gathering up the papers, ignoring their contents and continuing to collect them in a single pile.

'Well, they must be his lecture notes, mustn't they? We'll need to keep them separate. He'll need them separate, for his essays and his revision if nothing else.'

'Then,' Heather Brodie said, conscious that her tolerance of her sister and her annoying ways was now at a dangerously low ebb, 'he'll just have to separate them out after we've put them all together into one pile, won't he?'

'Of course,' her sister replied, aware of the unspoken reprimand, now wishing that she had never volunteered to help with the flat-cleaning, wasting a precious Saturday. She could have gone to the Botanics, checked out the Dean Gallery or simply cleaned her own flat, for that matter. It would have taken her mind off everything. And Heather simply did not understand the meaning of the word gratitude.

Feeling increasingly hot, and keen to get out of her sister's company before she said something rash, she abandoned the paper collection and strode into the windowless kitchen, turning on the fan extractor and hoping for a rush of cold air. It seemed impossible to keep cool nowadays wherever she was, modern thermostats must all be set too high.

How fortunate for me, she thought to herself as she set to work, picking up a pile of battered, slime-covered silver cartons from the table, that this generation chooses to live on carry-outs. So much less washing-up, but so bland, and goodness knows what it must do to the young people's health. No wonder the boy always looked so pallid, so thin and positively sickly of late.

Putting the cartons in the overflowing bin, she turned her attention to the sink, removed a couple of used teabags from the drain and lifted up a bottle of Fairy Liquid, the sole purpose of which seemed to be to act as a paperweight. Certainly, it had not been used for washing dishes. As she held it she noticed that an opened envelope with something inside it had stuck to the base of the bottle. Cautiously, she peeled it off. Now it was in her hand she was well aware that she should put it down again, or file it safely somewhere else, but she found that she could not resist the temptation to read it, to peek at it at least. The letter was addressed to Mr H. A. Brodie. The original India Street address had been scored out and, in Heather's neat script, the Raeburn Mews one substituted. Maybe the letter would contain a declaration of strong feelings, friendship, or a love letter perhaps, something life enhancing and real. Maybe he had won a prize! She needed distraction, and Heather was in another room after all, so no-one would ever know, and Harry might not even mind if he knew, and he would never know so it could do no harm to anybody, could it? A single glance might well be enough. Filled with anticipation, she wiped her hands on a foul-smelling dish cloth and took a sheet of paper out of the envelope.

'Heather,' she shouted, forgetting in her surprise that she was not supposed to be reading the boy's mail, 'What's this about? Was Harry going to have . . .'

Before she had finished speaking, her sister came into the room carrying another letter in an official-looking envelope. She took the sheet of paper from Pippa. Reading it, her expression changed to one of despair. She glanced at the name and address on the envelope that Pippa still held and sat down heavily on a nearby stool.

'What is it, Heather?' Pippa enquired, sitting down beside her on another chair.

'Nothing . . . nothing that I can't fix.'

II

Sunday

For some reason the fact that she had such a limited choice of clothes that morning, none of which remotely appealed to her, almost made her break down and weep. Instead Heather Brodie scolded herself roundly for her vanity, for her stupid shallowness, and in doing so managed to regain sufficient control of her emotions to continue sifting through her suitcase until she had got all that she needed. She looked disdainfully at the brown skirt and the blue shirt she had found. She had no recollection of packing them, and they would not go together at all. But she comforted herself with the thought that at least everything she was going to put on was clean, washed and ironed by her own hands. If only she had brought more clothes from India Street. Her make-up, too, would require attention if she was to appear confident and in control, if she was to seem to be the mistress of her own destiny.

The sound made by the flushing of the lavatory travelled through the thin plasterboard walls and alerted her to Pippa's imminent departure from the bathroom, but she waited until she heard her sister pad in her slippers across the corridor and close her own bedroom door before she made her move. Today, their usual insubstantial morning chitchat would be unbearable and was best avoided. Anyway, what did it matter how she had slept, or how Pippa had slept for that matter? That was all it ever amounted to, and her inability to feign interest might cause more offence and was almost bound to be misunderstood. She could feel her own nerves jangling, making her jumpy and prickly before they had even exchanged a word. A silly quarrel of some sort was inevitable.

As efficient as ever, within less than fifteen minutes she had showered, dressed and put her face on, but instead of leaving the bathroom and going into the kitchen in search of breakfast, she sat down on the lavatory seat and waited, listening for the tell-tale noises made by her sister as she exited the flat on her way to church. Soon the characteristic tuneless hum which invariably accompanied Pippa's removal of her waterproof from the coat-hook started up, interrupted by a thick 'Bye bye, Heather' spoken through the remains of the last piece of toast. Finally, a loud bang signalled that the front door had been shut.

In the peace and quiet that followed, Heather Brodie looked in the fridge. Seeing only goat's milk, she rejected the idea of cereal in favour of stewed apple with cream, a treat, if sprinkled generously with brown sugar. But once the bowl was in front of her, looking exactly as she had imagined it would, she found that she hadn't the appetite even to taste it and put down her spoon. Then, remembering with affection their mother's thrift, she carefully placed the bowl back on the fridge shelf, together with a twist of paper on which she had written 'untouched'.

The taxi driver, a bumptious individual sporting dark glasses against the grey, sunless northern sky, seemed determined to engage her in conversation. Though his overtures were met with monosyllabic replies, he continued pestering her relentlessly until, eventually, she responded. Talking to him would be less of an effort than not doing so, she thought. If she was lucky he would do all the work anyway. So, when he said in his matey Liverpool accent, 'You're going to St Leonard's Street are you? You work there then?'

She replied, 'No – no, I don't work there.'

'Reporting a crime at the police station are you?'

'Yes.'

'Theft, is it theft then? I've been burglarised myself, you know. I know just how it feels, them in your house and everything. Like a rape, sort of. First time it happened we were living in Portobello, and the next time it happened it was where I live now, Silverknowes. Know what I think? I think they ought to confiscate all of them thieves' possessions. That'd teach 'em to take other people's stuff, wouldn't it?'

'Yes, it would,' she replied earnestly.

'What they take of yours then?'

She racked her brain trying to think what to say, then a ready-made list forced itself into her consciousness: 'Em . . . a wallet, my husband's wallet, a computer, my jewellery case . . .'

'Your jewellery case?' he interrupted, sounding appalled on her behalf, 'was there much in it, then, by way of jewellery?'

'A necklace . . . a ring, a brooch or two, sentimental value . . .' she began, wishing that she had never weakened and entered this ludicrous conversation. Then inspiration came to her and she asked, 'And you? What did they take from you – in the first robbery, I mean – and in the second, of course.'

By the time the cab drew up outside the police station, the man was still busy listing his stolen possessions, occasionally adjusting their details, reminding himself that the music centre taken was a Sanyo, not a Panasonic, and that the CD collection nicked from Portobello, no, from Silverknowes, had belonged, not to his daughter, but to his wife. Stepping out onto the wet pavement, she gave the cabby a very generous tip, finding herself unexpectedly grateful for his incessant animated chatter, an endless stream which had kept at bay her own thoughts, her own demons.

When she told the man at the reception desk that she had come to see DCI Bell, the old fellow nodded and asked her in a bored tone what her visit was in connection with. For a second, she was stumped, unable to answer, and then she pulled herself together. 'To confess . . .' she said, marvelling at the words as she spoke them, almost overawed by their implication. Saying them out loud to another person for the first time, to a stranger, made them real in a way that, up to that moment, they had not been. Safely inside her own head, they meant nothing, like a daydream of some dreadful revenge or a song unsung. The receptionist looked almost affronted by her answer and she heard him mutter down the phone, 'Yes . . . a lady here wants to see DCI Bell, says she's come to confess something. No, I don't know what . . . course not . . . no, I didn't like to ask her.'

The only windows in the interview room were snibbed tight shut, and the smell of cleaning fluid in the place was overpowering. On top of its scent, some kind of floral air-freshener had recently been sprayed in the space, strong enough to take the breath away and burn the back of the throat. Her immediate instinct was to turn round and walk straight out of the room again, but, instead, as instructed, she took her place at the table.

Opposite her, and already seated, she recognised the female Sergeant who had interviewed her in the flat. She seemed to have aged in the last few days, with dark circles under her eyes, and appeared distracted.

When the male Inspector entered the room he looked straight through her, as if she was some lower form of life not needing to be accorded the normal courtesies. He had a wide choice of seats, and ostentatiously chose the one furthest away from her. There he slumped over his mug of coffee, staring into the middle distance, choosing not to meet her gaze. He looked unkempt, slightly sordid, she thought, as if he belonged in the cells rather than on the floor above them. Once he was seated, their DCI, the stout, officious woman, put down the telephone.

'Well,' Elaine Bell said, crossing her arms and sounding stern, 'I understand that you've a confession to make.'

'Yes,' Heather Brodie answered, sitting up straight, making herself as upright as possible, readying herself for the confrontation, the series of challenges, she was anticipating. To her relief her voice came across as strong and confident, as if it belonged to someone unintimidated by the setting or the situation.

'On you go then,' the DCI continued, as if encouraging her in something innocuous like a theatre audition or the opening speech in a school debate. Conscious that they were all now staring expectantly at her, Heather Brodie cleared her throat and said, 'I've come to confess to the murder of my husband, Gavin. I killed him . . .' Then she stopped abruptly, hoping that she had now said enough, enough for their limited purposes at any rate. What more could they need?

'How?' the DCI asked, leaning towards her, 'how exactly did you do it?'

She hesitated before answering, blinking as she gathered her thoughts. 'First of all I drugged him, gave him an overdose of his own drugs. Then I . . . I cut his throat using our kitchen knife.' As she said it, she made a horizontal slitting motion with her right hand as if she was cutting her own throat.

'But why?' Eric Manson demanded. 'Why did you do that? Cut his throat, if you'd already poisoned him?' The room was now in complete silence, the DCI's gaze fixed on her interviewee.

'Because . . . I lost my nerve. After I'd given them to him, I wasn't sure that the drugs would do the trick – kill him, I mean.'

'Why didn't you give him more?'

'He was comatose by then, he couldn't drink. Anyway, to tell you the truth, I didn't think of it.'

'What did you give him in the first place?' Eric Manson persisted.

'Em . . . the Nortriptyline and the Oramorph, a mixture of the two, but . . .' she said, now sounding slightly impatient, 'I'm not sure why you need to know all of this, though. It's like twenty questions, or something. I've already told you that I'm confessing to this. I'll plead guilty at my trial – to Gavin's murder, I mean. You needn't worry.'

Feeling oddly indignant that they felt the need to interrogate her, she glared at each of the police officers in turn.

'Right,' Elaine Bell said coldly, returning her glare. 'Let's get down to business, then, shall we? The Nortriptyline and so on – where did you get it from?'

'The bottles?' Heather Brodie began, 'over time, I mean. Every time we got a new prescription I'd collect it – well, draw off a little of the contents and store it for later use. I stockpiled the stuff. Quite a lot, well, enough, anyway. Actually, when the time came there was enough in the bottles.'

'How would you know what "enough" was, and which of his drugs to give him?' Alice asked.

Heather Brodie hesitated for a few seconds, and then replied, 'It wasn't difficult. Don't forget, I'd been giving him his medication every day for months and months. I know the effect each one has on him. Anyway,' she added, sounding more confident. 'I spent six years as a nurse before I married. A while ago, of course, but I haven't forgotten everything I learnt.'

'And the burgled stuff,' Eric Manson said, 'the wallet, the computer and so on, what did you do with that? And why, why did you do it, take your own things?'

'I took the computer and the rest of it so that it'd look like an "outside" job, then you'd be looking for a thief, someone who'd just come in. Obviously, once I'd cut his throat I knew that no-one would doubt that he had been murdered, so I needed to make it look as if someone had come into our house and killed him, someone who'd been robbing our house or whatever.'

'What did you do with the stuff?' the DCI enquired.

'I dumped it, in the first place I could think of . . . er . . . down by the Dean Bridge in amongst the bushes there. And some of it I put in the river. I threw the knife into the Water of Leith, the jewellery case, the wallet too.'

'Giving your husband an overdose of his own drugs . . .' Alice said slowly, 'poisoning him with his own medication? Didn't it occur to you beforehand that you'd be found out? Even if you hadn't finished him off with a knife?'

'I had thought about it beforehand, yes. But I don't agree. I reckoned I'd be all right. You saw the condition that he was in. There was nothing left of him, he was knocking on death's door. People would just think he'd died of the disease.'

'Then why did you do it?' Elaine Bell shot back at her. 'If he was knocking on death's door anyway, you didn't need to do it. You wouldn't have had long to wait, would you?'

Heather Brodie looked defiantly at the DCI and said in a hard, determined voice, 'You couldn't begin to understand, could you? You have no idea, no idea . . . I did it because I had had enough. *Enough*. He was supposed to die by last July, then by this June, but he just hung on – clung on like a desperate rat, drooling and dribbling, hissing and muttering, having "accidents", spitting . . . He'd hit me twice, lashed out at me like a madman, caught me once in the eye and the other time on the jaw. He wasn't human any more.' She hesitated briefly, letting the meaning of her words sink in. 'He'd become a beast, a miserable, vicious beast . . . an animal in nappies.'

'And the insurance policy?' the DCI asked, looking down at her notes.

'What?'

'Well, you wouldn't get any money, would you, if he died after February 2010.'

'Yes,' she hesitated, 'that's right, I wouldn't. But where did you find the policy?' She smiled politely at Elaine Bell, as if expecting an answer from her.

'In your desk,' Alice replied.

'It's his, it was his desk, actually.'

'And now,' Alice continued, 'why are you telling us all of this now? Why did you come here today to confess to your husband's murder, why not yesterday or the day before – or tomorrow for that matter?'

'Because,' Heather Brodie said, meeting her gaze steadily, 'things have altered, haven't they? You've all changed tack, and now you're after Colin, my Colin. You think he's involved – supplied the drugs, or whatever. My "accomplice". Well, he didn't. I told you, he didn't need to. I'd been thinking about how I would do it, if things got too bad, for weeks, if not for months.'

'Your toy-boy,' Eric Manson butted in, rolling his eyes heavenwards.

'How do you know we're after Colin?' Alice asked.

'Because someone at his work, a friend, told me that you'd collected him.'

'You're coming here today, confessing to us today . . . because you want to spare Doctor Paxton any more questioning?' Alice enquired, scepticism apparent in her voice.

'No, of course not. It's because I don't want him involved, I've told you. Because he's not involved. He had nothing whatsoever to do with it. He's not the one who killed my husband, I am. He had no idea I was going to do it. Probably wouldn't believe it if you told him.'

⸺

Once they were outside the interview room, Elaine Bell folded her arms again and turned to her Inspector, saying in a low voice, 'So, what do you think, Eric? Think she did it? Seems pretty believable to me.'

He nodded, his brow corrugated in thought. 'Aye . . . she knew about the overdose, the type of drugs used, about where all the "stolen" stuff was. Not a word of any of that has been in the papers. The only way she could know about it would be if she's the one – the one who did it, eh? How else?'

'Alice?' the DCI said, keen to get a further opinion. The Sergeant shrugged her shoulders. 'Yes, maybe. Maybe she did it, but I'm not sure . . . I'm just not sure.'

'Not sure about what, exactly?' Eric Manson retorted. 'She's just told us that she did it. So why don't you believe her? What's not to believe?'

'Her confession . . . I'm not completely convinced that it's true, it doesn't ring quite true. The gesture, the throat-slitting one – she used her right hand, did you see?'

'So?' the Detective Inspector snapped.

'So . . . you, Ma'am, when you were reading out your notes, told us that the Professor said in the P.M. that the killer was likely to be left-handed . . . It's on the board too.'

'Aha, that's right,' Elaine Bell confirmed. 'That's what he said, the killer's *likely* to be left-handed. Not *is* left-handed, only *likely* to be.'

'Anyway, maybe she's ambidextrous, dear – it's not that uncommon, is it?' Eric Manson said. 'You haven't explained how she knows what she knows. How could she know about the Nortriptyline and the Ora . . . Ora . . . the other stuff? We didn't tell her. How did she know where the computer was found, about the knife, the jewellery-case being in the river? None of that was in the papers. And McConnachie confirmed that the knife was likely to be the one that was used, and she identified it as her own too. How the hell do you explain away all of that, then?'

'I can't . . . unless, maybe, Paxton told her? If he was the one who did it, then he'd know all the details. He could have told her.'

'Yes,' Eric Manson answered belligerently, 'but why the fuck should we think he did it? He's not the one confessing

205

to it. And, as you said, his DNA's easy enough to explain away. One of his neighbours already confirmed that she saw him coming up the stairs after he'd seen the woman off that night. Other than his lying through his teeth and his having access to the drugs, we've got nothing on him, really, no real reason to suspect him. He didn't even try to suggest that Brodie could have taken the stuff himself. If he had known what went on he would have been clear about that, like she was, he would surely have told us categorically that the man could have taken the stuff himself.'

'True,' Alice conceded, 'but . . . I don't know what it is, something doesn't feel right . . .' her voice tailed off. 'Anyway, I thought Livingstone said it was him who threw the wallet in the river.'

'Did you see that smile – the smile she gave me?' Elaine Bell asked, recreating it in her own mind and shuddering theatrically as she spoke. Then she added, 'Alice, you wait here. I'm going to speak to the Super, he's here at the moment . . . and Eric, you come too, I want you to tell him what you think too.'

So saying, she disappeared down the corridor, bustling towards her office with her subordinate tagging along obediently behind her. As they disappeared from view, the interview-room door opened and, mobile in hand, Heather Brodie emerged, looking to the left and right, an anxious expression on her face.

'Could I make a phone call?' she asked meekly, catching the Sergeant's eye.

'To your lawyer or someone? Who d'you want to call?' Alice asked, surprised by the request.

'I'd like to call my son, my son, Harry. I need to call him. Now that I've spoken to you, got everything out of the way, I need to talk to him. He'll organise things for me, including a lawyer, he'll tell Ella for me, Pippa too. Is that all right? I'd rather they heard it from me.'

Looking at the woman, pale as death, it seemed rude, unkind to deny her this one thing. Without more thought Alice nodded her agreement, and then, before the first key had been pressed, she asked, 'Are you left-handed or right-handed?'

Heather Brodie was holding her phone in her left hand, her right index finger raised above the keypad. She paused momentarily before answering. 'Both,' she replied, 'I use both my hands. I can't remember the word for it . . . you know, I'm ambi . . . ambi . . . something or other. I'm lucky, I can use my left hand and my right hand. Why? Why do you want to know?'

'Just curious,' Alice answered.

A few minutes later Elaine Bell reappeared. The calm expression on her face vanished as soon as she caught sight of her suspect talking on the phone, and she said angrily to Alice, 'What the hell's she doing?'

'Er . . . I gave her permission. She's just letting her son know what's going on . . .'

'Christ Almighty! You let her? Have you forgotten that she's just confessed to murdering her husband? What the hell were you thinking of! Other members of the family may have been involved with it, there may be evidence in their control, stuff that they'll now destroy, get rid of . . .'

Shaking her head, the DCI walked straight up to the woman and calmly plucked the mobile phone from her hand, murmuring a curt apology as she did so. Heather Brodie looked stunned, but she said nothing, her mouth dropping open in amazement.

At that moment, Thomas Riddell, his jacket thrown nonchalantly across one shoulder, strolled past the assembled group, but he stopped in his tracks on catching sight of Heather Brodie, a warm smile lighting up his features.

'Heather . . . Mrs Brodie. I didn't know you were coming in today. You should have told me. What are you doing here?'

Seeing him, the woman frowned as if troubled, but did not reply. After a few seconds, Alice, feeling the need to fill the uneasy silence, answered his question. 'She's just confessed to her husband's murder, Thomas.'

Instantly, Riddell's smile disappeared and he looked, with panic in his eyes, at Heather Brodie's face; but she, as if ashamed, bowed her head, deliberately avoiding meeting his gaze.

'I don't believe it. I don't believe it for one second. Not for one second. What on earth are you doing, Heather? Why are you telling them these lies? Why are you doing this?'

As he was speaking he moved instinctively towards her, his hands outstretched as if he was going to touch her, but she shied away, ensuring that Alice remained between her and the distraught man,

'Thomas!' Elaine Bell's voice rang out, 'I need you to collect Mrs Brodie's sister. Go and bring her in right now, please.'

As he did not move, she insisted, '*Now*! And speak to the turnkeys on your way. See if there are any cells free below. And, Alice,' she added, 'you get the children, both of them, this minute. We'll just have to hope that we're not too late already!'

208

Racing across a red light from the Pleasance, Alice cursed her own crassness. It was so obvious if you thought about it for a single second, so blindingly obvious, but she had overlooked it, missed it completely. What a moron! What a fool she had been! By now blood-soaked clothes could have been burnt or dumped somewhere, or other elaborate lies concocted or, God forbid, Harry and Ella absconded, the pair of them going to earth completely. And she would be responsible for it, and possibly now remain a Sergeant for all eternity.

As she reached the top of the hill on St Mary's Street, she pushed her foot down on the accelerator, revving impotently, but nothing happened because nothing could happen. The car in front was jammed tight against its neighbour, as she was, as they all were *ad infinitum* into the distance. And neither the traffic lights nor a blue light could work magic. Gripping the steering wheel unnaturally tightly, she recreated the scene in her mind's eye, seeing again Heather Brodie's pleading expression, hearing the apparently innocuous question; but this time, when asked, she did the Right Thing and refused the request. She heard herself solving part of the problem by offering to phone on the woman's behalf instead, or at least arranging a lawyer for her.

Of course, she thought, it might still be all right. It was not impossible, all might not be lost. Suppose, just suppose, she had been right, suppose the woman had not killed her husband, had been making a false confession for some labyrinthine reason, then all might be not lost . . .

Yes, she reassured herself, it might still be all right. Stuck in the traffic, her engine now switched off, she began to analyse the roots of her unease about Heather

Brodie's guilt, trying to figure out if there was any real substance to her misgivings. No-one in their right minds was impressed by talk of 'intuition'. After all, everyone had it and often competing claims were made on the basis of it, none of which were capable of any form of rational justification. It was no more than witchcraft, really.

So, thinking about things properly, logically, what exactly had Mrs Brodie said? She had claimed to be ambidextrous, but had not appeared to be so, with her throat-slitting gesture or when holding her mobile phone. And, surely, an educated woman like her would have known the word for it, if she was indeed ambidextrous? If she was determined to confess and wished to be believed, the safest answer to the question posed about whether she was left or right-handed would be the very one that she had given, and she was fly enough to know that, so her reply might mean nothing.

What about her stated motive for confessing, the protection of her lover, Colin Paxton? Possible. But he had appeared to be telling the truth earlier, and a witness had seen him returning to his flat after their rendezvous. So, his involvement did not seem probable in any case. Anyway, could he not look after himself? He was articulate, competent, not someone easily confused. If he chose to do so, he was capable of shouting from the rooftops his innocence. She must know that.

But if she was not confessing to protect him, then who else could it be? And how, if she was not the murderer, did she know so much about the killing itself, about the disposal of the 'stolen' goods, the fact they had been dumped under the Dean Bridge and in the river, the fact of the overdose, the precise drugs used for it? Why had she phoned Harry, her son, expecting him to arrange things and to be the conduit for such shattering news to his sister and aunt? Was Ella not the competent, responsible one? The boy's childhood reports suggested that he would buckle under pressure, be unable to cope with that sort of shattering news. And he had seemed hostile to his mother, unwilling even to kiss her. Thomas Riddell had noticed his coldness too, remarked on it. Why had she chosen him, him of all people, to be the first to receive such dreadful tidings, never mind expecting him to pass them on to the others?

Thinking of Thomas Riddell, a picture of his anguished face as he heard the news of Heather Brodie's confession appeared before her, and she could hear his impassioned words ringing in her ears. Not very professional of him, she thought to herself primly.

And then, slowly, realisation dawned. That was the answer. Of course, he had not been professional, because his relationship with Heather Brodie went far, far beyond that. It was personal, possibly very personal. And he, obviously, like the rest of them, would know every single detail of the investigation, however obscure, however unlikely, and if he knew it, then so, too, might she. If she had asked him about it, then he, in his susceptible, over-enamoured state, might well have told her. Told her everything.

And that momentary hesitation when hearing about the insurance policy, the flicker of surprise, had been genuine. Because, as she had said, it was not her desk but her husband's. The files had become increasingly disordered, not because she had lost interest in them, but because her accountant husband could no longer attend to them, with the disease getting its claws further and further into his flesh. So, she might not even have known about the policy.

But one question remained: who the hell was she protecting with her false confession? Who had actually killed Gavin Brodie? Suddenly, and from nowhere, Una Reid's chilling question came into her head, her throaty, smoke-scarred voice sounding eerily triumphant: 'Why'd I bring his suffering to an end?'

Only someone who loved him would do that. His children or his mother. And, immediately, the answer came to her. She had no doubts, that must be it. Heather Brodie had broken the news to her son, rather than her daughter, because it was intended not for onward transmission to the others, but to let him know that she had confessed, was now shielding him and protecting him from the consequences of his crime. And how would he react to such tidings? Jesus Christ. What a God-awful muddle!

—

When Alice finally reached the door of the basement flat in Raeburn Mews, it was ever so slightly ajar, and loud music could be heard inside. She knocked sharply, then called out, but got no response. With trepidation she pushed the door further open and slipped inside. Unaccompanied drum music was reverberating in the small space, played at a volume high enough to hurt the ears, making the boy's flat feel like a mad house.

As she entered the sitting-room, the first person she saw was Harry Brodie. His thin torso was bare and he was holding a bread knife in his hand. He looked up as she came in, startled, and she noticed his knuckles blanch as he tightened his grip on the knife.

'What on earth are you doing in here?' he demanded.

'The door was open. We need to see you.'

'What?' he shouted, then he turned down the volume on the nearby speaker. 'What did you say?'

In the silence she repeated, 'We need to see you.'

'OK,' he said, moving towards her, the knife still in his hand.

'Could you put it down, Harry?'

'You mean the knife . . . sorry, it's just for the bread though – to cut the bread,' he replied, putting it down on a breadboard on the low coffee table beside her. A loaf, together with a pot of jam and a packet of butter, was also on the board. He looked at her calmly, expectantly, waiting for her to explain herself.

'Did you get a call from your mother?'

'No – why?'

'Sure about that? She said she was going to call you. I saw her do it.'

'No. I could have missed it I suppose, I've been having a shower. Maybe she called then. What did she want to speak to me about?'

There was no easy way to break the news.

'Because . . . she's just walked into the station and confessed to the murder of your father.'

'Fucking hell!' the boy said, dropping onto a chair as if his legs had buckled under him.

'You had no idea?'

'Of course I had no fucking idea!' he shouted, shaking his head. 'No fucking idea. I knew she was planning to put him in a home. I knew she had found another man. I knew she didn't love him . . . but, no, I didn't know that. It never crossed my mind that she'd do that. Ella, for sure . . . but not Mum. She just didn't care enough about

213

him. All his pleading was just water off a duck's back, I thought, and God knows, she wouldn't have had long to wait. Not Mum, though . . .'

'You talked about it – you, your mum and Ella? About taking your father's life?'

'Yes,' he said angrily, 'and don't look so surprised. We talked about it, but not with Mum any more. It didn't affect her, she'd somehow managed to stop "hearing" it. But Ella and I talked. Sometimes about very little else. Every time I saw him, every single time, he asked me to kill him. Ella too. Granny, probably, for all I know. Can you imagine that? I doubt it. But, yes, we talked about it. I think you'd find that anyone, anyone in that hellish position, would talk about it. And . . . think about it. Eat, bloody sleep and breathe it too. Jesus,' he said, hiding his face in his hands.

'Why would your mother phone you to arrange things . . . a lawyer, that kind of thing, not Ella?'

'What d'you mean? Why wouldn't she phone me? Maybe she rang Ella too, are you sure she didn't?' he paused before continuing. 'Probably not, though, because I won't crumble, but Ella will. She and Mum are really close, always have been. She'll not be able to cope. Anything happens to Mum and she goes to pieces, can't take it. It happened when we had a cancer scare, when Mum had a car crash too. Mum is Ella's Achilles heel, you see, and Mum knows that better than anyone.'

As Alice stood watching the boy, the door slowly opened and Ella slipped in with the child, Katy, holding her hand. Her face was red, tears streaming down her cheeks. The stealthiness of her entrance suggested that she had been outside, listening to her brother's words.

'It can't be true . . . not Mum,' she said, looking first at

Alice and then at her brother, waiting for either of them to deny it.

'I'm afraid it is,' Alice said. 'She came to the station and told us this morning.'

'But . . . but why? I don't believe she could do it. Mum couldn't kill him. She just couldn't bring herself to do it, even if she wanted to. I could, but not her. I even told Aunt Pippa that I was going to, and I meant it, I would have . . . if Dad was going to go into a home, and you said that he was, Harry, that he'd rot in there, it would be even worse for him . . . but Mum could never have killed him, any more than you, Harry.'

'When – when did you tell her that?'

'Who?' the girl asked, her voice quavering.

'Your aunt Pippa?'

'On the Friday . . . before he died.'

'What did she say?' Alice asked.

'She said not to be silly, not to think about such a thing. She kept saying that I was a mother now, had Katy to look after. She said that I mustn't worry, all would be well in the end.'

Pippa Mitchelson, Alice thought to herself. The one person left who had no alibi. And they had all known that and done nothing about it. Had somehow completely overlooked the timid spinster, seeing her only as a foil for the others.

—

'Only for a few minutes,' Thomas Riddell said, 'otherwise I'll be for the chop. I'm just letting you in to comfort Heather, nothing else. She needs somebody from her family. She was worried the boy might hurt himself when he got the news.'

'I understand,' Pippa said, 'and thank you very much, Thomas.'

Once seated beside her sister in the interview room, Pippa Mitchelson put her arms around her, rocking her gently as she had done before, long, long ago in their childhood years. Then she had been the confident one, the big sister, able to put things right, to soothe the younger one, take away her troubles. Until, one day, their roles had been reversed, and she had found herself the comforted instead of the comforter. Her new role, that of the less-worldly one, the lonely, unfulfilled spinster, had not been chosen by her, and by the time she had become conscious of it, it was too late. It fitted too well, too snugly and she could not shake it off. With her long fingers she swept a strand of hair from her sister's temple, rearranging it behind her ear and wiping away the tears that were glistening on her cheeks.

'It's alright, sweetheart, it's alright. I've just heard. Don't worry. Harry's fine. The female Sergeant brought both the children here. Katy, too . . . Ella's been speaking to that chief detective woman. But you needn't worry any more. Harry didn't do it.'

'Thank God!' Heather Brodie replied, sobbing unashamedly, 'thank God.'

'But what made you think that he had – that it was Harry?'

'I didn't . . . until yesterday,' Heather Brodie answered, 'but after those letters I knew. I thought he had finally listened to his father, put him out of his misery. He felt he owed it to him. That he couldn't bear the thought of him in a home.'

'What letters?'

'The Genetic Counselling Service one, I found it on

top of the hall table in his flat and I couldn't resist taking a look. They wanted to counsel him about Huntingdon's. He must have decided to have the test and heard he's got it. It must have been positive.'

'Why didn't you tell me, darling?' Pippa said, squeezing her sister's hand. 'When Ella was tested – and she doesn't have it, now does she? – she was called in. They call you in even if the result is negative.'

'Always? Do they really?' Heather asked, in a relieved tone.

'Always. What was the other letter? The one from the Abbey Park Lodge?'

'So, he still may not have Huntingdon's?'

'Yes, yes. But tell me about the letter.'

'It was the one you handed to me at the flat, from Mrs Drayton, the manageress. Our initials are the same, mine and Harry's. They'd put "Mr" before my initials, by mistake, so I thought it was for him and I forwarded it on to him in the flat. But it was meant for me. He must have learned from it that I was intending to put his father in there, into a home. I'd never discussed it with the children. I had to be the one to make the decision . . . I couldn't involve them in something like that.'

'I know. I knew you had taken that decision.'

'How? Who told you?'

'Ella, last week. Harry told her and she told me, you see. Anyway, you shouldn't have worried,' Pippa said, trying to reassure her again. 'Harry and Ella were together the night when it all happened, you knew that. Remember?'

'That's what I thought at first. But after that phone call, I worked out that Ella had spent the evening, and the night, with Vicky, Harry's girlfriend. That's what I thought Vicky said.'

'I don't know what she said, but maybe you got it wrong.'

'Maybe I did. I can't remember her exact words any more. But if it wasn't Harry, then who was it . . . God, not Ella – please, please God.'

'No,' Pippa said quietly, 'not Ella, darling. Me.'

'You?'

Thomas Riddell pushed the door open and advanced quickly towards the sisters, finding them both now sitting bolt upright.

'You'll have to leave now, Miss Mitchelson,' he said, looking at her anxiously and tapping her on the shoulder. 'You'll need to go into the other interview room. The Chief and Inspector Manson are both on their way, and they'll be here in less than a minute.'

Elaine Bell listened dumbfounded to her sergeant.

'Are you sure?'

'No, but I am sure that it wasn't Heather Brodie. And Pippa Mitchelson has no alibi.'

'OK, but that only gets us so far. Why? Why would she kill her brother-in-law?'

'Love, I think.'

'She was in love with the man?' the DCI interrupted, incredulous.

'No. Ella. She loves Ella.'

DI Manson came over to join them, shaking his head.

'She doesn't want one?' Elaine Bell asked.

'No, Ma'am. Says she doesn't need a solicitor. Wants to get everything over now. Right now.'

'Alright. Alice, you take the lead this time. I still don't fully understand what's been going on, but we can't wait.

Wouldn't want her to change her mind. But be very, very careful. Do it completely by the book . . . everything. Nothing must go wrong.'

Once they were all seated inside and the tape was running, Alice began, 'Miss Mitchelson, would I be right in thinking that you were not with your sister on the Saturday night?'

'Yes,' the woman smiled bleakly, tenting her long fingers and pressing their red tips together, 'you would be right.'

'But you covered for her?'

'That's what she thought, and she was right, of course. I always cover for her. I knew whenever she was going out to meet Colin. She would tell the children that she was going to meet up with me, and obviously I'd tell them the same. I had to, didn't I?'

'You always knew when she would be out of the house . . . when she was with him, anyway?'

'Shall we speed things up a bit, dear? Mr Riddell kindly collected me, but I would have come here myself. As soon as I'd heard about Heather's foolish, selfless act I had to, really, didn't I? So, shall I just tell you everything . . . would that be in order?'

The DCI and Alice exchanged glances, and then Elaine Bell said, 'Yes, you do that, please.'

'Well . . . where shall I begin?' the middle-aged spinster asked, shielding her tired eyes with her left hand, then answering her own question. 'At the beginning, of course. On Friday last Ella told me . . . she said that Harry had discovered from a letter that their mother was going to put Gavin in a home. She was crying, almost hysterical

219

at the thought. She said she couldn't bear it. Katy was beside her, she couldn't understand what was going on, so I put her on my knee as Ella talked and talked. She said that she was going to save her father, put him out of his misery like he wanted, like he kept asking her . . .'

She stopped speaking, looking into the distance.

'So?' The DCI prompted.

'Sorry. So I said not to worry. But I couldn't let that happen could I? Ella's a brave girl, a very unselfish girl, and she would have done it, you see. She has the courage to do it – to kill him. I knew she would . . .' her voice tailed off, but she began again, a tear running now down her cheek.

'I couldn't let that happen. Ella has everything to live for. She's young, beautiful. She's got Katy to look after. Her whole life is in front of her. And, goodness me, Katy needs her mother, doesn't she? Any child does . . . And what do I have to lose in comparison? No one needs me, you see. I had so much less to lose. I had to be the one. For Ella . . . Gavin too, in a way.'

'So?' The DCI repeated, mechanically.

'So I did it . . . on the Saturday. I knew Heather was going to be out with Colin. I had my key. I waited for Una to go, and then I gave him a cocktail of two of his drugs and waited. While I was waiting, I lost my nerve. I thought perhaps they won't work, perhaps the ones I chose were not strong enough. I couldn't wait any longer.'

Once more, she stopped speaking, staring straight ahead at the wall as if she was now alone in the room.

'You couldn't wait . . .' Elaine Bell prompted.

'So I cut his throat with a knife.' She hesitated briefly, shuddering. 'Blood went everywhere, a shower of blood all over me, all over everything. I wiped myself with my clothes and changed into some of Heather's things, I only put them back in her bag today. I took some of their possessions from the flat so that you would think it was a robbery or something like that. I dumped my own clothes later.'

'What did you do with the things you took?'

'I threw them away by the Dean Bridge. Except the photo, I took it out of its frame . . . the one of Ella, that was beside his bed. I kept it in my bedroom drawer . . . but after I heard about Heather today I brought it with me. I can show you it now if you like?'

The DCI nodded, and Pippa Mitchelson opened her handbag, removed an old-fashioned compact, a small hankie and her purse from it, and then a black and white print of her niece playing on the beach. Giving it a final lingering look, she handed it over.

'It's one of my favourites. She had such a wide smile, always happy. She was always happy . . . a carefree child.'

———

'Mrs Brodie,' the DCI began, 'you'll have got the news – that Harry's fine, and that he didn't do it. Sergeant Rice is talking to him now, then we'll release him. You're free to go too, of course. But there is one other thing that I'd like to ask you about.'

'Yes,' Heather Brodie said wearily, feeling drained of all life, her head still reeling from her sister's revelation.

'I have to ask you,' the DCI began again, 'did Thomas Riddell, our Liaison Officer – did he give you details of our investigation? Tell you about the overdose, for example, the type of drugs used, whether supposedly "stolen" stuff had been found, and if so its whereabouts and so on?'

For a few moments Heather Brodie hesitated, aware

that if she told the truth the kind auburn-haired policeman might lose his job, remembering how smitten with
her he was, how sweet to her he had been right up until
the last, and how she had used him. But then all the lies
she had told came back to haunt her. Lies to Gavin, to
Colin even, to Harry and Ella, the police . . . the list went
on and on, and sometime it had to stop. So, without further thought, she nodded.

When the DCI returned to her office, Eric Manson
looked at her enquiringly from his seat by the window.

'Yes,' she said shortly, lowering herself heavily into her
chair, 'it was Thomas.'

'Stupid bastard.'

'He's just offered his resignation.'

'Good. So he should. And the aunt, do we know yet
why she drugged the man *and* cut his throat?'

'Lost her nerve, apparently, that's what she said anyway. She wasn't sure about the drugs, she wasn't sure
they'd be strong enough. She gave him most of the bottle,
most of two bottles, in fact. She says he became uncon-
scious quite quickly, but carried on breathing. She knew
that Heather hoped to be away until the morning, but
might not be. She panicked and used the knife. Once
she'd done that, well, it could only be murder. So she
took the stuff to draw our attention away, make us think
just what we did think. At first anyway.'

Elaine Bell sighed, resting her head on her hands, then
adding, 'I've seen it all . . . or I thought I had, Eric. But
nothing like this in all my thirty years. And God alone
knows how she'll fare in prison . . . it'll be like putting a
sparrow amongst hawks.'

She shook her head, then she added, 'The poor bloody wretch.'

'Brodie?'

'No . . . well, yes, him too. But her, I really meant her. The whole lot of them, actually. Ever since the Mitchelson woman's confession and speaking to the child, Ella, I've been thinking about it. If it was my dad, if he'd been like that, what would I do? Fucking irony, isn't it? Keep a dumb animal alive in a state like that, and the RSPCA would be after you for not putting it down. But a person you know, asking to be put . . . asking for death? It's an odd, upside-down world we live in.'

'Aha. And ours is not to reason why,' the Inspector replied.

Her phone rang and she picked it up, mouthed 'The Super' and gestured for Manson to leave.

'Now, Sir. If that suits you, yes, that's fine by me,' she said, trying to sound bright and energetic. 'I'll be along at Fettes in, say, twenty minutes.'

Receiving her in his spacious office, the Superintendent looked confident, pleased with himself and, for the moment, with his subordinate too. With this case solved he would go out in a blaze of glory, whatever happened to her.

'I gather you've wrapped it up?' he said, pulling out a chair for her.

'We have, Sir. The woman's speaking to her lawyer now.'

'A right Lady Macbeth I expect, eh? But it's the appraisal you're concerned about, I appreciate that. Of course, we can discuss it, although I have now, as far as I'm concerned, committed my views to paper in their final form. But I can spare you half an hour or so to go over it. Would that do? I'll explain it, go through the basis for my firmly-held views, but my wife's due to pick me up in about half an hour or so. We'll have to stop when she arrives.'

He leant back on his chair, linking his hands behind his great bull-neck, beaming at her, convinced already that she would eventually slink out of his lair, tail down, accepting defeat. On her knee she had the brown envelope containing all the evidence she had compiled to present to him, illustrating why she should be upgraded, documenting her successes, staff improvements, initiatives, skills, everything she could find to persuade him to tell the truth. The truth would do. If he would tell that, then she would have a chance, and a chance was all she needed. Because at interview she would shine. She knew it, but with this appraisal before them, no one would include her on the shortlist.

'Just so I understand, Sir,' she said slowly, 'there's no question of actually changing it, the appraisal – just "explaining" it?'

He nodded complacently. After all, all the balls were in his court.

'No change whatsoever?'

'No change whatsoever, Elaine.'

What the hell, she thought, I've nothing to lose. He had no scruples, so why should she hobble herself with them? And he would not know whether it was a bluff or not.

'Did you enjoy your meal, Sir – the one in Claudio's on Friday? I know I did. I'll enjoy hearing your wife's impression of the place. She certainly seemed to like it, to be enjoying herself. So, we've half an hour or so until she arrives, is that right? Unless, of course, we finish earlier.'

For a second the Superintendant was speechless, working out the full import of her words. His complexion now puce, he said, stiffly, 'Good food, certainly . . .' He held out his hand for the envelope. 'Perhaps . . . there might be something in there that would help me revise my opinion . . . a little.'

———

'Well, that was a turn up for the books, eh?' the solicitor said to DC Littlewood as they were walking away from the interview room.

'How d'you mean?' the constable asked, opening the corridor door for the solicitor's portly figure and standing to one side to allow his bulk to pass through.

'Her confession to killing Gavin Brodie. Jim Nicholl, from my firm, he was the duty solicitor, remember? Only a few days ago when you lot were busy charging our cli-ent, Norman Clerk, with exactly the same crime. To be dropped now, I gather.'

'Oh, aye. And the cannabis, the assault and everything else, are they to be dropped too? I don't think so,' DC Littlewood said with grim satisfaction, remembering Alice's bruised face, 'so your "client" will be in Saughton for a wee whiley yet.'

'Nope, you're wrong there,' the lawyer replied, lurch-ing down the stairs and raising his voice to ensure it could be heard over the sound of his own heavy footsteps, 'not anymore. He's in the Royal now. He wasn't taking his drugs, you see. He had a psychotic episode and attacked one of the prison officers. Anyway, Jim will have to tell him the good news – as soon as he's safe to visit again.'

———

Heather Brodie was standing in the reception area with her son and daughter beside her, all of them waiting patiently for the police lift they had been promised. But, catching sight of the lawyer, Heather rushed over to speak to him. Ella, lifting up her small child, followed behind her. Only Harry remained where he was.

'Hello? I understand you're looking after Pippa – my sister, Miss Mitchelson. She will be alright, won't she?'

'That's correct, my firm will be representing her. Not me personally, for various reasons, but don't you worry, we'll do our best for her,' the lawyer said, putting on his overcoat and straining to button it up.

'But . . . she will be alright, won't she? She won't be kept in prison?' Ella asked anxiously, her face blotchy, stained by tears, and the little girl in her arms distracting her by fingering her mouth.

'Hard to say at this juncture,' the man replied, glancing through the glass door at the rain hammering down and bouncing off the pavement in St Leonard's Street, unfurling his umbrella in readiness for the dash to his car.

'How d'you mean?' the girl exclaimed. Her brother had joined the group and was now standing behind her.

'Well, looking to the long term, we'll have to see what the prosecution will accept, won't we?' he replied, distracted, having just noticed that two of the spokes of his umbrella were poking through the material. The twins must have been playing spaceships with it again, he would look like a down-and-out or some kind of comic tramp.

'But,' Heather Brodie persisted, deliberately putting herself in front of him to stop him leaving, 'everyone will appreciate that she didn't do it for herself, won't they? That it was a mercy-killing. So they're bound to be lenient with her, aren't they? She only did it because she had to do it. She'd nothing to gain from killing Gavin, everything to lose.'

'Well, I'm not sure I'd quite go along with that . . . no, I can't quite go along with that,' he replied, impatient to leave, snapping the popper shut on his now-closed umbrella, having decided not to expose himself to ridicule by using it. This would be no legal-aid job, and the tattered mess would create quite the wrong impression. Better to accept a soaking.

'Why not? It's true!' Harry said.

'A mercy killing? No, that's not what she described to me, or the police, I gather. She said that she did it for Ella – not really for Mr Brodie.'

'So?' the boy demanded, unable to conceal his frustration.

'Well, that was her fatal mistake – purely from a legal perspective, you understand. You see, if Ella had done it for her father, killed him as he had begged her to, that clearly would have been a mercy-killing, a culp. hom., the Crown would likely accept a plea to culpable homicide and she would have got . . .' he paused, thought briefly and then continued, 'well, who knows? Maybe even probation if she was lucky. But this? This is quite a different kettle of fish.'

'So what is it then, if not a mercy-killing?'

'I'll have to speak to Senior Counsel, obviously, but it looks much more like murder to me.'

—

Driving home that evening, Eric Manson put on Classic FM, and found himself bathed in the haunting sound of Albinoni's 'Adagio for Strings', the solemn and moving music a strangely fitting accompaniment to his mournful frame of mind. It was true, they had solved their case, but he could not celebrate that. Not that bloody catastrophe, no. No nips or pints for him in the pub this evening, no banter, no knees-up for having cracked this one.

Feeling his eyes becoming hot, tears prickling at their edges, he shook his head violently from side to side as if such a movement might shake away his grief, then turned the radio off, forcing himself to concentrate on the road ahead. It must have been the sad music, and he must be over-tired too, that explained it. Or maybe, he was getting a cold from that sickly baby sneezing all over him. Anyway, nothing like a bout of righteous anger to drive the blues away, he decided, egging himself on by thinking about all the hours that they had spent on the Brodie woman's lies, not to mention her fancy-man's contributions. Wasting all their precious time and muddying the waters terribly. But that poor teacher, that poor bloody woman. Unworldly, a holy fool. In some ways too good for her own bloody good. Too good for her adulterous sister, for sure.

And, Christ, the fucking coven was supposed to be having another of their interminable gatherings in his house that evening, monopolising Margaret and marginalizing him again. Witches to a woman. But if they saw him in a miserable mood they would scent his weakness immediately. A single glimpse of his bloodshot eyes and they would know that he was wounded, vulnerable, and take strength from the fact. But he had not given up yet, oh no. Margaret would stay his, stay married to him, because he would see them all off, and any fancy man too. Tomorrow, he would be feeling better, stronger, somehow he would sort it all out. She *must* still love him.

He traipsed up the garden path, feeling lower than ever, and came to a halt on the doorstep, breathing in, pulling his shoulders back and forcing his mouth into a confident grin. So fortified, he strode into his hall, and as he did so, all the lights in the house were switched on and a raucous cheer went up. He saw that his hallway was crowded with people, with his friends and with his family, and, bewildered, he stood blinking in amazement at them all. As he waited, struck dumb, Margaret elbowed her way through the assembled throng towards him. Her face shining with delight, she planted a huge kiss on his lips, and as he responded the crowd erupted, clapping and whooping at the pair of them.

'Surprise! And happy thirtieth anniversary, my darling,' she whispered in his ear. Glancing at her he was struck by how pretty she looked, dazzled by her figure, now shapely in a cream outfit with the navy embroidery on the collars. It was her going-away dress.

'What do you think?' she said twirling round like a model in front of him. 'I tried out lots of new outfits, but I didn't like myself in any of them. So I dieted for weeks and weeks, very difficult when you're trying out new recipes for a party too, and yesterday, for the very first time, I managed to do up all the buttons on this!'

Tears welled up in Eric Manson's tired eyes, and he felt that his legs were about to give way, but he put his arm around his wife for support, kissed her cheek, then took a long draught from the champagne flute that had been thrust into his hands. Opposite him, a glass in her hand too, stood Elaine Bell. She gave him a quick thumbs-up, which, smiling wanly, he returned.

———

Walking along Henderson Row, Alice, too, was finding it difficult to get the events of the day out of her head. She could still see Pippa Mitchelson's figure in the interview room. The woman had seemed so awkward and vulnerable in there, so utterly incongruous in such a setting. In a classroom of small children she might, possibly, wield some authority, but outside it she had none. She seemed almost bemused by the world, like a nun released from her convent too late, no longer able to survive in changed times. She spoke like the schoolteacher she was, in an unhurried, measured way, a manner suited to the times tables or dictation, but not to the confession of a killing that she had carried out.

And listening to the lone spinster, most of Alice's sympathies had been with her, because she had so obviously lost her way. Love had led her astray, had been her only motive. And the sight of her, stricken, when, for a second, she re-lived the moment when she cut the man's throat and was sprayed with his still-warm blood, would remain with her forever, Alice thought, however much she might wish to forget it. Handing her over to the turnkeys, watching them laugh uproariously at their own in-jokes while manhandling her, listening to her old-fashioned expressions of gratitude as her cell door was opened for her, had been heartbreaking. Now she was just another body in the system, waiting to be processed like the rest of them, and there was nothing to be done to change that, nothing she could do. Pippa Mitchelson's life was over, whatever sentence was pronounced on her.

Once she saw Ian, she told herself, her mind would stop racing and she would be able to distance herself from the Brodies, get everything back into its proper place, into perspective. Finally they would be able to talk freely, in private, and she would tell him about the woman's tragedy, the man's tragedy, in fact, the whole bloody family's tragedy. The very act of telling their story, of putting it into words, would help to make it all easier to understand, to accept. Things would fall into place, as they usually did. And, embracing one another at last, they could smooth any ruffled feathers, reassure each other and find the way back to their old, comfortable world.

Of course, and naturally enough, he would give her more news of the boy. This child who had, somehow, entered their lives through a back door, and had no mother. Only a father.

When she had considered children at all, and idly at that, she had only ever imagined her child, their child. She had wanted their child, never someone else's. Not some other woman's child. Loving their child would be easy, it was unimaginable not to love such a wondrous new being. But what did she know about children? Nothing. Despite her best efforts, the squalling baby in the surgery had found no comfort in her arms. So how would she manage? And, as importantly, would she, could she, love this unknown boy? Because if he became part of their family, in fact, made them into a family, she would have to. And what would happen to them, all of them, if, for some reason, that never happened? Perhaps there was no way back to that old, comfortable world?

Pushing her head through the sheets that separated the two studios from each other to enter Ian's part, she heard a high-pitched laugh and saw, sitting on the only chair in the unheated space, a dark-haired little boy. One of his hands was bright blue, as if it had been dipped to the wrist in a pot of paint, and the other one was bright red. Seeing her, he instantly held them both up to show them off, and then clasped them together, marvelling loudly to himself as parts of them turned purple. He then clamped one onto each side of his face and, as if life was for laughter, giggled again at her, showing his magically perfect little milk teeth and creasing his fat red and blue cheeks.

Then, as if it was the most natural thing in the world, he wriggled off the seat of his chair, bent forwards to splay his hands on the stone floor, admired their imprint and toddled across to her. When she stooped down beside him, wanting to be nearer his level, he looked with his innocent eyes into hers and then, saying nothing, held out a red hand for her to clasp in her own. Taking it, feeling the slimy, warm paint between their palms, she realised with pleasure that all her attention, all her being, had, for the last few minutes at least, been focused on the small child, drawn completely into his world, his life as he lived it moment by moment.